finding THE cure

CASSANDRA GIOVANNI

Show n'ot Tell

Show n'ot Tell Publishing

Connecticut, USA

This is a work of fiction. Names, characters, places, and incidents are products of the author's imagination. Any resemblance to actual persons, living or deceased, events or locations are wholly coincidental.

PUBLISHER'S CATALOGING-IN-PUBLICATION DATA:

Giovanni, Cassandra

Finding the Cure

ISBN: 978-0692452585

1.   Romance—Fiction. 2. College—Fiction. 3. Cancer—Fiction. 4. Photography—Fiction. 5. Death—Fiction. 6. Arizona—Fiction. I. Title

Cover Art: Gio Design Studios © 2015

Edited by: Lara Johnson & E.S. Tom

Being a daddy is a chance to be the strongest super hero in the world, and the living guardian angel who never lets you down.

Prologue

I wrapped my fingers around the steering wheel, and it squeaked with the pressure as my knuckles turned white. The sound echoed through the car as my grip continued to tighten. I used to wonder if it was harder to know you're going to die, or just dying without the ability to say goodbye. The tears began to stream down my face as I sped down the highway. The guardrails were just silver blurs as I hammered the gas.

I shouldn't have wondered it. My life was cruel punishment for the thought. The question should have been what's harder, never getting to say goodbye or knowing that every breath could be goodbye?

My chin trembled as my eyes fell to the speedometer.

I was going too fast.

The highway was too straight; a never ending path in front of me that I wanted to drive on until I fell off the edge of the Earth.

I already had, hadn't I?

My eyes lashes fluttered, the drops of tears weighing them down.

Never getting to say goodbye.

I knew that evil. God, did I know that evil. The look on Dad's face as the phone slipped from his hands, the words forming at his lips never reaching my ears.

I read them.

I knew them.

The shock hit my body, and I desperately wanted to feel something—anything besides the rolling waves of pain. That numbness weighted down my limbs as the physical ache coursed through my veins. The anger and pain crushed down on me until my chest was so tight I couldn't breathe. Then I had Dad— he was always there, despite his own pain. His warmth overtook the shocking cold of loss. He broke the edges that hardened on my soul.

Knowing that every breath could be goodbye.

Now.

That was now.

I lifted my foot off the gas, letting the car slow until I pulled over and stopped. My head dipped between my shoulders as my chest heaved with a sob. I let my hands drop to my lap, red lines marking them where my skin had met too tightly with itself. The tears puddled in my palms.

I knew he was going to die. There was nothing that could stop it. I had to watch it. The pillar of strength when Mom died was withering into nothing in front of my eyes. The numbness that hit me when Mom died was a constant part of my life; it never left. I had just gotten better at hiding it. The chains around what was left of my heart tightened with each passing day. Each day meant there was one less breath. Who would save me now?

My eyes rose to the black sky above me.

There was no cure for Dad.

There was no cure for me.

Chapter 1

I took a deep breath as I grabbed the handle of the door to the bookstore.

Finally, I was free—*free*. I walked in, running my fingers over the books on the sale rack. Normally, I was here to get something for a dreaded course at my college but it was the last day of the semester, and I was here for me. I stopped in front of the New Adult section, running my fingers across the bindings until I found a title that looked good. I pulled the book out and looked at the cover. I couldn't help my eyebrow raising as I looked at the two individuals, sparsely dressed and entangled.

"Ellie, nice to see you! What can I help you with? I thought college was out for a while?" Stew came around the corner, and I found myself holding the steamy cover to my hammering chest.

I looked over his shoulder to see if the nameless boy who always seemed to be there to smirk at my suffering due to Stew's attentiveness was around.

He wasn't.

I took a deep breath as I shook my head, moving the book to my back. "Uh, yeah...I mean...I'm good, and yes, it's out for a bit."

Stew leaned against the shelf, flashing me his braces as he pushed his thick glasses up his nose.

"So here for pleasure?" he asked, looking around my shoulder to see what book I was holding behind my back.

I shuffled backwards as I lifted my shoulders to shrug. "Yeah...nothing in particular."

He stepped forward, keeping pace with me as I tossed the book behind me into a pile of sale ones. "There must be *something* you had in mind?

I shook my head. "No, not at all."

I actually did have something in mind, but he was never capable of actually finding the books I needed. Over the past several months I had gotten used to looking up what aisle it would be in while he walked away, leaned too close to a computer screen with, his brow furrowed, hunting and pecking his way around the keyboard. I always had the book in hand by the time he figured out how to use the search bar properly.

"You have to have *some* idea what you're looking for, El. Come on! One year studying your butt off, and now you have some time to read something you like and you have absolutely no clue what you want?" Stew pushed, walking in time with me as I headed through the store.

I gritted my teeth, looking over the shelves and my eyes landed on nameless boy, smirking at me as he put a book back on the shelf. I widened my eyes at him and mouthed the words, *help me please!*

He sucked in his lower lip as he attempted to contain his laughter. He jumped down from the ladder, and I squeezed my eyes shut as I stopped at the shelf I was next to.

"How about a New Adult romance?" Stew suggested, and my face went red as I thought of the book I'd been holding when he walked over to me.

"Stew," a deep voice made my eyes shoot open; "I think it's time for your break," Nameless boy said, covering his smiling lips with his hand as he looked between us.

"I was just helping my favorite customer out," Stew replied, and it sounded like he was pouting behind me. My jaw tightened as I fought the urge to thrust my elbow into his gut.

"Don't worry, bro. I can handle it from here," Nameless boy said, narrowing his green-blue eyes at Stew.

"Yeah," Stew huffed. I looked over my shoulder and shot him a sympathetic smile as he nodded at me saying, "Nice to see you."

"You too," I replied watching as he walked away. I turned to face Nameless boy, looking up at his slender frame. He dropped his hand, sticking it into his jean pockets as he smiled at me. "Thanks for finally saving me."

"I've been watching him do that for months...it's been quite entertaining."

I narrowed my eyes at him, breathing in through my nose before pushing passed him. "It hasn't been entertaining for me. Good way to drive away customers."

"That's why I finally decided to save you," he said as he followed me through the bookshelves to the classics section.

I turned, walking backwards. "Oh, how kind of you."

Nameless boy raised his eyebrows up and down quickly as he leaned against the book shelf, tapping his fingers on the wood. "So what can I help you find?"

I shrugged, looking around the store. Suddenly I had no clue what I wanted to read. His smile and eyes seemed to be a deadly combination for my brain cells.

Finally, I replied, "I like Jane Austen, but I've read all of her books."

Nameless boy nodded over his shoulder. "So you're a romance novel buff?"

I followed him as we made our way a few shelves down. "Not exactly...I just admire her writing. I like her sense of humor."

He looked over at me, his smile enhancing his strong cheek bones and jaw line. "You don't seem to find things very funny."

I blinked at him. "If you're referring to the fact you let Stew torture me for months, that isn't funny."

"It's the kind of thing Miss Austen would've found amusing."

"Yeah," I shot back. "I'm sure *you'd* know that."

He stopped, crossing his arms so they bulged slightly. He had an Adam Levine build; lean muscles with his sex appeal focused on his confidence as he looked down at me. "Stereotyping are we? And you haven't even seen my tattoos."

"Tattoos?" I repeated, my chest tightening with pressure.

He winked at me, flipping his arms over to expose the tattoos on either forearm. "Have you read any of Austen's unfinished work?"

I nodded as I stared at the koi fish on either arm. One danced in moonlit water, while the other danced in water shimmering with the light of the sun.

"You have, or you're that amazed by these?" he asked, tapping his arm with his finger.

I shook my head, my breath sticking in my throat as I tried to make my vocal chords work. I swallowed. "Uh...yeah, I've read them."

I fought the urge to hit myself in the head. I was acting like as much of an idiot with this guy as I did with Stew. My eyes moved from his tattoo back up to his face. He scratched his five o'clock shadow before reaching behind me.

I tried not to shiver as the warmth of his body washed over me. "Here it is."

He handed me a book with a disturbing cover of a girl with half her face gone.

I raised my eyebrows. "You're joking, right? *Pride and Prejudice and Zombies?*"

"Judging a book by its cover isn't a good thing to do," Nameless chastised me, shaking his head. "It's actually very good."

I looked down at the book and back up to his soft lips and then his eyes. "Fine," I began as I narrowed my eyes at him, pushing my shoulders back and standing taller. I was pretty sure my 5'2" frame and all hundred pounds of me couldn't be less confrontational. "I guess I'll trust you, but only because you saved me."

"Are you trying to intimidate me?"

I fluttered my eyelashes at him. "Is it working?"

His shoulders rose as he chuckled. "Not really."

My stomach growled, and my whole body tensed as Nameless' brow furrowed at me.

"I...I forgot to eat today," I stuttered out, looking down at the book in my hands.

I watched from the corner of my eyes as he looked down at his watch then back at me. "It's almost four. You forgot to eat all day?"

I curled my toes inside my ballet flats as my hands tightened around the paperback binding. "Uh...sometimes I do that."

I chewed on the inside of my lip as he looked at my small frame, and I knew he was thinking I was too skinny.

I knew he was right.

"How about I get you a muffin and coffee from the cafe?" Nameless suggested, cocking his head at me. His expression warmed me, and I didn't feel the judgment I expected.

"You really don't have to."

He held his hand out for the book. "It's my way of making up for letting Stew torture you for months."

I let the book drop in his hand, trying to ignore the rush of heat from the touch of his fingertips against mine.

"I suppose I could allow that," I replied, and we headed to the cafe across the way.

"Do you hate me because I let him bug the shit out of you?" he asked as he pulled a stool out for me to sit.

I hopped up into it, replying, "You still have a chance to redeem yourself."

"What type of coffee can I get you?" he asked, leaning on the table. His smile toyed with my emotions, making my empty stomach dance with butterflies.

"White chocolate mocha latte with a blueberry muffin," I answered as he pushed my book towards me with one finger. "Please."

"I'll be right back, start looking through that—you don't have to buy it just because I suggested it," he commented before turning to the counter.

I glanced down at the book, flipping through the pages and catching bits and pieces here and there. It wasn't like I could concentrate on anything within it when I was waiting for him to come back.

"So," Nameless began as he easily slipped onto the stool and pushed the coffee and muffin my way; "how often is sometimes...if you don't mind me asking."

I stared down at the muffin, my mouth watering from its freshly baked scent. I pulled off a piece and popped it in my mouth.

"I'm sorry," he replied, sticking his head in his hand and tangling his fingers in his hair. The top was longer than the sides, sticking between his fingers as he squeezed his eyes shut and shook his head. "I shouldn't have asked. I have no—"

I cut him off. "Don't worry about it. You're not the first person to tell me I'm too skinny."

"Probably the first stranger to, though," he answer, his chest rising as he sat back in his chair, holding his biceps as he stared at me, obviously uncomfortable.

I offered him a soft smile before taking a sip of the drink and then answering, "Not really."

"Well...I just—"

"I don't do it because I think I'm fat."

He nodded, looking down at the table as he tapped his fingers on it. "So," his eyes met mine; "You do know you're beautiful...even when you're eating."

I choked on the piece of muffin my mouth. "Thanks?"

His ears turned red, but he kept his eyes locked on me. "You're welcome."

I looked down at the muffin, picking at the wrapper before letting my gaze back up to his. "I really do just forget to eat...and not on purpose. There's—" I paused, looking at the muffin before continuing; "There's just a lot of things in my life that distract me. Honestly, half the time I don't eat, and the other half I just jam something down because I know I should."

He ran his teeth over his lower lip as he nodded. "Your friends don't say anything?"

I shrugged. "I don't talk about it. You're the only one who's ever really asked. My friends are too involved in being in college and partying to really care. I guess I don't really know if I'd call them friends anyways."

"Sometimes that happens...friends drift apart as they become adults—or don't become adults," he commented as he leaned in. "I get it."

"Some situations force us to be adults sooner than others," I replied. I pursed my lips as I realized I said too much. I shook my head as I stood, grabbing my coffee and book. "Thanks for this, and the book recommendation."

"Sure," he replied, his jaw tightening as he looked at me.

My shoulders relaxed, and I found myself smiling at him. "Thanks for listening. You're easy to talk to...almost too easy."

He laughed, standing and walking with me to the register. "I can honestly say you're the first person to say that."

I handed him the book and he scanned it. "Well, you were."

I swiped my debit card, and he stuck the receipt in the book before holding his hand out to me. "It was good to meet you—"

I took his hand, and a tingle rushed up my body. "Ellie," I replied, trying to not sound as breathless as I was.

"Trent," he replied. "I can make a list of books you might like for the next time you come in?"

"I'd appreciate that," I said, biting my lip and watching as his eyes lingered on me.

"I'll see you in a few days?"

I nodded. "Sounds good."

Chapter 2

"Brought another book?" the nurse greeted me as I passed the lobby desk.

"You know how much Dad likes it when I read to him," I replied, watching as she gave a soft nod and smile.

I paused outside the door, looking at Dad's skeletal body as he watched the television. I swallowed down the pain in my throat before walking in and leaning down to kiss him on the forehead.

"How are you feeling today?" I asked, sitting down on the edge of his bed as he turned the television off.

He breathed in deeply, the bags under his eyes dark as he smiled weakly at me. "I'm good," he said, tilting his head. "You seem more cheerful than usual."

I nodded, trying to ignore the gnawing in my stomach as I looked at the fatigue that caused his eyes to droop. I squeezed his hand. "I got a new book at the bookstore."

"I'm guessing Stewy didn't annoy you too much this time?" he laughed weakly, and I watched as he leaned forward to cough.

My breath caught as he finally settled back. I ignored it, biting the inside of my lip before replying, "I came very close to telling him off, but his boss saved me."

Dad leaned back, wiggling his bare brows at me.

"Come on, Dad!"

"So he *was* hot."

I looked at the ceiling as I shook my head, warmth creeping up my limbs and to my face. "He bought me a coffee and a muffin."

"Oh, a gentlemen."

"I'm not going to talk to you about my love life," I replied wrinkling my nose at him as I ran my hands over the brown paper I wrapped the book in to hide the death-like cover.

"So what book did he suggest?" Dad asked, nodding to the covered book in my lap.

"You'll laugh," I cocked my head; "*Pride and Prejudice and Zombies.*"

"Zombies?" Dad repeated, his forehead creasing as his brow lifted into it. "You've got my attention."

"It's a funny twist on a classic— I'm surprised I like it," I replied.

I watched as Dad's eyes fluttered, and he winced as he sank deeper into the pillows behind him. "Read it to me?" he asked.

The lump formed in my throat making it impossible to swallow as I watched his rough breathing. I leaned over, kissing his forehead before replying in a whisper I wasn't sure he heard, "Of course."

I moved to sit in the chair beside him, and his hand found mine only going limp after he fell asleep. I closed the book slowly, my eyes washing over him. I put my head on the bed as the tears rushed over my cheeks, pooling beneath my hand as I cried silently against the beeping of the machines that monitored the weathered strings keeping him alive.

Every day was the same thing.

Trying to fight a losing battle.

Trying to ignore the death surrounding me.

Trying not to die inside for his sake.

I looked across the room to the picture of Mom and Dad, my lip trembling as fresh tears tumbled down my cheeks. When I got home, it would be to an empty house; one haunted with memories of happiness struck down by death once, and now, so close to destroying everything.

I stood, wiping my cheeks before leaning down and kissing his. "Love you, Daddy."

Chapter 3

I yawned as I rolled over, jolting awake as the book on my chest slammed onto the floor. I rubbed my eyes as I sat up, my body aching all over as I stood, grabbing a sweatshirt from my bedside chair and yanking it over my head. I headed to the door but stopped as I walked passed my mirror. I turned looking at myself.

I rubbed the dark circles under my eyes. I wasn't sure when I fell asleep, but I was sure of one thing I needed to go to the bookstore again. I glanced over at the clock, 9:00 AM. I stopped moving, my eyes glued to those numbers. I never slept that late; I usually wasn't able to sleep more than a few hours at a time. I ran my hand through my hair before grabbing a t-shirt and a pair of jeans and heading to the bathroom.

I took my time getting ready, because I didn't want to be the first one at the bookstore, and I wasn't even sure *he'd* be there...Nameless boy. I tapped my fingers on my steering wheel to the pop music I never listened to anymore. He wasn't nameless any more—Trent.

When I walked in the door he was standing at the registers leaning on his arm, and he smiled up at me.

"Don't tell me you finished it already?" he asked as he came around, stopping in front of me.

I laughed as I looked up at him. "Is there an alarm somewhere that says I'm coming in so you can greet me at the door?"

He smirked, placing the book he had in his hand on the bargain pile. I swallowed as I saw the cover— it was the one I had put there the day before to hide it from Stew.

"Not exactly," Trent said, leaning back on his heels as he looked at me.

"Wait," I narrowed my eyes at him. "Where you watching for me?"

He shook his head. "Not at all," he crossed his arms; "I have spidey senses."

"You don't look like a comic book guy," I replied, laughing at him.

"What kind of guy do I look like then?" he asked. "Should we get you breakfast while you analyze me?"

I fought against the smile on my lips, but gave in as we fell into step next to one another. "Did you eat yet?"

"I was waiting for you," Trent replied. "Same as yesterday?"

"Surprise me," I replied, watching as he walked around the counter.

"Don't look so shocked," he said as my jaw dropped. "I have to multitask." I blinked at him and he began to brew the coffee. "So what kind of guy am I?"

"Maybe it's the tattoos, but I see you more as the musician type."

"I guess you can judge a book by its cover," Trent commented. "So how was the book?"

I leaned against the counter, watching him as he skillfully steamed the milk. "I actually really liked it, and I think my dad enjoyed hearing something different."

I looked down at my hands, picking at the edge of my nail polish as I waited for him to question why a grown woman was reading to her Dad.

"So you live with your dad?" Trent asked, and my eyes rose to meet his. Today he was wearing a dark blue button up with the sleeves rolled up so I could see the artwork on his forearms. The color intensified his eyes as he slid the coffee across to me and he began to make his own.

I swallowed, looking down at the cup as I tried to figure out what to say. It was an easy question, but it was still difficult to answer. "Not exactly."

He looked over at me, his eyes racing over my face, but he didn't press the subject. "Well," he began, grabbing a scone and handing it to me and then grabbing his coffee and scone before coming back around to me. "There's another one; *Sense and Sensibility and Sea Monsters.* It's by the same author."

"I'll take it," I replied as we sat down on the stools.

"Don't let me forget to get it for you before you leave."

I bit into the scone, and leaned back in the chair as the frosting and cranberries melted into my tongue. "This is amazing."

"It's my favorite," Trent explained.

"So," I asked between a sip of perfectly brewed coffee. "Are you going to give me one book a day?"

He paused, the coffee cup covering the smile on his lips but it reached his eyes, making them wrinkle at the edges. My heart hammered in my chest as I waited for him to answer. "I assume you don't always stay up all night reading."

I shrugged, cocking my head at him. "Sometimes I sleep."

His eyes dropped down to his coffee as he placed it make down on the table. "Is this like the other sometimes?"

My lips suddenly felt parched, and I found myself looking around the store. I shook my head, "No, I sleep. I'm not that crazy."

Trent leaned forward, his gaze locked on me again. "I didn't mean it like that."

I looked down at the now empty napkin, smeared with spots of left over frosting. "Just making sure," I whispered.

He coughed, and my eyes went back to his face. "I like to think I can read people pretty easily. I don't think you're crazy...I think you're a private person—much like myself."

I clenched my jaw, rubbing the back of my neck. "So that book?" I reminded him.

"Oh, yeah," he said standing. I hopped off the chair, and he smiled over his shoulder at me.

"What? You think it's funny I'm short and have to hop off your chairs made for giants?"

He put his hands up. "No, not at all," he replied with a smirk. "I actually think it's kind of cute."

I stopped walking and he turned to face me. "Are you trying to inflate my ego?"

He widened his eyes, crossing his arms so my eyes moved to his flexing forearms. "No," he shook his head; "that's big enough as it is."

I blinked at him. "Don't get me started. Tight t-shirts and now a button-up...those tattoos. You're the one with the inflated ego— all mystery and smoldering hotness."

He smirked down at me, grabbing a book from the shelf without looking at it and handing it to me. "So you think I'm mysterious and hot?"

A tingle crept across my neck and to my face. *Did I really just say that?*

A group of girls walked in, looking over at Trent and me and immediately burst into giggles.

I nodded towards them. "They sure do."

His jaw tightened. "They're also ten minutes late for their shift."

"Uh oh, hot boss is all angry," I teased, walking passed him and knocking shoulders with him. "Now are you going to check me out like they were checking you out?"

Trent caught up to me, reaching over and grabbing the book from my hand as he slipped passed me. His eyes ran up and down my body. "Checked out, now would you like to purchase this book or continue making my employees jealous?"

I leaned over the counter, pushing my chest up. "I think jealous is more fun."

He looked over my shoulder at them and the smile slipped away. "You know they're always trying to figure me out. It gets tiring."

"Maybe they're just trying to figure out why you haven't asked any of them out yet, when they're fluttering their eyelashes at you and talking sweetly."

Trent scanned the book. "How do you know they do that?"

"I've seen it."

"Well, there's an easy explanation for why I haven't, besides the fact I'm their boss— I'm just not interested."

My mind raced over the many reasons he wouldn't be interested. I swiped my card, concentrating on entering my pin as I managed to ask, "Already have a girlfriend?"

The sound of the receipt printing echoed throughout the store, and I cringed at the sound of it against the silence where his answer should be.

"You could've just asked me that instead of bringing them into it," he replied as he tucked the receipt into the book and handed it to me.

"Answer the question, Mr. Mystery," I shot back, grabbing the book.

"You got it wrong, it's Mr. *Smoldering* Mystery to you El," Trent replied, leaning over the counter.

My heart pounding in my chest as I bite my lip.

Trent's eyes slipped down to my lips before he replied, "No girlfriend."

"So do they talk behind your back?" I asked as I leaned forward towards him. I narrowed my eyes. "What's the juicy gossip on you?"

"Well, there are rumors I'm in the mob."

I snorted as I laughed at him and his eyes widened. "It's that bad boy exterior, but I think you have a heart of gold beneath those perfect pecks."

"Or," he replied, dragging out the word. "I'm just a mobster with perfect pecks."

"And I'm a Russian spy."

He pointed a finger at me as he stood up. "You cover your accent well."

I cleared my throat, standing and putting my shoulders back as I narrowed my eyes at him and tried on a Russian accent. "I have caught zu admitting zur illicit activities. Zurrender now."

We burst out laughing again, and he shook his head. "Oh, man, you suck at that."

I shrugged. "Well, you suck at being a mobster!"

Trent scratched the back of his neck. "I guess I should get back to my real job, seeing I suck so badly at being a mobster...and before one of my employees tackles you for flirting with their hot boss."

I rolled my eyes. "There's that inflated ego again."

He walked passed me, leaning down to whisper in my ear. "Will I see you tomorrow?"

The feel of his breath on my neck sent shivers down my spine. I looked at him through my bags. "Do you want to?"

He winked at me. "I'll see you tomorrow, Ellie."

"Wait," I replied, stopping him in his tracks. "I have to hang out with some college buddies tomorrow."

His eyes faded, looking passed me as he pursed his lips and nodded. "Well, let me know if you like the book."

I stared at his back as he disappeared into the stacks of books, and the high his presence created faded.

I had enough emotional strife in my life, why was I adding more to it by falling for this guy?

Chapter 4

I dropped the mascara into my makeup bag, looking down at my watch to see what time it was. Erica would be here any minute now. She was always the timely one, and unfortunately, also the one I could stand the least. My pulse quickened as I made my way down the three steps in to the living room. I pulled open the curtains, dust pluming off of them as the room filled with light. I dropped onto the couch, leaning my head back against the pillows before finally deciding to turn the television on. I couldn't remember the last time I actually turned the thing on. I flicked through the channels, looking down my nose at the screen until I settled on the home shopping network. There was nothing on anyways. I chewed the inside of my lip as I looked at the book sitting on the coffee table. It only took me two hours to finish this one.

My mind drifted back to Trent, and his dismissive attitude when I said I was doing something today. My eyes wandered over the room, reminding me of exactly why Dad wasn't here and how crappy he looked. The doorbell rang, and I jumped as my heart pounded, the sound rushing through my ears.

"Ellie!" Erica squealed as I opened the door. She tackled me into a hug that crunched my spine.

"Miss me much?" I asked, my face tightening with the fake smile as I laughed awkwardly and closed the door behind her.

"Yes!" Erica said, clapping her hands before flipping over the back of the couch and staring up at me. "So Andrea and Morgan are going to be here in a few minutes, but I have no idea what we're going to do! Did you have any plans?"

I shook my head, holding my arms to my side as I stared down at her. She was more comfortable in my home than I was. She looked at the ceiling, her hair spread out behind her and draping over the side of the couch.

"Your hair looks nice," I finally said.

She spun around, patting the seat next to her and looking over her shoulder. "Blonde totally fits me, right?"

"Sure does," I replied, running my fingers through my own honey blonde hair.

"I wish it was natural like yours, though." She pouted before her eyes drifted passed mine to the window and widened. "Oh! They're here!"

I opened the door as Andrea hopped out of her Jeep, linking arms with Morgan as she came around the car.

"Hey!" Andrea said, pulling me into a hug when she reached me. "You look so good! I love, love your outfit!"

"Thanks," I replied, wondering if Morgan's hug would be the one to break one of my ribs.

"You and your skinny jeans!" Morgan added, and I cringed as she hugged me, waiting for a crack. When she pulled away I was happy I could still breathe. "You were honestly made for them! My hips are just way too big to rock them."

I rolled my eyes as I looked at her. She was curvy with thick brown curls that cascaded over her shoulders, enhancing her perfect caramel skin.

"I'm sure you could pull them off," I replied, shutting the door behind them. Morgan sat down on the coffee table across from Andrea and Erica.

Morgan blinked at me, shaking her head. "They're called skinny jeans for a reason, El."

"By the way," Erica said, turning and looking at me standing at the door still. "That shirt makes you look—" she used her hands to signal to my chest. "Nice."

"Like seriously, El, how do you stay in such fabulous shape?" Andrea asked as I finally sat down on the armchair, pulling my knees to my chest.

"I forget to eat."

They all laughed. "You're so silly!" Erica said.

I sucked my lower lip in as I looked at my hands, running my fingers over the holes on my knees. "Yeah, I'm always the comic."

"So!" Andrea began, flipping her straight black hair over her shoulder. "What are we doing today?"

"I've got an idea," Morgan said, looking around the room and pausing for effect. "Go get coffee at the bookstore down the street."

My head shot up. "Bookstore?"

Morgan leaned forward, "Yeah," she dragged her teeth over her lower lip. "I had to go in at the beginning of the semester to pick up a book, and there's this totally hot guy working there."

"You think he still works there? It's been months since you last went there," I pointed out, my mouth drying as I thought of going to the store with them in tow.

"I drove passed this morning. He was totally there," Morgan replied.

"That solves it!" Erica stood up. "I haven't had a date a while!"

"What's a while?" I shot back, grabbing my purse and following them out.

"Nope!" Morgan said, turning and walking backwards in front of us as she dangled her keys in our faces. "I called dibs by mentioning it!"

I slid into the backseat of the jeep, grinding my teeth as I looked at the three girls. What if one of them was more Trent's type? I cringed. "How do you know he doesn't already have a girlfriend?"

Andrea glanced over at me, fluttering her eyelashes. "That doesn't mean anything, and" she glanced at the other girls; "as for dibs, I say whoever gets the guts up to flirt with him first wins."

"I'm in!" Morgan and Erica answered in unison as I stared at the stitching of my purse. I rolled down the window, feeling hot even though I had a skimpy blue tank top on. At least I looked good right now. I let the breeze rush through my hair as the girls sang along to the song on the radio. I didn't know the words, but I put my hand out the window and let it tap to the beat. When we got to the bookstore I froze, staring at the door.

"Ladies, let the games begin!" Morgan called as she jumped out of the car. She waited for me to get out, linking arms with me and leaning over to whisper. "This guy is gorgeous—all smoldering musician hotness."

I laughed. "I'm sure he is."

"Don't you come here a lot being a literature major and all?" Morgan asked as she held the door open for me.

I shrugged, trying to keep the smirk off my face as Trent's eyes slowly rose from the person he was cashing out at the register to me. His lips twitched at their edges, hinting at a smile before he handed the bag of books to his customer. He leaned back on his heels, sticking his hands in his back pockets as he looked from me to the other girls around me.

"I'll do it," Erica commented, fluffing her hair.

"Do what?" I asked, turning to face her.

She looked over my shoulder at Trent, narrowing her eyes at him. "I'll talk to him."

She pulled out a lip gloss, smearing the goo over her lips. I glanced over my shoulder as dizziness set in. I wasn't sure if it was because I hadn't eaten or the panic that was coming over me. Trent moved to the bargain books and was organizing the titles; he looked over from the corner of his eye before continuing to ignore us.

What if he likes her? What if he hates me for bringing them here?

"What are you going to say?" I asked looking back at Erica.

We were exact opposites, and I stuck my tongue in my cheek as I wondered what he would like better. She was busty, all soft curves and butterflies, while I was all hard edges and raw scars that never got the chance to heal. I was pretty sure I would pick posies over rose thorns.

She leaned over, whispering in my ear. "If he knows any good sex books."

My eyes widened as my jaw dropped, and I had to reach for the bookshelf to steady myself. Trent looked up at me, his eyebrows drawing together as I fought the nausea rolling over me. Maybe she was butterflies and fifty shades of slutty.

"He's already checking me out," Erica whispered to me before sauntering over to him.

I squeezed my fists at my sides as I fought the urge to rush out the door and never return. I watched as Trent listened to what Erica was saying. His lips remained in a solid line as he nodded and then signaled to the other side of the store. Erica smirked over at me, giving a thumbs-up as she followed him.

I wanted to melt into the bookshelf. What had I done in a past life to deserve this?

"Erica might be making a move on smolder, but I," Andrea commented, waving her cell phone in my face; "got rebel without a causes' phone number."

"Who?" I asked, laughing at her.

She nodded over her shoulder to the guy manning the coffee bar. His black hair hung in his eyes, curling around his ears in surfer curls. Visible tattoos crawled up his arms, disappearing under his t-shirt sleeves and reappearing at his neck.

"You don't think that's a bit much?" I asked, scratching my neck. "Maybe...like just a little?"

Her chest rose as she stared at him, shaking her foggy eyes. "Hell no, I want to know where else they go."

My eyes crossed as I gagged. "Seriously?"

"Well," she asked, running her fingers over the books and pretending to read the back of one. "When was the last time you got laid?"

My hand moved too quickly over a book and I swore as my finger burned. I stuck my finger into my mouth sucking on it.

"That long?" Andrea asked, smirking at me and holding out a book. "You might need one of these."

I hit the book out of her hand and flopped back onto the shelf.

"Wow, a really long time," Andrea continued, crossing her arms at me. She nodded behind me, and I turned to see Erica sulking back.

I was glad to change the subject from me. "Didn't go well?"

Erica sighed. "Turns out he has a girlfriend. He wouldn't stop talking about how beautiful she is."

My pulse sped up, and I felt heat wrapping its way out of my belly to my limbs.

He lied.

I was an idiot. Just like the friends who adopted me in my freshmen year of college.

"Actually," Erica commented, cocking her head at me. "She sounded a lot like you, El—but he said she reads a lot, and you don't do you?"

Morgan rounded the corner with several books in hand, and I wondered if she really wanted to come to the store to see Trent, or if she needed books. She held them to her chest as she looked from me to Erica and Andrea. "Do either of you pay attention at all?" she asked.

Erica leaned back, crossing her arms as she looked at Morgan. "What?"

Morgan rolled her eyes. "Ellie is a *literary* major—historic, I think, with a minor in graphic design."

I nodded; flustered by the fact Morgan knew my major and had nailed it to down to the historical part.

"That means books, right?" Andrea asked as her and Erica shared a blank expression.

"No," I snapped. "It means I'm studying to be an astronaut."

"Whoa!" Erica threw her hands up. "Take the bitch down a notch."

"She hasn't been laid in a while," Andrea commented, and my back straightened as I felt someone standing behind me.

"You finish the book I gave you yesterday?" Trent's voice cracked into my skull, and the girls' eyes widened as they stared at him behind me.

I turned slowly, looking up at him.

He leaned against the bookshelf, staring down at me as he tapped his fingers against the wood. His brows rose expectantly.

"Yeah," I replied, breathless.

He ran his tongue over his teeth. "I figured as much, so I picked this one out for you this time."

He handed me a book, and I mouthed the word *sorry*. His chest rose with a silent laugh, and I narrowed my eyes at him.

"You all set?" Trent asked Morgan, looking at the books in her hand.

"Sure," she replied, the book covers hidden by her arms.

"You know him?" Erica hissed at me as we followed Morgan to the register.

"Maybe," I replied.

"Why didn't you say you were dating him?" Erica practically spit at me.

"I'm not!" I hissed back. "Just because he recommends me books doesn't mean I know his life story."

"So he didn't tell you he had a girlfriend?" Erica asked, her frown tipping up into a smirk.

I grit my teeth as I shook my head, stepping up so Trent could cash me out.

"So," he said as the girls walked away. "They don't seem like a group you fit into."

I looked at the ceiling, letting the breath I had been holding out. "You're telling me."

"Do you have to hang out with them again anytime soon?"

"I haven't figured out a way to avoid it since my freshmen year...and I'm almost done with college, so you tell me."

He handed me the book, receipt tucked into it. "You should stand up for yourself more often."

"Then I'd have no friends at all."

Trent looked over my shoulder and then back to me. "Just because you tolerate them doesn't make them your friends."

I looked over my shoulder at them.

Maybe he was right.

Chapter
5

I walked up the steps of the hospital with my new book in tow. I hadn't even looked at it to see what it was, but I was sure from Trent's previous picks it would be good. I needed a good alternate reality to lose myself in after today. We drove into Phoenix after the bookstore, heading to the Arizona Mills outlet to look for something for Andrea's date with Tattoos. The superficial conversation left me feeling empty, and Trent's words echoed in my mind, making me wonder if I ever had real friends at any point in my life.

I was pretty sure I hadn't. We moved around so much for Dad's jobs that once we settled, and I found a group to fit into, we were picking up and leaving. No one ever stayed in touch. When I reached Dad's room I flopped on the chair next to his bed.

He pursed his lips at me as he sat up. "How was your day, honey?"

I looked at the ceiling, blowing my bangs out of my face. "Don't ask."

Dad ran his hands over his bald head as he looked at me. "Something go wrong with the girlfriends?"

I sighed, leaning forward and kissing his cheek. "I'm just wondering about the *friends* part of that." I looked down at my hands before letting my gaze meet his serious one. "They're all pretty self-involved. It's easier to get along with them during school because we don't actually talk that much."

"Most people your age are pretty self-involved," he replied, squeezing my hand and cocking his head. "Not many have to deal with the things you have."

"You know I've never been good at keeping friends."

Dad licked his lips, his eyes drifting as he considered his words. "El, do you think it might be superficial because that's all you allow? You don't let people in."

"I don't think I'd want to let these girls in," I said, breathing in through my nose before continuing. "Erica dyed her hair the same color as mine...and apparently the dye went to her head...At any rate, Morgan brought up the idea of going to the bookstore."

"Uh oh."

I nodded, leaning forward and tangling my hands in my hair. "Apparently, she thought Trent was really cute, so then it became some sort of bizarre competition to see who could get a date first."

"Blondie has new confidence?" Dad assumed, and I narrowed my eyes at him.

"It's not funny!"

"It kind of is," Dad replied. "I'm not sure what competition it was with you wearing...uh...that."

I pulled the front of the tank top up, the ruffle traveling down the middle fluttering with the action. "Dad!"

"It's not skanky or anything...just a little low cut."

"That's beside the point— Erica asked him where the *sex* books were!"

Dad burst out laughing, and I stuck my chin out. "Oh, sorry... not funny...at all."

"It gets better."

"Ha — this is good."

"I'm glad you're getting amusement from my suffering—"

"Sorry, continue," he said, gathering himself and putting his hand over his mouth to hide his smirk.

"Andrea and I were standing talking, and she asked me when the last time I got laid was—and Trent walked up behind us!"

Dad leaned forward as he started laughing again. "This is better than television."

"Dad!" I snapped, standing and slapping him softly. "You shouldn't find this funny."

"It is...besides the part where you're talking about getting laid. I don't need to know about that," Dad snorted.

One of the nurses walked in. "Laughter is the best kind of medicine," she said as she handed Dad a cup with pills in it and a glass of water. "But...you should take it easy. No overdosing."

"Not possible," Dad retorted, and I rolled my eyes as he smiled at the nurse. Dad held his arm out for the nurse to check his blood pressure. "Probably a bit high...El, I mean come on. If this girl has to ask for a sex book, how good could Trent actually think she is? Not exactly the best pick up line in any book."

The nurse burst out laughing, and I put my head in my hands as my face burned.

He did not just say that!

I looked up when silence finally filled the room and crossed my arms as I sunk back into the chair.

"Old man still has a sense of humor!" the nurse commented, patting him on the back. "Everything looks good. We're on track to start physical therapy tomorrow. I hope you're ready!"

"I'm not *that* old," he fired back, winking at her as she placed her stethoscope back around her neck.

"Of course not, Paul. Tomorrow," she said, pointing from her eyes to his. "You and me. You'll be back on your feet soon."

He nodded at her. "Thanks to you...and my girl here."

The nurse squeezed my shoulder as she walked by. "Laughter is the best cure."

"So..." Dad began, cocking his head at me. "What's bugging you so much about this, besides the superficial?"

I looked down at my sneakers, bouncing on the tip of my toes. "What if he thinks less of me because I'm friends with them?"

"He saw you with them, right?" I nodded. "Then I'm sure he knows. You wear your emotions on your sleeve. I guarantee he could see you don't exactly fit in with them."

"So I should go back?"

His lips curved up to one side, and he gave a slow nod.

"Okay."

"Now," he said, looking at the bag at my feet. "What's tonight's read?"

I grabbed the bag, sliding the book out. My mouth dropped open. "No shit."

Dad reached over and took the book I'd hid from Stew, his own jaw going slack before he started cracking up again. "A bit risqué, huh?"

He held the book up, and I grabbed it, pushing it down into my lap cover down. "He..." I shook my head. "I'm going to give him hell tomorrow."

Dad reached for it again, stealing it back.

"Dad! Seriously!"

He opened the front cover and turned it so I could see the inside. There, written in a half cursive scribble, was a phone number with an arrow →

Don't judge a book by its cover, or its friends.

Trent.

Chapter
6

I parked in front of the bookstore, tapping my fingers against the steering wheel of my Subaru as I stared at the door.

You promised Dad. I reminded myself. *After this song is done.*

I closed my eyes, continuing to tap my fingers to the beat, my feet joining the symphony. I had been listening to a lot of pop that last few days, channeling my anxious energy towards something happy. I was usually a metal only girl, but the pop seemed to be taking away some of the edge I always had about me. It was hard to be miserable when Adam Levine was serenading you. As the final lyrics I knew by heart came to an end my pulse rushed in my ears, and I let my eyes slowly open.

You can do this.

In my anxiety over the way the girls acted and the fact I realized I had no valuable relationships, I had forgotten that Trent told Andrea he had a girlfriend. I swallowed as I grabbed my purse and got out of the car. I needed to figure out if this was some kind of game, or if Trent's attention to me was all in my head. I pushed my shoulders back and took a deep breath before heading to the door. I paused when I got there, my hand frozen on the metal warmed by the morning sun.

You can do this.

I breathed the dry air into my lungs before stepping into the air conditioned building. Despite having lived all over the US, I enjoyed the heat of Arizona the most. Dry heat was much easier to deal with than the humidity of Florida, and I was never a fan of the stale air AC systems produced. I paused in the front, quickly assessing the store. Trent was at the front, kneeling down as he grabbed some books from the return rack. I was caught off guard by the way his jeans pulled perfectly around his ass and the shape of his back muscles against the tight t-shirt.

Stop staring.

I shook my head as I turned to the bargain section of cookbooks. I concentrated on rifling through them, but the thought of Trent didn't leave my mind.

Cookbooks, El. Cookbooks.

There always seemed to be a plethora of them on clearance, and I wondered how good they could be if the store was always selling them at cost. I picked a slow cooker one up and flipped through the pages.

"You cook?" Trent's voice echoed behind me, and I bit the inside of my lip to keep from smiling as I turned to face him.

He leaned against the shelf behind us, one leg crossed behind the other as he smirked down at me. He was never completely shaved, and today was no exception. It was amazing to me that overnight he seemed to have grown twice as much facial hair as yesterday.

I shook my head slowly, the book still in my hand.

He nodded to it. "Then why are you looking at a really bad cookbook? *Fifty Shades of Crock Pottery?*"

I looked down at it, my heart hammering as I glanced back up at him, cocking my head. "I was interested in how you hog tie a chicken."

Trent burst out laughing. "You seem to be in a much better mood today."

I put the book down, staring at it for a moment. "I'm glad you're still talking to me after yesterday."

I watched Trent step forward, tipping on his toes as he put his thumbs in his pockets. "Why wouldn't I be?"

I swallowed. "You have some time to talk?"

He nodded. "Follow me."

We walked to the back corner of the store, where there was a 'hidden' nook with a loveseat and several other comfy looking chairs. It was meant for those customers who wanted to read a few chapters before purchasing.

Trent sat down on the loveseat, patting the cushion next to him. My stomach fluttered as I stared at the space next to him. His smile softened and he moved over a bit more. I sat down next to him, and turned, pulling my knees up to sit Indian style. He put an arm over the back of the seat, his fingertips inches from my shoulder.

"So what's up?"

"I'm sorry about the way my friends were yesterday...hitting on you and such."

He looked down at his lap, pressing his lips together before looking up at me. "Is that what they were doing?"

"You found it amusing?"

He shrugged, tapping the couch with his fingers. "I found your jealousy more amusing."

My body tingled, and I had to control the shudder threatening to move through my body as his fingertips grazed my shoulder.

"Jealousy?"

He nodded slowly, pursing his lips as if he knew exactly what I was thinking. "It was all over your face."

My chin tucked in as I narrowed my eyes at him. "What does your girlfriend think about this?"

"This?" Trent repeated. "What exactly are you referring to?"

"You sending me home with a kinky book with your number written in it!"

Trent scratched his chin, his eyes moving to the books behind me. "Oh, that. Did you read the book?"

I shook my head. "I was mortified! My dad saw it!"

He leaned closer to me, his arm flexing against the back of the couch. "You judged it by its cover."

I leaned in. "I wasn't going to risk reading it to my dad with a cover like that."

Trent nodded, his arms going into his lap. He flipped them over. "Would you risk bringing the bad boy home to your dad?"

I followed his eyes up from his tattoos to mine. "Bad boy would have to not have a girlfriend."

He shook his head. "I don't."

"Then why—?"

"I had to get that chick off my back somehow."

"Ahh," I said, tapping my fingers against my ankles before looking up at him. "I don't know how I've spent so much time with those girls. I...I just don't have many valuable relationships...or any, honestly."

"You're obviously close to your dad," Trent commented, his hands moving forward and falling over my fidgeting ones.

"Yeah...but I guess I never really thought about the relationships I have with other people. They never last that long, but the one with those girls has been almost three years. It's a record...still, I always feel lonely around them, like I'm a shadow in their presence."

Trent's hands stayed over mine, their warmth spreading up my arms and heating my face. "Are you lonely now?"

I smiled, shaking my head. "No, it's nice."

His eyes raced over my face. "I'm glad to hear that. So you're still in college?"

"Yeah," I replied, leaning on my free hand. "I've been going full-time all semesters for the past three years. This summer I decided I needed a break."

Trent's eyes widened. "That's a lot of work, but I'm glad you decided to give yourself a break."

I shrugged. "I wanted to—" I swallowed as the words caught in my throat *spend time with dad before... there's no time.*

Trent cocked his head. "What?"

"It's complicated," I finally managed to say.

He looked down at his watch, moving it back and forth over his wrist. "I get complicated. Uh—so what's your major?"

"Historic literature."

"What are you going to do with that?"

I shook my head. "God only knows. I have a minor in graphic design, so maybe I can do something with that. I do a lot of photography and painting...artsy stuff, about as useful as my major, I guess."

"I'm sure you could find something in graphic design."

I shrugged. "I don't know that I like the idea of being stuck in a high rise in Phoenix."

He smirked, his lips twitching, and I narrowed my eyes at him. "You'd look good in a pencil skirt."

I rolled my eyes. "So what about you? Are you in college?"

"Nah. I already have a bachelors in management, and here I am...managing a bookstore," he answered, his jaw clenching. It relaxed into a smile as he said, "Not a fan of being stuck in a high rise in Phoenix."

I smirked at him, and he narrowed his eyes. "You'd look killer in a suit and tie."

We both laughed, our eyes locking on one another. It faded as our heads leaned towards one another. Trent's hand found my cheek, and I closed my eyes breathing in deeply as his warmth spread over me. My phone ringing caused us to pull apart, and I looked down at it as Trent leaned forward, raking his hands through his hair and entwining his fingers at his neck. I felt his eyes turn to me as I started down at the phone.

"Ellie?" he asked as I felt the blood drain from my face, and my body went numb. "Ellie?"

My body snapped into action as I jumped up, picking the phone up and running towards the door.

"Ellie Abela?" the voice on the other end said.

I made some sort of choking noise in response as I pushed the door to the store open and rushed to my car.

"You need to come now," the nurse said.

The choking noise repeated as I fumbled with my keys. I dropped my phone on the seat before jamming the key into the ignition. I looked up to see Trent standing at the door, holding it open as he stared at me. I shook my head, the tears streaming down my cheeks as I slammed the car into reverse and then sped out of the parking lot.

Chapter
7

Three days.

Three days of silent Hell. I found no comfort in the steady beeping of the machines surrounding Dad. They signaled he was alive but just barely. His heart beat was slow—too slow, they said. The nurses came and went reassuring me if anyone could pull him out of this, it was me. They all knew who I was and guilt rolled in my stomach as I realized I barely knew one of their names. For months they had been keeping him alive, and I barely knew their names to thank them.

In that moment I was too much of a zombie to try to memorize each of them. I hadn't left the hospital in three days, and I barely left his side. I watched him now, pale with lines running into his arms and monitors hooked up to him in too many places. He was supposed to start physical therapy, but the chemo treatment he'd had that day had knocked him on his ass. The fatigue was so much he hadn't woken up at all. His eyes fluttered across his cheeks, and I leaned forward, squeezing his hand. Words failed to come out of my mouth.

"Ellie? Is that you?" he murmured, and I put my head on his chest. His hand raised and slowly patted my back. "Woohee, that last round was tiring."

I nodded into his chest as the tears rushed down my cheek onto his white gown.

"Ellie, look at me," Dad ordered and I followed. His shaking hands cupped my face. "You look like a ghost, honey—so pale and drained."

I closed my eyes, my chest rising with a pained laugh. "You should talk, Daddy."

He moved my bangs away from my forehead, pressing his lips against them before I sat back in my chair.

"How many days?" he asked.

I held up my fingers, still struggling to speak.

"Is that how long it's been since you've been home?"

I nodded.

He wrinkled his nose. "I could tell. You should go home and sleep in your own bed...and shower."

I rolled my eyes. "I do not smell."

His eyes widened at me. "That's what woke me up."

I laughed, shaking my head in my hands. "You're insane," I said, my nose and eyes tingling.

"Paul," the nurse said, coming in the room. "You're up!"

Dad nodded. "Just trying to get my daughter to go home and relax."

"I'm not leaving until the doctor comes in and says you'll be okay."

Dad locked eyes with the nurse, and she smiled. It was the same nurse who had come in when Dad was making perverted jokes last week. She nodded over her shoulder, saying, "I'll go see if he's available."

"I'm going to the bathroom," I explained. "But I'm coming right back."

"Brush your teeth while you're in there," Dad joked, and I looked at the ceiling before walking out of the room.

When I returned the doctor was already in the room.

"Ah! Ellie, your father is doing quite well right now," he said, closing the chart and putting at the end of the bed. "His heart rate is much stronger, and his other vitals are showing recovery." He looked up at me and frowned, stepping forward. "I'd like to speak to you privately, though. Step outside the room with me?"

I tried to inhale, but the air caught in my throat as I nodded. I stepped outside, putting my cold hand to my forehead to keep myself from fainting.

Here comes the day count.

Dr. Williams placed his hands in his pockets, pursing his lips before he spoke, "Listen, Ellie, your father has expressed some concerns, and I can see he may be correct about feeling the way he does."

I opened my mouth, but no words came out. I could hear my heart pounding as I stared at Dr. Williams' brown eyes, framed by serious gray eyebrows.

"I'm not sure I understand where you're going with this," I finally managed to say.

"You look as if you're having some difficulties yourself. Your weight is a bit low for someone your size. The nurses told me you haven't eaten since you've been here. This sort of situation is extremely stressful, and being anxious or depressed is completely natural. We can help you with that," he said, taking a pad out of his pocket and clicking his pen. "This is a prescription for a moderate anti-depressant. It should help with some of those things. I also think counseling would be a good idea."

I put my hand up, blocking the paper. "No, no, I'll be fine. We've been dealing with this for years."

Dr. Williams sucked in his lower lip before continuing, "We all deal with these things differently, but your father is right in saying that if you continue like this...he won't be the only one in the hospital. You're weak, Ellie. It will do your father no good if you're sick as well. You need to take care of yourself for *him.*"

I nodded, pursing my lips as I controlled the tears threatening to pour from my eyes yet again. *Stop, being selfish,* was what I was hearing. I took the prescription he pushed into my hand.

"Your father will be fine. You should go home—sleep, take a relaxing bath—but most importantly eat. Do something that makes you happy, takes your mind off of this. Your happiness is the best medicine for your father—for any father, a daughter's happiness is the greatest cure."

I looked down at the scribbles that said *Zoloft.* "Thank you, Dr. Williams."

I watched him walk away, my eyes following him over my shoulder. I tucked the prescription in my back pocket and went back to Dad. He was looking down at his hands, a guilty expression tugging at the edge of his lips as his concerned eyes met mine.

"So," I said, sitting on the edge of his bed. "You're tattling on me now."

He grimaced, his eyes darting away from me. "I know you get so wrapped up in worrying about me that you forget yourself, but you can't, Ellie." He put his hand over mine.

"Yeah, I know," I whispered.

"Go home, El."

I leaned forward and kissed him. "Love you."

"Love you more, princess," he replied.

I stood, turning at the door and he smiled. "Call him."

Chapter 8

I stared at the book, the number sitting there as a perfect taunt. Dad wanted me to call him. I looked at my cell phone; it was kind of late. I looked at the ceiling as I fell back on my bed.

Nine wasn't really *that* late.

I sat up, dialing the number. I kept my eyes closed as I counted the rings. *He's not going to pick up.* Just as I was about to give up, he answered.

"Hey, I'm sorry to call so late—"

"Ellie?"

"Yeah."

"It's not late—how are you? What happened?"

I ran my hand through my greasy hair. I hadn't showered yet.

"Something came up," I replied as my stomach rolled.

"I kind of got that. Where are you now?"

"Home."

"When was the last time you ate?"

"I...Ummm..."

"That long?"

"Trent—"

"Where do you live?"

"Sunrise Circle," I replied.

"Number?"

"1020."

"My sister is asleep, so I'll see if my neighbor can come over for a bit to make sure she doesn't wake up," Trent explained, and I heard the jingling of his keys.

"No—Trent, you don't—"

"I'll be there in half an hour. You like pizza?"

"Trent—"

"What toppings?"

"Hawaiian," I caved.

"See you soon, El."

I put my phone down, staring at the screen as it went black. I looked down at myself before shooting up. I needed to change—no, I needed to shower.

Trent was coming over.

Now.

Holy shit.

I went to my closet, ripping shirts off their hangers. I didn't want to look like I was trying too hard, after all, it was nine. Nine twenty five now.

Crap. Just pick something.

I grabbed a black t-shirt, pulling it off the hanger and the first pair of pants out of my drawer. *Yoga pants?* My phone buzzed on my bed.

Trent - Be there in twenty.

I squeezed my eyes shut before bolting out of the room and going to the bathroom. When the door bell rang I had just pulled my hair into a messy pony tail at the top of my head.

"Hey," I said opening the door. I was greeted by the strong smell of pizza and Trent's warm smile.

"Hey," he said, looking down at my shirt. "Parkway Drive?"

I closed the door behind him, and we settled on the couch. "Yeah, they're one of my favorite bands."

"No shit," Trent said as he opened the box and handed me a slice. "I wouldn't have pegged you for a metal girl."

I bit into the pizza, leaning back into the cushions as the cheese hit my tongue. "What kind of girl did you peg me as?"

He shrugged as he chewed. "Something more calming...Nick Jonas or something."

I raised an eyebrow. "Hell no. I do like Maroon 5, though."

"Now, I can see that..." he looked down at his pizza, smirking.

I elbowed him. "You like them too!"

He laughed. "You caught me."

Silence filled the room as I finished my piece and Trent handed me a bottle of soda.

"Thanks for doing this," I said after I took a sip.

"So..." he said, rubbing his hands over the top of his jeans and looking over his shoulder at me."Are you going to tell me why you disappeared?"

I stared at the soda as I screwed the cap back on.

"I get if it's private, El...But you had me worried."

I locked eyes on him. "My dad...he's sick. Cancer."

"Is he okay right now?" Trent asked, putting his hand on my knee.

I breathed in through my nose, putting my hand over his. "Yeah, for now."

"I'm sorry," Trent whispered, and I looked up at him before leaning in and letting him wrap his arms around me. He put his hand on the back of my neck, pulling me tighter into his embrace, and I let his cologne drift over my senses, fogging them.

"Every day I wake up wondering if he'll be okay...if this will be the day they tell me he can't take any more treatments...that there's no reason to fight anymore."

Trent nodded. "You shouldn't have to deal with this all alone."

I pulled away, and Trent slipped his hand into mine. "There's no one else...my mom was killed in a car accident by a drunk driver when I was sixteen."

"I get it...it's just my sister and I. My mom has drug issues, and my dad left right after Allie was born. When I turned twenty one I fought my mom to get custody of Allie...Then we moved as far away as we possibly could. She was just two. I know it's not the same, El—but I do get where you're coming from in a way."

"You're a lot braver than I am," I replied, looking down at our hands. "I can barely take care of myself, let alone anyone else."

Trent's hand tilted my chin. "You're just as brave, El."

"No, you're strong...truly strong."

"I try to look like it," he responded. "I just did what I had to do."

"My dad told the doctor to give me a speech about my eating habits," I admitted, leaning forward and taking another piece of pizza.

Trent grabbed another piece himself. "Tell your dad I'm going to fatten you up."

I laughed through a full mouth. "If you bring me pizza on a regular basis I will be."

"So tomorrow, why don't we have a real date?" Trent asked.

I looked over my shoulder at him, smiling. "I'd like that."

"My place, some real cooking and a movie?"

"I'd like that," I replied.

Trent finished his soda, looking down at his watch.

"You should go," I commented, seeing it showed it was ten thirty. "I'm sure your sister will be upset if she wakes up and finds your neighbor is there and not you."

"Are you sure you'll be okay?" he asked, cocking his head.

"Yeah," I replied. "This really helped. Thanks."

He wrapped his arms around me when we reached his truck, and I closed my eyes as I breathed him in, memorizing the comfort he wrapped me in. He pulled away, kissing my forehead. "I'll text you my address. How does tomorrow at eight sound? My sister will have gone to bed, so it can just be us."

"Sounds good," I replied, my heart beating hard in my chest as he stared down at me. I gave him a smile and finally pulled away as my brain clicked back on, telling me that logically, he wasn't going to kiss me, and I wasn't brave enough to do it myself. I waved as he got into his truck, and he winked at me, waiting to pull into the street until I had the door to the house open. I closed it behind me, pressing the back of my head against it as I shut my eyes. I pulled my lips into my mouth as I breathed in through my nose. The calm left me and I found myself squealing before dropping onto the couch and pulling the blanket over me. I stared at my phone; suddenly wishing one of my girlfriends was someone I could share this moment with.

I shook the thought from my head as I sunk deeper into the couch and turned the television on.

I couldn't wait to tell Dad.

Chapter 9

"Wow!" Dad said, rubbing his hands together as he looked at me. "You got yourself a date! Way to go!"

I blinked at him. "Most dads would be upset that their daughter had a boy over the house all alone."

Dad chuckled as he looked over at me. "First of all...you're what twenty? I'm pretty sure at this point you're grown up enough to make your own decisions, and two...you're you."

"Ha ha," I said, and stuck my tongue out at him.

"So," Dad said, leaning towards me. "Is that what you're wearing?"

I looked down at my dark wash jeans and v-neck graphic t-shirt. "Yeah? I mean it's just dinner at his place."

Dad shook his head as his nurse, who I now knew was named Angie, walked in. "Ang, she's wearing that to her date."

"You finally nabbed a date with bookstore hottie?" she asked as she handed Dad some pills and pulled her stethoscope from around her neck. "Good for you."

Dad nodded, and I cringed. "And she's wearing *that*."

"Dad!" I hissed.

Dad picked up his pudding cup from the bed side table and pulled the spoon out, flicking it at me.

I stood, throwing my hands up as I stared down at the brown blob on my shirt. I took the napkin Angie held out to me as she bit her inner lip to keep from smiling.

"Nice, Dad, nice."

"Now if he says anything you can say your Dad got overexcited with his pudding cup!" he replied, smirking at me.

I shook my head as I wiped it, making it even worse. "I don't have anything else clean! I was going to do the laundry tonight!"

"You have a debit card, don't you?" Dad asked. I nodded. "You have money in your account right?" I nodded again. "Go buy yourself something like that blue shirt you wore the other day...buy yourself a few things and then bring them back here. I'll choose!"

I laughed. "You're some kind of fashion expert now?"

He stuck his chin out, puffing his chest. "I watch Project Runway. I know what the in thing is."

I rolled my eyes. "Okay, I'll trust you."

He used his hands to shoo me out, and I leaned down to kiss him. The truth was he knew what the fashions were from the time I was a teenager; without Mom around, he felt he needed to keep on top of it for me. He was determined to be Mom and Dad at the same time. I smiled to myself as I drove to the mall. He did a pretty amazing job at it.

I wandered through the mall for an hour before I settled on three shirts, a few large accent necklaces and a white cardigan that matched them all. When I got back to Dad's room he shooed me into the bathroom to try each on and show him.

"That one! Yes, that's it!" Dad said when I walked out in the turquoise v-neck that had a diamond shaped embellishment in the center of the chest. The material was soft and flowed from the gathering directly below the embellishment.

"Is it unanimous?" I asked, turning to face Dad's second shift nurse, Joe.

"For sure," he replied, giving me a smile.

I looked down at the shirt, running my fingers over the folds of fabric. "Are you sure it's not too fancy for dinner in?"

"No," Dad said, looking to Joe for support.

Joe shook his head. "Not at all. As long as you're comfortable."

I breathed in, letting the air slowly out of my lungs as I looked at Dad. "I should get going then?"

"Mascara? And some of that cat-eye liner you do sometimes?" he suggested.

"Fine!" I mumbled as I grabbed my purse and went in to put some makeup on. When I came out I put my hand on my hip. "Better?"

"Much! Right, Joe?"

Joe blushed as he looked down at Dad's chart. "Yeah."

I widened my eyes at Dad and he shrugged. Joe was a few years older than me, but it was obvious he was uncomfortable with the situation.

"Here," I said as I slipped a small black device from my purse

"What's this?" he asked as I handed him the recorder.

"The book we were reading. I taped me reading it for you."

I leaned down and kissed him.

"Clever girl," he said as he looked down at it, and then back up to me. "Now go have fun— just not too much."

I laughed,

Chapter 10

I licked my lips as I walked up to the front door of Trent's apartment, rubbing my sweaty palms against my pants as I stared at the cotton ball bunny on the door. The nervousness coursing through my system ceased as a laugh rose up my throat at the adorable and awkward caricature.

Trent opened the door with a smile. "You found it okay?"

I held up my cell phone. "GPS works miracles. Cute bunny, by the way."

He laughed as he shut the door behind me. "You should see the creator of it; she'll melt your heart."

"Your sister, I'm guessing?"

He nodded, putting his hands in his back pockets as he nodded into the living room. "So this is it—it's small, but this is our humble abode. Living room," he pointed over the half wall; "the kitchen and dining room." He nodded to three doors to the right. "My room, bathroom and," he pointed to a door covered with butterfly stickers. "Allie's room."

"I thought that was your room," I joked, smirking over at him. I let my eyes linger on him. He was wearing a plain black t-shirt which pulled at his shoulders, accentuating his slightly muscled arms.

"I'm more Ninja Turtles and Captain America, personally," he shot back. "You hungry?"

My stomach growled the response. "So you can cook?"

He smiled over his shoulder as he walked into the kitchen, pulling a casserole dish out of the oven. "Cook books work wonders."

"Did you get *Fifty Shades of Italian?*" I asked as he reached in again, bringing out garlic bread.

He rolled his eyes as he brought the two dishes to the kitchen table. My mouth salivated as I looked at the spaghetti and meatballs.

"First rule of cooking," he began handing me a bottle of water; "anything with the words fifty shades in it is not going to be a good cook book. Unless you want to have meatballs smothered all over you?"

I squeezed my eyes shut as I shook my head. "No thanks."

He laughed, and I opened one eye. "Good, because my food is much better in your belly."

"This is amazing," I said after taking a bite and leaning back in the chair. "I can't remember the last time I ate anything this good. My dad isn't much of a cook."

"My mom wasn't either," Trent explained, and I watched as he carefully wrapped his spaghetti around his fork.

"How long has it been since you started taking care of your sister?"

He paused, shrugging. "From the time she was born. Mom was straight for the pregnancy, but the second she could get high she was."

I swallowed, losing my appetite despite the amazing food in front of me. "I would say sorry, but I don't feel like that does the situation any justice."

He reached over, putting his hand over mine. I looked up at him and he smiled. "I love my sister more than anything in the whole world. It sucks that my mom and dad were such messes, but I have her, and I'm glad for that. I think that things happen for reasons..." his voice drifted as he watched my eyes fall. "Well, most things."

He sighed, pulling his hand from mine to rub his forehead. "I'm sorry—that seemed insensitive."

"No," I replied. "I believe I'm the person I am today because of all the things I've been handed, as shitty as they've been...and I like the person I am, despite my flaws."

"I like that person too," Trent replied, and I couldn't help laugh as I took another piece of garlic bread. We ate in silence, but it wasn't an awkward silence. It was a silence that acknowledged there was nothing anyone could say to make our pasts different.

Trent cleared his throat. "You still feel like a movie?"

"Definitely," I said, patting my stomach. "If I can move after all this food."

Trent popped the DVD in before sitting down next to me, putting his arm over the back of the couch. I leaned my head on his shoulder and his arm fell to rest on my waist as the movie began to play. I tried my best to stay awake, but the comfort of being in his arms quickly lulled me to sleep.

"Hey," Trent whispered as my eyes fluttered open.

"I'm sorry," I replied, looking up at him, my hand on his chest. I could feel his heart beating beneath my touch. It began to race as he moved my bangs out of my face, his hands tracing the shape of my cheek before stopping at my chin. His thumb paused over my bottom lip as he leaned down.

"T-Trent!" Allie rushed into the room and we moved apart as she crawled up into his lap. Her wavy dirty blonde hair fell into her eyes as her lower lip quivered. "I had a bad dream."

He pulled her tighter into his lap, wrapping his arms around her. "It's okay." He mouthed the words *sorry*, and I shook my head smiling.

Allie looked up at me through sniffles. "I'm sorry, Ellie," she said as she rubbed her eyes.

I reached forward and rubbed her back. "No, sweetie, it's fine. Why don't we have Trent read you a story to get those boogey men to go away?"

"Will you stay?" she asked, pulling her teddy bear closer to her.

"If you want me to?"

She nodded, and Trent stood, carrying her into her room. He placed her on the bed, taking a book off the nightstand. Allie looked up at me, patting the other side of the bed for me to sit next to her. Trent began reading in a low voice, and I had to try to stay awake as the rumble of his voice sunk into me. When Allie finally drifted off he placed the book back on the table and kissed her forehead as we stood.

"It's late, huh?" Trent said as he closed Allie's bedroom door behind us.

"Yeah."

"I'll walk you to your car?" he said, slipping his hand into mine.

We walked in silence to my car where Trent wrapped his arms around me, kissing the top of my head. "Did you have a good time?"

"Yeah, I did."

He pulled away, pushing my hair behind my ear. "How about a real date next time?"

"I don't know," I said, and I watched as his smile froze on his face. "I'm pretty fond of our impromptu dates."

"Dinner and a concert? Friday night?" he suggested.

"Sounds good," I said, leaning up on my toes.

His hand slipped out of mine, and my chest tightened. "Goodnight, Ellie."

I squeezed my empty hands against my side as I looked up at him. "Night."

"I'll text you what time I'll pick you up on Friday, okay?"

I nodded, slipping into my car.

I wasn't tired any more, and my mind raced as I watched him close the door behind him before backing into the street.

Why hadn't he kissed me?

Chapter 11

"I told you he likes you!" Dad said as he reached over and squeezed my hand. "And I see you did some laundry?"

"Ha ha," I shot back. "I finally did some this morning. I kind of had to; otherwise I'd be walking around naked pretty soon."

Dad's smile wavered as he traced the pattern of the pools of blankets around him. "Speaking of things that need to be done, you haven't brought in a catalog for more courses yet. Shouldn't you be picking your next semester's classes soon?"

I looked down at my lap. "About that...I was thinking maybe I would take next semester off."

I let my eyes slowly rise in anticipation of his anger, but instead he rubbed his neck, his cheeks puffing out as he continued to look at his lap. "Is the reason me?"

I swallowed, blinking too rapidly as I fought the wave of nausea washing over me. We both danced around the fact he wasn't getting any better, and I didn't want to think about it anymore than I wanted to admit it.

"No, of course not," I replied, my dry mouth causing me to swallow yet again. "I just need a break."

"Real life might not be as pleasant without school to distract you," Dad commented, and I watched as he licked his parched lips.

"Let me go get you some water," I said as I stood. Dad stopped me, his hand on my arm.

"We need to talk, El."

His eyes met mine, and I felt my legs quake beneath me. I sat back down. "What?" I whispered so low I couldn't hear myself. Maybe I just mouthed the words.

The room shrunk around me as my eyes blurred, concentrating on him as he gave a firm nod. "I'm not taking any more treatments."

My jaw shook, and I couldn't keep my gaze on him. It fell to his hand over mine, blurring with tears. "What are you saying? You're giving up?"

"No, El. I'm in remission, well, partially. The last treatment knocked me on my ass, but apparently it knocked the cancer on its ass too."

"You're what?" My eyes snapped up to his, and he gave me a smile that was too weak for what he was saying.

"Yeah," he replied. "But if it comes back...El, which it will— I can't do any more treatments. I just want to live the rest of my days without being trapped in a hospital bed, too weak to enjoy life. I know at some point I'll end up like this again, but the chemo will kill me at some point too."

"So partial remission?"

He nodded, leaning forward and catching my tears on his thumbs. "It means it's weakened, but it will come back, El."

"How long do we have?"

Dad's chest rose as he shrugged. "We just don't know. Months, years, it just depends on how strong it is when it comes back. I want to concentrate on getting back on my feet so I can at least be home with you. I want to see you graduate."

"I'll go to the school tomorrow and see how many credits I am away from graduating. I want to balance out school and spending time with you, how does that sound?" I asked, fighting the sickening feeling in my stomach as I smiled at him.

"Sounds like a deal," he replied. He reached forward and rubbed my cheek. "I can't wait to have eyebrows again."

Despite the tightness in my chest, I found myself laughing as he moved his hairless brows up and down.

"We could always pencil some on," I suggested, reaching down into my purse and pulling an eyebrow pencil out.

He blinked at me a few times before looking straight ahead and pursing his lips as he contemplated it.

"Wouldn't be the first time I wore makeup," he finally said, and we both laughed. "You remember?"

I nodded, holding my stomach as I thought of the many times I put nail polish and mascara on him when I was a kid. "Mom," I managed to say through hiccups. "Couldn't. Believe. You. Let me!"

"The mascara was waterproof too! I couldn't get that crap off!" Dad added. He leaned forward with the laugh, and his body suddenly racked with a cough. I reached forward, patting his back as he tried to catch his breath.

"Could go for that water now," Dad managed to say through the coughing fit, and I nodded, turning out of the room to get a cup.

My head spun as I headed down the hall, the walls seemed to close in on me as I found the fountain and then rushed back to him.

When I got back the coughing calmed, but he was pale as I handed him the water. I smiled as I sat on the edge of his bed. Dad wouldn't look at me, and the raw feeling inside my heart raged through my veins, causing the burning pain of worry to heat and simmer.

It just reminded me when physical therapy was over, and when he was home, it was only a matter of time before we were back here.

Chapter 12

Just dinner and a concert. I reminded myself as I yanked on another shirt, cocking my head before ripping it back off over my head. I huffed, flopping back on my bed and dialing the number.

"You don't give up, do you?" Trent said when he picked up the phone. "I wasn't responding to your direct question because it's a *surprise.*"

"Why does it have to be a *surprise?*" I whined, blowing my bangs up out of my eyes.

"I want our first date to be amazing," he replied, chuckling as I pouted even though he couldn't see me.

"This isn't our first date," I shot back as I sat up and looked around my bedroom. Half my closet was spread out on the floor. "And I don't know what to wear."

"Clothes usually work," Trent replied. "But then again—"

"You're an ass!"

"I didn't picture you as someone who spent hours in front of a mirror trying on different outfits."

I ran my tongue over my teeth as my cheeks burned. "I just want to look amazing."

"You always look amazing, El. Just wear what you normally wear."

"Fine," I replied, dragging out the word.

"Bye, Ellie."

"Bye, Trent."

I tossed my phone on the bed before standing and looking at the few shirts still left on their hangers. What would Dad tell me to wear?

I smirked as I pulled a navy blue button up off the hanger, buttoning it up just enough so that what little cleavage I had showed. I traded my yoga pants for a pair of fashionably worn skinny jeans with holes in the knees and finally slipped on a pair of leopard print flats. I cocked my head at myself, pulling my hair out of the ponytail at the nape of my neck and running my hands through it to form a braid.

Cat-eye liner. I smiled to myself as I went into the bathroom and put on the makeup Dad preferred. Silver and gray that picked up the turquoise in my hazel eyes. I took a picture of myself in the mirror, wondering if I nailed Dad's look for me or not.

I sat on the couch, turning on the television for the second time in three weeks. I tried to get Dad to cancel the cable numerous times because I never watched it, but today it was coming in handy. I put my feet up on the coffee table, my feet tapping a nervous beat against the wood.

Just dinner and a concert.

I looked up at the ceiling.

When was the last time I went on a date?

Mark...over a year ago.

I rubbed my hands over my jeans, stopping at the holes on my knees and running my fingers over the sparse fibers. My stomach rolled as the thought echoed through my brain.

Over a year.

Holy shit.

I pulled off the blazer I decided to put over the shirt I was wearing. It was way too hot in here. I stood and went to the thermostat. I shook my head as I looked at the number *62 Degrees.* It was perfectly fine, actually kind of chilly. I started as a knock came on the door.

I stopped at the mirror by the door and glanced at my reflection. At least I didn't look like I was sweating, but I felt like it. When I opened the door Trent wrapped me in an unexpected hug, and I found myself unable to control the smile on my face. I blushed as he looked down at me.

"See, I told you you'd look amazing," he commented as his hands slipped down my arm and our fingers entwined.

I shook my head, grabbing my purse from the table and closing the door behind me. We fell into step together as we headed to his truck.

"So," Trent began, opening the passenger side door for me and leaning against it. His button-up fluttered in the breeze, causing the cotton undershirt to lift so the skin of his hip bones showed. I moved my eyes up quickly, and prayed he didn't see. His lips curled at their edges as he continued; "How have the past couple of days been?"

I shrugged. "Fine."

He shut my door and then walked around to his side. He slide in, and the truck roared to life. "Fine?" he repeated. "What does that mean?"

I looked down at my jeans again, fighting the urge to run my fingers over the holes. Instead, I clasped my hands in my lap. "I finally had the guts to tell my dad I wasn't going to enroll this semester—but he really wants to see me graduate so I went down to the university and signed up for two classes. I usually take four or five, so hopefully that will balance things out."

Trent nodded slowly, and I watched as his jaw tightened.

"What?" I asked.

"Do you know how much time he has?"

I looked out the window, watching the desert landscape I loved so much slipping passed us. "You know that saying; live everyday like it's your last?"

I saw Trent nod out of the corner of my eye. "Well, I live everyday like it's the last day I'm going to see everyone I meet."

Trent didn't respond, and I watched as his hands tightened on the steering wheel.

Finally, he spoke, "I don't think that's a bad thing...it just sucks the reason you do is because that's the way your life has been."

"I look forward to every day that I get to see my dad. The good thing is he's in partial remission."

Trent glanced over at me, the smile returning to his face. "That's good, right?"

"It's like most things...a mix of good and bad."

"You're being very cryptic today," Trent replied, his brow furrowing.

I ran my fingers over the bumps of my braid as I thought of what to say. "I'm sorry—I'm just not used to talking to anyone about any of these things...even my dad and I hover around it but don't really talk about it. It means he's alive, for now—but the cancer will come back," my breath caught in my throat, and I struggled to finish the sentence; "and my dad has chosen to forgo any future treatments."

Trent reached over, snaking his fingers in between mine before squeezing. "I'm sorry. I can't imagine what you're feeling right now."

"I can't either...because I have no idea what to feel."

Anger, sadness, pain—it all seemed to be one singular mass inside of me, raging for attention, but over the years I got used to muting it out.

At some point, I figured I would implode, or become completely immune to feeling anything.

Trent nodded as he turned into the parking lot of a fancy French restaurant; one I knew existed, but never thought I would go to. He put the car in park before turning to face me, his eyes on our hands as his thumb rubbed over mine and caused tingles to shoot up my spine. His eyes lifted to mine, and the tingles turned to sparks that heated my face.

"I know this is a weird thing to say on a second date, but no matter if we just end up friends—I'm not going anywhere. I'm going to do my best to make you feel happiness."

"Thank you," I whispered, and his hand lifted from mine, moving my bangs out of my eyes and settling on my cheek.

His eyes raced over my face as we leaned in, our lips grazing one another in a single, deep kiss that left me light headed. He pulled away, smiling. "I'm really hoping for more than friends, though."

I laughed, shaking my head. "Me too, because I'm pretty sure I couldn't forget that kiss."

I watched as his tongue moved over his lips, and my mind went places it really shouldn't go on a second date.

"Good," he replied. "Now, dinner?"

I looked around the restaurant as the hostess seated us. "Are you sure we're not dressed to casual for this placed?" I whispered as she walked away.

Trent smirked, nodding to the couple across from us. The man was wearing a t-shirt and plaid shorts and the woman wore a tank top and short shorts. "Nah, I think we're good."

I laughed into my hand as I looked down at the menu. "Have you been here before?"

"No, but Stew recommended it. Apparently, he brings all his hot dates here," Trent said, moving the lime sticking out of his glass of water around the rim.

"Oh, so Stew has moves!"

Trent shrugged. "I'm just glad they didn't work on you."

I laughed. "I'm pretty sure I was too busy staring at nameless boy AKA you."

"Is that what you called me?"

"In my head," I replied, smirking at him. "Trent is a much better fit, though."

He took a sip of his water before cocking his head at me. "Thanks. Beautiful still fits you fine, though."

I raised an eyebrow. "Is that what you called me in your head?"

He nodded as the waiter came over. "My name is Paul; I'll be assisting you tonight. Can I interest you in our special appetizer tonight, tomato basil crostini? It pairs very well with our signature Pinot."

Trent looked over at me, and I only hoped I wasn't drooling from the sound of it.

"That sounds amazing, we'll take it."

I blushed as I looked up at the server. "No wine for me, though."

The waiter turned to Trent. "Your ID, please."

Trent showed it and then coughed as the waiter walked away, rubbing his neck. "Do you not drink?"

I opened my mouth to speak but nothing came out as my face heated to what I assumed was various shades of pink. "I'm not old enough."

Trent's eyes widened. "Oh...can I ask—"

"In four months I'll be twenty one."

He leaned back in his seat, visibly relieved. "I thought maybe I was robbing the cradle or something."

I looked down at my napkin, playing with the edges before looking at him again. "How old are you?"

"Twenty-five," he admitted.

I put my hand on my forehead as I leaned forward, my stomach sinking. "Does that make you—?"

He cut me off. "Doesn't change anything for me—you?"

I shook my head, my shoulders relaxing as the tension faded from my muscles.

"Well, now that is out of the way—what are you thinking for a main course?" Trent asked as he thumbed through the menu. "Everything looks so good!"

"What does duck taste like?" I asked, stopping at the Poultry section of the menu.

Trent looked at the menu, his forehead wrinkling as he looked at the different options for duck. "Not a clue."

"You willing to try?"

Trent shook his head. "I'm not one to try new things."

I narrowed my eyes at him as the waiter came over with our appetizer and poured Trent's wine. "Have we decided on the main course?" the waiter asked.

"You first," I said to Trent.

Trent narrowed his eyes back at me. "I'll do the stuffed pork loin."

"Very good choice," the waiter said, and then looked at me. "You miss?"

"I'll try the Duck a l'Orange."

"Excellent choice, it's my personal favorite," the waiter said as I handed him my menu.

Trent chuckled as he followed suit.

"You shouldn't be laughing," I said as I picked up a piece of the crusty bread."

Trent took a sip of his wine before leaning forward. "And why is that?"

I swallowed the piece of deliciousness I was chewing before replying. "Because I'm making you try some."

Trent froze, his own piece of food stopping as he blinked back at me. "Why would you do a thing like that?"

I smirked as I ran my finger over the top of my glass of water. "Because it said it pairs nicely with Pinot."

Trent's eyes drifted as he thought. His lips turned downward as he shrugged. "I guess that's a valid point."

I laughed as I took another bite of food.

"Have you always lived in Arizona?" Trent asked as he took his first bite of food.

I was already on my second piece as I shook my head, covering my mouth to answer, "I've lived a couple of different places. We moved pretty much every two to three years. Before this we lived in Connecticut."

"Miss the snow?"

"Not at all...I do miss some of the scenery—like the ocean, but I love the rain and God knows we get enough of that here during monsoon season! If I want to see snow I can always drive up to Flagstaff."

I watched Trent wipe his mouth with his napkin, and my body flushed as I thought of how his lips felt against mine. I took a sip of water and glanced away, hoping I wasn't blushing yet again.

"That's one of the things I like best about Arizona," Trent said; "You have the desert here in Phoenix, mild weather in Sedona and then snow in Flagstaff—and the variations in plants is amazing!"

"Definitely, so what about you, have you always lived in Arizona?"

Trent shook his head, his eyes drifting, and I remembered him saying his sister and him moved as far away from their mom as possible. "No, we lived in Colorado prior to moving here, towards Denver. I got my degree from the University there."

"Which do you like better?"

Trent looked at me. "Definitely here...how did you end up here?"

I shrugged. "Dad hated the unpredictable New England weather, and Mom loved the scenery here. My dad's job took us all over the place. He was a scientist. At any rate, my mom actually ended up opening a gallery up in Sedona—she was a photographer."

I glanced out the window, the setting sun cascading its different colors across the horizon. I smiled as I thought of Mom snapping pictures; she couldn't have resisted such a beautiful scene. She thought most things in life were beautiful—it just depended on the angle and getting the light just right.

"Do you do photography?" Trent asked. His eyes stayed trained on mine, and I found myself biting my lip at being the center of his attention.

"I did for awhile. It was hard after Mom died...my dad ended up turning the dark room in our house into a study, so I stopped. I think it was too painful for him."

"You should try again; maybe you could get into a gallery over in Sedona and follow in your mom's footsteps—make a few bucks while you're at it."

I shrugged, looking down at the now empty plate from the appetizer. "I don't think my dad would approve of me setting up a black room again."

"Why not just do digital—instant gratification," Trent suggested.

I glanced out the window as the sun completely disappeared over the horizon. "I could use a hobby."

"It's settled then; tomorrow we head into Phoenix and get you a camera. As long as you're okay with Allie tagging along. I told her I'd take her to the toy store this weekend."

My gaze returned to him, and I admired how the dim light placed him in shadows. It made me wish I already had a camera. "Sounds good, as long as Allie is fine with *me* tagging along."

"Absolutely," Trent said as he took his last sip of wine.

"Another glass?" the waiter asked as he set Trent's meal in front of him.

"I'm set," Trent replied, smirking over at me as my duck was placed in front of me.

"What's that look for?" I asked as I cut off a piece, and held it up. "You think you're getting out of it because you finished your wine?"

Trent's lips twitched as he looked at me. "I'm not, am I?"

I shook my head. "Do I have to air plane this to you?"

Trent leaned forward; his tattoo's stretching over his arms. "You have to feed it to me."

I leaned forward too, my cleavage pushed up, and I watched as Trent's eyes drifted. His ears turned pink as I raised an eyebrow at him, and his eyes came back to my face.

"How is it?" I asked as I watched him chew.

Trent swallowed. "Like chicken...except not chicken—it's greasier, and duckier."

"Duckier?"

Trent shrugged as he cut into his pork. "You try and see for yourself."

I took a bite, chewing slowly as I savored the taste. It was more flavorful than chicken, and had a much stronger taste. "Agreed," I replied as I cut another piece. "Duckier."

"Speaking of ducks, what's your favorite animal?"

I laughed as I swallowed the piece I was eating. "Chihuahua."

"Chihuahua?"

"Yeah, what's wrong with cute little dogs?" I shot back as I watched him laugh.

"That's not a dog! It's a glorified rat!"

I looked down at my plate, concentrating on spearing the Brussels sprout. "Jerk!" I huffed.

"I'm sorry...I expected something like, I don't know, a horse."

I finally looked back up at him. "I do love horses, but I've always wanted a dog. Just hard moving around so much, it wouldn't be good for a pet. Anyways, now that you've ridiculed my favorite, what's yours?"

He pouted, looking down at my plate. "Ducks."

I took another bite and smiled at him. "Quack!"

"Well, that's just cruel," Trent replied, hiding his smile with his glass of water.

I shrugged. "I can't help it that your favorite animal is so delicious."

"Dessert?" the waiter asked, and I shook my head.

"Are you sure?" Trent asked.

"Yeah, thanks."

"Your check, Sir," the waiter handed him the black bi-fold.

"Where to next?" I asked as we headed out into the cool night air. It wasn't sweater weather, but it hardly ever reached sweater weather even in the dead of what was called "winter" everywhere else.

Trent looked over his shoulder at me. "It's a surprise."

I rolled my eyes as I opened the truck door and hopped in. "I hate surprises!"

"Some surprises are good."

I pouted at him, and he shook his head.

I settled in my seat, smiling as Trent's fingers wrapped around mine.

Maybe a surprise was just what I needed.

Chapter 13

I rolled down the window, leaning my head against the side as I stared at the stars passing above us.

"Do you miss her?" Trent asked, and I turned shaking my head in confusion. "I mean...your mom?"

"Yeah..." I swallowed before continuing; "It's been such a long time that sometimes I need a picture to remember her face...and I really hate that."

"I bet you look like her?"

I leaned my head back against the seat. "Not really...I have her eyes, but the rest is more my dad."

"Luckily," Trent said, smiling at me. "I look nothing like either of my parents."

I looked down my nose at him, and I wondered how sensitive a subject his parents were.

"Does it get lonely? Raising Allie all on your own?" I finally asked.

Trent tapped his thumbs against the steering wheel, his eyes racing over the road. "Yeah...it's confusing and frustrating," he sighed; "and expensive, but epically amazing to watch her grow up."

I smiled, moving closer to him. "How do you do it?"

"I surround myself with people I trust—neighbors and other parents, mostly," he replied. He ran his hand through his hair, stopping to rub his neck. "I could never let my mom raise her—hell; she didn't know who she was half the time."

I leaned over and kissed his shoulder, and he smiled down at me.

"Was the court battle hard?" I asked.

He shrugged. "My mom knew she had issues she had to deal with...she knew she wasn't in a good place."

His jaw clenched, and I watched as his eyes stopped moving, losing focus. "My dad was what made it bad. He came back into the picture when he heard I was trying to get custody. He wanted Allie so he could live off the state free..." he scoffed. "He's heartless."

I sat there, my stomach feeling empty despite the full meal we consumed only a half hour before, wondering what I could say. I had two amazing parents. Despite my fading memory of Mom, I knew she loved me and I remembered her and her warmth fondly. Trent had none of those memories.

"Thank you..." I said, and my voice quiet against the hum of the engine. I looked at my hands and then up to him. "For telling me."

He parked the car and I slid over as he wrapped me in his arms. He kissed the top of my head. "Of course—you told me about your dad, so..."

I pulled away and looked at the familiar parking lot. "Why are we at the bookstore?" I glanced around, seeing there were hardly any spots left. "And why is it so packed?"

"We hold concert nights once a month for area artists," he replied.

"How did I not know that?"

He shrugged as we fell into step together. "You always come here for something for school and then scoot out. Plus, you're always trying to get out as quick as possible to avoid Stew."

"Speaking of which, will he be here?" I asked as he held open the door.

"Probably," he replied, leaning down and whispering in my ear. "This is where he picks up all his 'hotties'."

The smile and laugh in my throat froze as I stared at the packed store. The cafe area had been turned into a concert venue. At the back corner was a stage with a stool and microphone. There were people both standing and sitting, either in the lounge seats that had been brought up front or on the stools that were typically there. Trent led the way, his hand on the small of my back, and I smiled to myself as his employees glared at me as we passed.

"Here we are," Trent said as he picked up the card that said reserved and moved it off the table.

I jumped onto the chair, watching him chuckle as I did so, but he didn't take the seat across from me. My mouth opened to ask where he was going, but nothing came out as he smirked and moved to the stage. I stared as he grabbed the guitar and sat on the stool. The buzz in the room died down as everyone watched him adjust the microphone. He coughed as he scratched his chin before taking a deep breath and saying, "I know everyone's been anxious to see if I can actually sing or not."

There were some whispers of affirmation that ceased as soon as he began strumming the guitar. The air in the room seemed to disappear as we waited for him to sing, and finally, he did. His voice resounded through the room, raw, yet strong and airy; with touches of the blues, the words were drawn out with passion. His voice softened with the guitar and then came back just as strong, fierce and methodical. He kept his eyes down or closed as he sang, and I knew he wasn't used to performing in front of a crowd. I leaned forward, closing my own eyes as I sunk into the music.

Since Mom died music was my therapy, even more so when Dad was first diagnosed. I often lost myself in the hard rhythms of metal music with its deep riffs and passionate vocals, but this was different. My eyes fluttered, locking on his, and he smiled through the words of his song. His voice pulled me in and instead of losing myself and becoming numb, I found myself— felt myself. My heartbeat pulsed through my ears, and the pain melted away, leaving room for utter bliss I didn't know existed anymore. In that moment, I forgot the raw edges of impending loneliness and loss that haunted my every breath.

When his set was done he stood and bowed to a standing ovation that included me. He winked at me shaking my head before he was swamped by people who wanted to talk to him. When I finally managed to push my way to the front of the room he was zipping his guitar into its case.

"Wow," I commented as he stood up.

"You like it?" he asked as he slung the case over his shoulder and wrapped his arm around my waist.

"You rock!" I said as we made our way to the door.

We were stopped several times by people wanting to talk to Trent, wondering if he had a CD they could buy, or a website they could download music from. He gave a generic response that there were business cards at the counter and continued towards the door.

"Wow," I repeated as we finally made it outside.

"You think they will be more or less scared of me?"

I laughed as I looked up at him. "On one hand, you have a soulful voice which isn't very intimating...but," I dragged out the word; "on the other hand, you're even more mysterious now."

Trent put the guitar in the backseat of the extended cab, before hopping in next to me.

I sighed, pressing my head against the glass to look at the stars. "I don't want this night to end."

Trent moved the center console up, and I moved over to put my head on his shoulder. "It doesn't have to end just yet."

"What about Allie?" I asked as he put the truck into gear and headed out onto the street.

His hand moved to my thigh, and I closed my eyes as warmth spread over me. "She's sleeping over a friend's house."

"So where to?" I asked.

"I'd love to drive to Sedona and look at the stars from the air port...but it's a bit of a haul from here."

"The stars look amazing from my backyard," I suggested, looking up at him.

"Perfect. Sedona some other time? We'll make a weekend of it?"

My stomach fluttered at the thought. "That sounds good—especially after I have my camera."

He smirked down at me. "Tomorrow."

I smiled and closed my eyes. When I opened them Trent was pulling into the driveway.

"Hey," he whispered. "Tired?"

"No," I replied, but my eyes were heavy.

He kissed my forehead. "We'll see each other soon enough?"

My eyes fluttered as I sighed. "Mhmm..."

"Do I need to carry you in?" he said, his chest rumbling with a laugh.

I shook my head and slipped out the door into his arms. When we reached the front door he pressed his forehead to mine.

"Thank you," he said, his breath washing over mouth.

"For what?" I asked as my lips tingled from the closeness of his.

His thumb slid over my cheek. "For one of the happiest nights I've had in a long time."

"I can say the same to you," I replied.

He leaned down and pressed his lips into mine. He didn't pull away like the first time, and I slid my hands to the back of his head as the kiss deepened. He pulled away slowly; his lips achingly close to mine.

"I'm not tired anymore," I whispered.

He kissed me lightly once more. "I'll pick you up at ten?"

I nodded; my head fuzzy from the kiss. "Okay."

He moved my bangs out of my eyes before finally pulling away.

Chapter 14

I opened my eyes to the sun streaming in through the curtains. I reached for my phone, rubbing my eyes as I stared at the time. I froze as the digits shown back at me: 10:00AM.

What time did Trent say he was coming?

10:00AM.

Shit! I stood, looking down at my wrinkled yoga pants and over sized sweatshirt. I looked in the mirror, and my hair was an absolute rat's nest; not to mention my eye makeup was smeared across my temples.

I closed my eyes, grinding my teeth as the doorbell rang. My neck flushed, the heat traveling up to my face and ears as I stumbled out of my room and to the door.

"Hi," I said, and my voice was hoarse as I stared up at Trent.

He tipped on his toes, his hands in his pockets as he attempted but failed to keep from laughing. "Sleep in?"

I put my hand on my forehead as my stomach rolled. "I never sleep in. I actually meant to wake up early enough to go visit my dad first."

I stared over his shoulder at Allie, the window in the back of the truck rolled down. She waved at me, and I smiled, waving back.

"You want to bring Allie in?" I asked, swallowing. My face continued to burn as he smirked at me. "I promise I'll be like ten minutes. Just let me shower, and I'll be right out. You can watch some cartoons or something? Or I can give her a canvas and some of my paints?"

Trent chuckled, scratching his chin. "Then *Allie* will be the one needing a shower."

I gave in, laughing. "It's the only thing I have in the house that I could remotely think about a kid wanting to do."

Trent shook his head. "You underestimate the power of a television."

"Ten minutes?" I asked.

He nodded. "Take your time."

"Remotes on the coffee table," I said before turning and heading up the small set of stairs that led to the bathroom and bedrooms.

~~~

I stopped at the top of the stairs, staring into the living room where Allie and Trent sat watching television. Trent was pointing to the screen and whispering something in Allie's ear. She giggled in response, cuddling closer into his arms. My body warmed, and I smiled as I made my way into the room.

"Hey," I greeted them, and Allie turned to face me, her tiny hands grasping the top of the couch as she peered over it at me.

Her brown eyes widened with her smile. "You look pretty."

Trent turned and nodded in agreement. "I didn't mind the pajamas, though."

I raised an eyebrow at him, shaking my head.

"You need to see your Daddy first?" Allie asked, jumping off the couch and coming to stand in front of the table with a picture of him and me. She cocked her head at it, putting her hands on top of the table as she stared at him. "You look like him."

"Thank you," I said, kneeling down next to her. "I can go see him tonight after we go shopping."

"Are you sure?" Trent asked, and I looked up at him.

"Yeah."

"We can swing by if you need to let him know what you're doing."

"It's alright. He'll be fine," I replied, swallowing as I thought about breaking our routine. "He'll be glad I'm actually doing something."

Allie's hand snaked into mine, and she stared up at me, a soft smile on her face. "Where does your daddy live?"

I found myself swallowing again as I tried to think of an answer that would make sense for a four year old. Trent saved me as he leaned down and swept her into his arms. "Daddy's don't live with their daughters forever."

Allie pouted down at him. "You mean we won't always live together?"

Trent shook his head, pouting back at her. "I know it's hard to believe, but someday you're going to think your brother is really icky."

I covered my mouth with my hand as I smiled at them.

Allie put her hands on either side of his face as she leaned forward shaking her head. "No, no, Trent. I'll never think you're icky."

Trent looked over at me. "I hope she remembers that when I tell her she can't have a boyfriend."

Allie giggled. "Boys are icky! Except you Trent, right, Ellie?"

I nodded as I followed them out to the truck. I watched as Trent carefully buckled Allie into her seat and handed her a book from a small bin on the floor before smirking over his shoulder at me.

"You're positive about your dad?" he asked as he held open the passenger side door for me.

"Yeah, he'll be glad I'm spending the day with other human beings, especially ones that are so cute," I replied, leaning up and kissing him on the cheek.

"What's that for?" he asked, his hand resting on the small of my back.

"I just felt like it," I replied, breathing in his scent as I stared at him.

"Hey!" Allie called from the backseat. "What you guys doing?"

I ducked my head, blushing before I jumped in the truck and buckled up. I turned to look at Allie. "Hey, did you notice we have very close names?"

She nodded enthusiastically, her fingers running over the book in her lap. "Who chose your name?"

I looked at the car ceiling, scrunching my lips to the side as I thought. "I'm not sure. I suppose my mom and dad came up with it together." She beamed at me, waiting for me to ask, "Who chose yours?"

She pointed at Trent as he turned the truck on. "Trent did!"

I looked over at him and he shrugged. He looked in the rear view mirror before pulling out into the street, and he waited until Allie was engrossed in the book before leaning over and whispering. "Dad took off a few days before she was born. Mom was too distraught to really make any decisions, so she asked me to name her."

I slipped my hand into his. "I think you picked a great name."

"Says the girl with the same exact name except with an E."

I moved to pull my hand away, but he tightened his hand around mine, smirking over at me. "So did you do any research on what type of camera you want?"

I looked ahead, chewing the inside of my lip. "My mom was a Nikon. Maybe I'll choose the same side."

"There's a side?"

"My mom used to say you're either a Nikon or a Canon," I explained, my mind drifted to when I was ten and she showed me each of the lenses, carefully explaining each of the types and what they did.

"Ah, so you're a Nikon?"

"We'll see," I replied as I took a deep breath.

"So you paint?" Trent asked as he merged onto the interstate.

"Yeah, I used to paint my mom's pictures. I hid it from my dad, though. I was afraid it would be too painful for him. Our basement is filled with them now, though."

Trent nodded, and his eyes were distant as he thought. Finally he spoke, "Have you ever thought about bringing them into Sedona or one of the galleries in Phoenix and selling them?"

"No, actually...I don't know if they're any good," I said.

Trent squeezed my hand, bringing my gaze back to him. "I'm sure they're great."

"You should buy one!" Allie commented from the back.

Trent glanced at me from the corner of his eyes, his brow rising into his forehead causing wrinkles to crease across it. "What do you think?"

I laughed. "I'd like that."

"Will you help me pick one out?" Trent asked, looking at his sister in the rear view mirror. I watched her scrunch her nose as she closed her eyes and gave one big nod.

"Trent paints on people sometimes," Allie explained, her chin pointing out as she closed her book.

"You what?"

Trent's chest rose as he sighed. "I don't paint on people. Sometimes I sketch out tattoos for people—and sometimes I sell my designs to shops. She's got an eye like a hawk," Trent explained, shaking his head. "We'll be out, and she'll recognize one of my sketches on someone and think I actually did it."

"Ah, so," I replied, turning his forearm and running my fingers over the koi on his right arm. I traced the outline, watching as goose bumps traveled over his skin after my touch. "Did you design these?"

My eyes drifted from the tattoo to his face. His breath seemed to catch in his throat, and his eyelashes fluttered against his cheeks as my fingers hovered over his skin. He blinked hard, coughing. "Uh, yeah."

I smirked before leaning over and whispering, "Something wrong?"

The skin on his neck reacted the same way to my breath against it as his arm had to my touch.

"Wait until I find what drives you crazy," he shot back.

I smiled over at him.

I was pretty sure I would love it when he did.

Chapter 15

"Has the great dilemma been solved?" Trent asked as I picked up the Nikon and peered through the lens again.

"Yeah," I replied, handing him the floor model. "Look how much crisper the lens is."

Trent looked through it, and then glanced at the lens. "It is, but this doesn't have a stabilizer in the lens like the Canon does."

I blinked at him, my hand frozen mid motion of taking the camera back from him. "Did you research them?"

He shrugged, looking through the lens at me. "Maybe."

"So you're leaning towards the Canon?"

"That's about the only detail about the things that made sense to me."

I took the Nikon back, placing it on its display. "If you're doing rolling shots of cars or stop action shots, then the stabilizer is going to be your best friend inside the lens, but;" I explained, turning and crossing my arms over my chest. "The Nikor lens is going to be your best friend any other time."

Trent smirked, putting his hands up so my eyes drifted to the tattoos on either forearm. I tried not to get distracted by them, but my mind drifted to how I could capture them in a picture, along with the rest of his presence.

"Is there something I can help you with?" a store associate asked, looking between us and Allie playing at our feet. "Your daughter?"

I shook my head and Trent nodded. The associate stood awkwardly looking at his hands.

"So what's it going to be?" Trent asked as he picked Allie up and put her on his hip. Her eyes were starting to get heavy, and she cuddled into his shoulder.

"The Nikon D3300."

The associate pulled out a set of keys and knelt down to the case. He moved his shaggy hair out his blue eyes as he looked up at me. "Any preference to color?"

"Red," I replied, biting my lip as I felt my pulse rushing in my ears. I hadn't spent that much money on one thing...ever. My stomach dropped as I stared at the box he was handing me. I wondered how Dad would feel about me spending that much money.

"Buyers remorse?" Trent assumed, cocking his head at me as I looked down at the box, glued to the spot. "You haven't even swiped your card yet."

"I didn't ask..." I stopped mid sentence. How bad would it sound if I admitted I felt the need to ask my dad first? I was an adult, yet I still counted on him for money, or on the savings account I'd had since I was a kid.

I had never spent any of the money from that account on anything but school supplies or Christmas presents for other people.

I closed my eyes before putting one foot in front of the other.

Maybe this could pay for itself.

Chapter 16

I tapped my hands against my legs as I watched the floors tick by. Their red numbers were a stark contrast against the black background, reminding of my camera sitting at home with the charger blinking as it pushed energy into the battery. I already decided the first picture I wanted to take with it would be of Trent. I smiled as I leaned back against the cool metal of the elevator. My mind drifted to him sitting on a chair, one hand in his hair, the other pointed up so his tattoo showed. When the door to the elevator opened I stood for a moment, blinking at the floor ahead of me. I finally reacted when it started to close, sticking my arm out so it paused, opening back up again.

"Hey, Princess," Dad said as I walked to him and gave him a kiss. "I hear you had quite the day?"

The smile on my lips dropped as I stared at him with my mouth open.

He slipped his legs over the side of the bed, placing his feet into his slippers as he stood.

"Dad, be careful," I squeaked out as I reached for him.

He shook his head at me as he used the bed to move across the room, and then walked the few steps to the couch by the window. He sat down and patted the seat next to him, smiling at me. "Tell me about your day."

I sat down, pulling my knees to my chest as I turned to face him. "First, you tell me what you were insinuating."

He rubbed his head where fresh hair was beginning to poke out in patches. He closed one eye, chewing on his lips before he answered, "There something you left out about book hottie?"

I tilted my palms up, shaking my head in confusion.

"One of my nurses mentioned seeing you at the mall this morning with him and his daughter?"

I tipped my head back, looking at the ceiling before letting my chin drop to my knees. "She's not his daughter...well, technically, I suppose she is."

"Huh?"

"It's his sister, he adopted her...his parents," I paused, swallowing as I wondered what I should say; "aren't very stable people."

Dad's nostrils flared as he exhaled, reaching forward and squeezing my hands. "I wouldn't have cared if she really was his daughter...but wow...that's amazing that he'd be willing to do that."

My skin tingled as I nodded. "His mom has drug issues and his dad took off. I think he's just happy he's able to take care of her. Makes me feel silly for being so weak."

Dad shook his head, his lips pursing. "How are you weak, El?"

I swallowed, looking down at our hands. Dad's were finally starting to get some color back to them, and I could even see the hair growing back on his knuckles as I ran my fingers over them. "I can barely take care of myself."

"El, look at me," I did; "you've spent far too much time worrying about me to worry about yourself. That doesn't make you weak."

I inhaled, letting the air go stale in my lungs before exhaling. "I feel like I've failed you...spent too much time concentrating on school, and not spending enough time with—"

"You've been trying to distract yourself from the truth—you've been trying to live a normal life while..." he paused, the words seeming to leave him. I knew what he was thinking *while your dad is dying.* "It's hard to deal with what we've gone through, El, and I don't blame you for any way you've handled it. I'm not going to lie, I'm looking forward to spending some more time with you—but that's only because I'm selfish. There's so much I'm going to miss..."

I looked at the ceiling as my nose and eyes pricked.

"Don't say that, Daddy," I whispered, my voice cracking.

He reached forward, his thumbs catching my tears. "No matter what, Ellie, I'm going to miss things with you. It doesn't matter how long I live—I'll never have had enough time with you."

My body shuddered as full on tears raced down my cheeks, and Dad pulled me into his too frail arms. We sat there until well after the tears died away. Dad kissed the top of my head, his voice quiet as he whispered, "I love you, princess."

I nodded, swallowing as I tried to avoid the tears returning.

He rubbed my back before I sat back up. "So, how was your day? What's Trent's sister's name?"

I gave in, smiling as I played with the laces of my sneakers. I glanced at him, shrugging. "Allie. And today was good—I...I bought a camera."

Dad's jaw dropped open, but there was a smile on his lips. "You did what? You spent money on yourself?"

I leaned forward, nudging him softly in his ribs. "Shoosh!"

"Nikon, I hope?"

I nodded.

"Mom would be proud," he replied. "Speaking of Mom, are you ever going to sell any of those paintings you hid in the basement?"

My mouth dropped as I stared at him smirking.

"You think I didn't know?"

My mouth opened and closed, my jaw clicking but no noise coming out.

"I knew," Dad said, squeezing my arm. "I figured you didn't say anything because you didn't want me to."

"I thought they might upset you."

"They're gorgeous, why would they upset me?"

I leaned back, looking up at the tiles on the ceiling as I shook my head.

"If you're interested, I still have some contacts over in Sedona. I'm sure they'd be willing to feature you if you're willing to cut them a percentage?"

My chin fell back to my chest as I stared at him. "Do you and Trent, like know each other?"

Dad's eyes raced over my face as he shook his head. "Not sure what you're saying?"

"He suggested the same thing earlier today."

Dad pointed to his bald head. "Great minds think alike. I already like this guy!"

I rolled my eyes. "He's coming over tomorrow with Allie to be my first sale."

Dad smirked, wiggling his bare brows. "I'll make some calls. Next weekend you'll have to make a trip to Sedona."

I looked straight ahead as my muscles tensed.

"Sure."

Chapter
17

I rubbed my eyes as I dropped my messenger bag on the couch and headed to the kitchen. I opened the fridge first, looking at the three bottles of salad dressing, a few other condiments and soda. There probably wasn't much more in the freezer. I opened it and stared at the bags of veggies before picking up a very frost bitten piece of chicken and cocking my head at it. I was pretty sure *that* was not edible. I sighed, going back to the fridge and popping open a can of soda before opening the cabinets. They were just as sparse. I grabbed the container of chocolate crème filled cookies and made my way back to the couch. I closed my eyes as I chewed, letting the gritty chocolate coat my mouth.

I really needed to go grocery shopping.

My eyes shot open as my cell phone rang in my bag. I could hear my pulse rushing in my ears from being woken up abruptly, and shook my head as I fumbled in my bag to grab the cell phone before it stopped ringing.

"Hello?" I answered, breathless, without checking the caller ID.

"Hey, did I catch you at a bad time?" Trent's voice instantly brought a smile to my face.

I dusted the crumbs off my lap as I replied, "No, just had my first Intermediate Algebra class, and it kind of wore out my brain."

"What would you need algebra for with a literature degree?"

I sighed. "It's the minor that calls for it. Apparently, you should know math if you're going to do graphic design.

"If you say so," Trent said, and I could hear the smirk on his lips. "I'm pretty decent at math, if you need any help."

I looked down at the textbook, my stomach hardening with the frustration I felt during the class and after when the teacher tried but failed to help me. "You might get sick of seeing me every day."

"I highly—" Trent began, and I heard the muffled sounds of Allie. "Hold on...yes? Okay, I'll ask her...Allie would like to know if you'd come to her school play, it's this Friday at 6:00."

"Sure thing," I replied. "I have a feeling I'm going to need a break by then."

"Ask her! Ask her!" I heard Allie saying in the background.

"Is there something else?" I asked.

"She'd like it if you came to the school potluck. They do it before the play so all the kids have a nice dinner first," Trent explained, and I heard Allie go silent as they waited for my response.

"Of course. Should I bring something?" I asked as I looked down at my cookies—the only edible item left in the house.

"You want to poison the whole school with your kinky cooking?" Trent teased, and I bit my lip to keep from smiling.

"What's kinky?" Allie asked, and I burst out laughing as Trent stuttered out a response.

"Um...well...nothing...I—it's a bad word."

"Why were you smiling then?" Allie asked, and I struggled to keep the tears from my face as I doubled over.

"I...it's an adult thing."

"If you say so. Seems like you like whatever kinky is," Allie commented, and I heard Trent choke.

"Go pick out a game...we'll play a game after I get off the phone with Ellie," he said, and I imagined him sitting on the couch, tilting his head back in exasperation.

"So, you like it kinky?" I said through hiccups.

"Wouldn't you like to know," Trent shot back.

I stopped laughing, caught off guard by his retort.

Awkward silence followed. Finally, Trent coughed. "Uh, what were we talking about?"

"Algebra."

"Right," Trent said, and I heard him release a relieved breath. "It'd be my pleasure to help you with your homework, if you want."

I rubbed my forehead, pulling my knees to my chest as I looked down at the messenger bag. "I doubt I'll pass without some help...but I don't want you to feel like you have to. Besides, I'll probably frustrate the hell out of you."

"I have a four year old. I'm used to being frustrated," Trent replied. "But Friday is a long time away. You don't need another book, do you?"

I laughed. "I'm pretty sure my brain won't be able to handle anything else, but I do need to go grocery shopping...so I could stop on my way by."

"What did you eat today?" Trent asked, and I heard the sounds of pots and pans.

"Cereal...a granola bar...and some cookies," I replied, looking at the now empty package of junk food. "I'm going for super healthy."

"Do you want to join us for dinner? Maybe bring a few paintings for me to look at—this way I can try them out in the house first?" Trent suggested.

My stomach growled, and I was glad he couldn't hear it.

"Sounds good," I replied. "What time should I be over?"

"Why don't you pick out the paintings you're interested in selling and text me when you're on your way over. I used the slow cooker today, so whenever you're ready will be fine."

"You even use a slow cooker?" I said, my voice feigning shock.

"I'm a single parent, the slow cooker is my savior, and besides pulled pork is amazing," Trent shot back.

"Pulled pork?" My stomach growled again. "I'll be over in twenty minutes."

"That's my girl."

I smiled as I hung up the phone, heading down into the basement. Most houses in Phoenix didn't have basements, but my parents had given up the money to have one put in our house. After living on the East Coast for so long, there was no way Mom could live without one. It also gave her a good area for a nice, cool dark room. I ran my fingers over the door that led to that room. I hadn't been in it in years. I continued to the corner where I stored my paintings, away from the sump pump. We learned quickly one of the reasons basements were less common was due to the monsoon season where it rained—a lot. I loved the monsoon season. It was a unique feeling of electricity, fear and wonder to sit on the back patio while a thunderstorm raged around you, especially in the flat deserts of Phoenix. I looked down at the canvases, standing up against the wall wrapped in black trash bags to hide their contents. I pulled the first one out of the bags. It was a three-piece set depicting a dark night, lightning striking in the background and illuminating the desert. It was one of my favorites. I put it back in the bag and moved to the next one. I swallowed the lump rising in my throat as I ran my fingers over the paint. I closed my eyes as I slipped it back into the safety of the black bag and placed it to the side.

The last picture Mom took.

I shook my head, quickly going through a few more and choosing two others to bring with me.

Chapter 18

Trent was waiting for me when I pulled in the drive way. He was leaning against the wrought iron railing, and as he looked up the shadows from the setting sun perfectly framed him. I grabbed my camera, jumping out of the car.

"Don't move!" I yelled as he began to lean up to come towards me.

He laughed, leaning back over, and I snapped the shot. I looked down at the camera. It was even better than the one I pictured in my head. He was smiling, his mouth partially open as he looked down, and the lighting...it was perfect. I smiled down at the small preview. I couldn't wait to see it larger.

"Can I come kiss you now?" he asked, and I shrugged.

"If you want to," I replied, and he hopped down the steps, pulling me into his arms.

I let my arms fall around his neck, and he tilted my chin up to kiss me.

"How was your day?" I asked as my hands slipped down his chest into his own.

"Interesting," he replied. "Can I help with the paintings?"

"They're in the backseat," I said, and I waited for him to grab them so we could walk up the steps together. "What do you mean by 'interesting'?"

I held the door open for him, and he placed them against the wall. His hands went into the back of his hair, muscles curving beneath his gray t-shirt. I pursed my lips as I fought the urge to take a picture of him, but gave in as my eyes raced over how perfectly his tattoos framed his downward glance.

"Hey!" he replied, looking up at me, his arms dropping and crossing over his chest. "Are you just going to take pictures of me all the time now?"

I shrugged, and he pulled me into his arms, grabbing the camera and holding it away from me as he kissed me.

"Can't be taking pictures of me if I'm kissing you," he whispered in between breathes.

"I can hear your lips smacking," Allie called from her bedroom.

Warmth spread through my body as I looked up at him through my bangs. His lips were a tease, so close, but so far away as he smiled at me. "I guess we'll have to be quieter around her."

"How exactly do you do that?" I asked with my hands on his neck.

He leaned forward, one eyebrow higher than the other as he whispered. "Like this."

His lips grazed mine, slowly moving against mine in a way that left me more breathless than the deep kiss we'd just shared.

"Okay," I replied, breathless as he pulled away.

"So," he said, and I narrowed my eyes at his cocky smile. "Dinner or paintings first?"

"Dinner!" Allie said as she came into the room.

"Hey, Allie," I greeted her, leaning down.

She wrapped her arms around me. "I tried to give you some privacy," she said into my ear.

I stood up, covering my smile with my hand. Trent's brow furrowed as he mouthed the word w*hat?*

I shook my head as I followed her to the table. Trent opened the slow cooker, spooning the contents into a bowl as the smell filled the apartment.

Allie saw my face and nodded. "It's the best thing he cooks," she said, leaning forward and taking a sip from the straw coming out of her cup of water.

"Smells like it!" I replied, my mouth watering as he placed the steaming bowl in front of us along with a bag of chips and buns.

"Do you want me to help you?" I asked Allie as she leaned forward to grab a bun.

She shook her head. "I'm a big girl."

I smiled between her and Trent as I watched her take just the top of the bun and put it on her plate. She spooned a small amount of the pork onto the bun before taking a spoonful of coleslaw and putting it on it as well. Trent gave her a handful of chips on her plate, and I watched as she folded the bun in half. She looked between Trent and me.

"Aren't you going to make your own?" she asked.

"Oh," I replied, smiling at Trent as he handed me a bun. "Yes."

"She won't eat until we all have food on our plates," Trent explained as he started making his own sandwich.

"How polite of you," I commented as I piled a generous portion of meat onto my bun. Trent raised an eyebrow. "I'm hungry," I hissed at him. "All I have in my house is stale Oreo's and soda."

Trent gagged. "You do need to go grocery shopping!"

"I like Oreo's!" Allie said as she bit into her sandwich. She swallowed before continuing, "But Trent says they're bad for you."

"They are," I replied, scrunching my nose. "And besides, this," I took a bite and chewed slowly; "is so much better!"

Allie nodded as she took another bite. "What you going to make for the potluck?"

"Well, your brother is afraid I'll poison everyone."

"That's mean," Allie said, turning to face Trent. "I'm sure her food isn't *that* kinky."

Trent choked on his sandwich, tapping his chest as he swallowed. He coughed, leaning forward to take a sip of his water.

"Hey, you said it," I replied, looking through my lashes at him as I popped a chip in my mouth.

Trent recovered and opened his mouth to speak but nothing came out.

"I think you made him speechless," I said to Allie.

She blinked at him. "Is kinky really bad?"

It was a good thing Trent wasn't chewing, because I was pretty sure from the shade of his face that comment would have made me need to give him the Heimlich.

"It's just not a word we should be using. Trent was a bad boy using it in front of you," I replied, putting my hand on her arm and trying to make my face serious.

I was pretty sure the thing on my face was a smirk, though.

She turned slowly to Trent, crossing her arms. "You're not going to use that word again are you?"

Trent shook his head, covering his mouth with both of his hands as he leaned forward.

"Good," she said with one firm nod before turning back to her chips. "Trent's making mac and cheese!" She leaned forward, cupping her hand over her lips so only I could see them. "It has *bacon!*"

I widened my eyes. "How will I compete with that?"

Trent shrugged, leaning back. "You could bring soda; that might be safe for you."

I narrowed my eyes at him. "How do you know I can't cook?"

"It was your choice of cookbooks that led me to that conclusion."

I threw my hands up. "I was trying to look like I hadn't come in just to see you! That was the first book I picked up!"

Trent leaned forward, grabbing a bun to make another portion. "Now the secret comes out."

I rolled my eyes. "Your ego—" I used my hands to show an over sized head.

He smirked as he took a bite of his sandwich. "You know you want more of this."

"To what are you referencing?" I shot back. "The food, yes."

He winked at me, and I had to fight the shiver running up my spine.

Chapter
19

I stared at the sign, surrounded by beautiful cactus that seemed to sway naturally around its beautiful engravings; *Agave Healing Center.* I wished I could say I never saw the sign before, but I had, far too many times. This was only Dad's latest relapse and round of chemo. I swallowed as the bump formed in my throat, growing in such a way I thought I might choke. According to Dad this would be the last time he was here. I closed my eyes, letting the warm mid-morning sun warm my suddenly cold body. Dad had only been at the center briefly for therapy visits, but the chemo had never knocked him down so badly that he would be staying here for several weeks. I let my eyes flutter open as I heaved a sigh. At least I knew the place was nice, and the nurses were even better than the ones at the hospital. They already knew him by name, and of course, playful personality. I looked into the passenger seat where one of my smaller paintings sat in one of those black plastic bags.

My pulse quickened as I stared at it. *He'll like it.* I reminded myself as I grabbed it and headed to the guest check-in.

"Ellie!" the girl behind the counter greeted, and I froze in my tracks with the hot black bag pressed hard against my chest. Morgan came out from behind the desk and wrapped me in a huge hug. I blinked at her in her hot pink scrubs.

"Hey," I replied, the word drawn out as I tried to keep my puzzled expression off my face.

"Scrubs are not that flattering," she said, smiling at me over her shoulder as she went back around her station. "So what are you here for?"

My mouth dried as I stared at her. "Umm...could ask you the same thing?"

She shrugged. "I've worked here over the past few breaks, but money is tight at home, so I decided to work more hours here and drag out school a little bit more. Gotta do what you gotta do, though, right?"

"Yeah," I replied, leaning on the counter for support.

"So you?"

I ran my fingers through my ponytail as I struggled with what to say. "Visiting."

"Of course, why else would you be here?" she asked, looking at her nose and making a face I assumed she thought was adorable. It just made her look ten years old. "So where can I direct you to?"

"Paul..." I swallowed, my nails digging into the canvas. "Abela."

Morgan looked up at me, her brow creasing before she typed in the name. "Isn't that your father?"

My eyes went down to the painting in the bag as I picked at its edges. "Yeah."

Morgan clicked on a few pages before, coughing. "So it looks like you probably know your way around?"

I nodded, still concentrating on the bag, as if it was the most interesting thing in the room.

Her voice was soft as she answered, "It looks like his room is in the left wing. It's on the opposite side from the office visit section of the campus. Martha should be back any second, and I can show you the way if you'd like?"

I thought about saying no, but as I looked around me I realized the place was just too big for me to deny her. I didn't know the left wing at all.

I smiled, and it felt like my face was cracking. "Sure, I'd appreciate that."

Morgan smiled back at me before looking down at a file on the desk. She flipped through the pages, but her eyes didn't move, and I knew she was only pretending to be distracted. Her head swung around as she heard sneakers on the floor. "Here she is. Martha, I'm just going to take Miss Abela to see her father. Can you cover the desk for me? It's her first time on the west wing."

"Of course," Martha said as she put her coffee mug down and sat in her chair.

Morgan nodded over her shoulder and we fell into step with one another. She coughed before speaking, "The west wing is even prettier than the office visit part of the campus. I'm sure your Dad's comfortable."

"The whole place is nice," I replied, keeping my eyes straight ahead. Of all places for Morgan to be working, she was here, right here, in the very place Dad was staying. I didn't know how I'd missed her so many other times. She seemed so comfortable here; she said she'd been working here awhile. I wondered if I walked right passed her without knowing it before. I cleared my throat, glancing over at her. "So how long have you worked here?"

"Two years," she replied, smiling over at me. It faded and I watched as her eyes fell to her shoes. "Listen, El, I wish I'd known—why didn't you tell me?"

We stopped, and I turned to face her. My insides twisted as I stared at her pale face, eyes racing over mine. "I didn't tell anyone."

Her head tilted as a sad smile twitched at the edge of her lips. "But we're friends, right?"

Friends? I always called her one, but I never really treated her like one. I never treated any of the people I hung out as friends, more like acquaintances to pass the time.

"Yeah, of course," I finally said, leaning back on my heels.

She reached forward, putting her hand on my elbow and squeezing. "You shouldn't have to go through this alone—I know it's a lot. I mean—I know we're not close...but I get it." She looked down before continuing; "I'm going to school for physical therapy. I'm going to be interning here soon."

"Physical therapy?" I repeated, letting my gaze meet hers.

She gave a soft nod. "Yeah, I want to help people."

"I didn't know," I whispered, shaking my head.

Superficial. That was the way I would have described Morgan and the girls we hung out with before that moment, but she seemed so in her element here; so caring and down to earth.

She shrugged. "No one ever asked."

"And yet you were the only one that knew my major."

"Eh," she said, smiling as we began walking again. "I'm the only one who pays attention."

"Apparently, including me," I said, and we both laughed lightly.

"So how long has your dad been fighting?"

We rounded the corner and I smiled at the glass paneled hallway looking out at a beautiful garden.

"That's the healing garden," Morgan explained, noticing where my eyes had drifted.

"It's amazing," I replied as we continued down the hall. At the end was an entrance that said *Healing Wing - Left.*

"The secretary should be able to let you know if your dad is in his room or out and about. It depends on what his schedule is today," Morgan explained as she rubbed her hands together. "Good seeing you."

As she turned I finally spoke, "Three years."

Morgan turned, cocking her head. "Three years?"

I nodded. "It's tiring."

Her eyes drifted to the door behind me, her tongue poking into her cheek. "I believe it."

"Thanks for showing me the way," I paused looking down at my painting as my hands finally loosened against it. I locked eyes with her. "And I'm sorry I didn't tell you. It would've been nice to have someone to vent to."

"I know you have that amazing hunk of a boyfriend, but I'm still here for you if you ever need to talk," she said, smirking at me.

My face burned, and I knew I was blushing. "How do you know about that?"

She put her hands up, looking at the ceiling. "I may have or may not have been at that concert he gave...you two were so into one another you didn't even notice the room around you."

I laughed, rubbing my forehead. "Yeah..."

"It was cute...I've got to get back, but see you soon?"

"I'd like that."

And for the first time, I meant it.

Chapter
20

Dad linked his arm into mine, smiling over at me as we walked out into the healing garden. I placed my hand over his, and he shook his head.

"You're always so cold, El!"

I looked at the sky as I shook my head. I flinched as his cane scraped against the pavers, the harsh noise bringing back the reality of how cold I usually felt internally.

"I actually had to shave today!" Dad joked, and I swallowed as we settled on the wooden chairs beneath the shade of a tree.

"Your hair is coming back good," I said as I glanced over at him. His hazel eyes, hauntingly similar to mine, sparkled as he wiggled his eye brows.

"It's a lot more impactful now isn't it?" he teased, and when I tried to laugh, it sounded more like I was drowning. "Alright, what bee is in your bonnet?"

"Seriously, Dad, you're not old enough to be using that saying," I shot back, looking into the distance at the rolling mountains, their tan dotted with cacti that looked black from where we were.

"You're avoiding the topic. Did your date go poorly? I'm sorry I didn't ask, with moving here, it just slipped my mind," Dad said, his soft tone creeping in and unfreezing the parts of me that reminded of why he was here.

I rubbed my forehead with my freehand. "No, it was amazing. It's just..."

I stopped, the words choking in my throat.

"What?"

"Morgan runs the front desk. It was just awkward...and it's..."

"Hard coming here," Dad completed my sentence.

I looked down at my hands, weaving my fingers in and out from one another as I nodded.

"I know it means you're on the mend, but—" the words died in my throat, and I found myself biting the inside of my lip.

Dad's hand found my knee, squeezing. "I know."

I stared down at his hand, his wedding band glinting in the sun. I covered it with my hand, letting the warmth of the metal melt into my palm. I glanced around me, watching as a black butterfly with white stripes fluttered by us before settling on the flower of a desert lily. Its black wings contrasted against the orange red petals, and I wished I brought my camera.

"Mom would've loved this place," Dad said, leaving out the reason we were here.

"It's really beautiful."

"So that date...it went well?" Dad asked.

"Yeah," I replied, glancing over at him. His hair really was coming in. It was almost half an inch, creating a fuzzy blonde gray glow to his head. "He brought me to this amazing French restaurant."

"Fancy!"

I nodded, smirking as I leaned over and knocked shoulders with him. "I even ate duck!"

His face dropped, and he blinked at me before shaking his head. "How could you! A cute little duck?"

I stuck my tongue out at him. "I tried something new, you should be proud of me!"

"Are you on quack?"

I rolled my eyes, and he laughed before saying, "Go on...what else?"

"He can sing—I mean really sing," I replied, my chest lightening as I remembered the soothing cadence of his voice. "It's amazing."

Dad cocked his head at me, and I felt my face burn with warmth. "You really like him, huh?"

"Maybe..."

"I'd love to hear him sing sometime, you know, if you feel comfortable with him meeting me," Dad said, and I watched as he pursed his lips. His eyes were on the distance.

"Of course I'm comfortable with you meeting him. I'm pretty sure you couldn't embarrass me any more than I embarrass myself on a regular basis," I replied letting a smile lift my lips.

His focus stayed on the distance, and I swallowed. "He knows; if that's what you're concerned about."

Dad's eyes slowly moved back to me, and he blinked a few times before speaking, "You told him?"

I nodded as I put my hand over his. "Are you mad?"

My chest tightened, and I reminded myself to not tighten my grip as I watched his lips angled downwards. He shook his head, his eyebrows rising into his wide forehead. "No, just surprised...I'm glad, though. You should talk to someone about it. I know it's hard to talk to me about it."

I opened my mouth to deny it, because I never had any issues talking to him about anything. He closed his eyes, shaking his head, and I realized it didn't make him feel bad. I relaxed, slouching in the bench and putting my head on his shoulder. He kissed my head, wrapping his arm around me, and I closed my eyes.

I wouldn't take any breathes for granted today.

Chapter 21

"Hey," Trent said, reaching over and putting his hands over my wringing ones. "You alright?"

I breathed in and out through my nose before nodding. I didn't remember the last time I went to anything like this, let alone with my boyfriend. My eyes flicked over to him before going back to my hands. *Is he my boyfriend?* I squeezed one hand over the other, stopping the wringing, but soon my foot began to tap.

Trent put his hand on my knee, applying pressure as he widened his eyes at me. "Really?"

"Fine," I said, throwing my hands up. "I'm nervous!"

"Think how I feel!" Allie commented from the backseat, and I turned my head to look at her.

The tension in my muscles relaxed as I watched her kicking her feet at the air with a stern look on her face. It was so adorable that I couldn't help but laugh. I leaned forward, putting my hand on her knee much like Trent did with mine.

"I'm sorry, honey. I didn't realize you were nervous! Didn't your brother practice your lines with you?"

"Yeah, but what if I forget them, El? What will I do?" she asked, her eyes searching mine.

"You won't. You're going to nail it," I replied. "I'm certain of it."

"You will," Trent said, tossing her a smile. "If I can sing for a whole hour in front of a crowd of people, than you're definitely going to nail this!"

Allie scrunched her lips to one side, her noise wrinkling as she stared at his back. "But you're so good! And you practice all the time! You sing me to sleep every night." She held her fist up, putting her fingers up as she counted; "For one, two, three...four...five! Five years! That's a lot of days!"

We reached the school and Trent parked the truck before looking over at her. "You're being very brave, but Ellie is being even braver, you know why?" She shook her head, and I looked over at him, my lips pursed and eyes narrow. "She's feeding people her cooking."

My mouth dropped open, and I smacked him. I flinched as I did, and Trent grabbed my hand, flipping it right side up so he could see my knuckles; two of which were swollen and purple.

"Did you punch something?" he asked, and I closed my eyes as his fingers brushed over the marks.

"I had an accident," I began as he leaned forward, his eyes signaling for me to go on; "I was in a rush, and when I went to turn the light switch on that's under the cabinets I rammed my hand into the edge of them."

Trent's lips parted, but he shook his head without saying anything. I blushed as I pulled my hand away from him and pushed the door open to get out. I opened the door to get Allie, and when I reached across her to unbuckle her, the frown still on her face deepened.

"That's a good boo boo," she commented as she put her arms around my neck so I could take her out. "Trent you should kiss it since her daddy isn't around to do it. Trent always makes my boo boos feel better that way."

I placed her on the ground, and she slipped one hand into mine and one into Trent's. I was pretty sure Dad would chastise me for always rushing and not paying attention. He worried one day I would be cooking dinner and accidentally cut a finger off. I rolled my eyes at the thought. I wasn't *that* careless.

"So that's why you were late!" Trent whispered over to me. "Are you typically accident prone?"

I shrugged.

"Good thing you don't have any weapons."

My jaw clenched along with the muscles in my back as I stood straighter. My mind drifted to the gun in my glove box. I not only had a permit to carry, but to conceal and carry. I just never really felt the need to. Dad asked me to get the permit when he first went into the hospital, and I was spending a lot of time alone in the house. I never felt it was necessary because we had a good alarm system, but nevertheless, I still went and got the permit. I even went to the shooting range at least once every two weeks to keep my aim sharp.

Trent's lips pressed into a thin line as he glanced over at me. "Do you?"

My neck gave an involuntary twitch as I kept my eyes ahead. "Why would I?"

Trent didn't have a chance to press me further because the door to the school swung open, and we were greeted by a middle-aged woman with yellow blonde hair and a crooked smile. "Trent! Allie! There you are!"

"Sorry, Miss May—my girlfriend, Ellie, had a little accident when she was cooking and it held us up," Trent explained. "Miss May, this is my girlfriend Ellie, Ellie this is—"

"Hey!" Allie interrupted; "I want to!"

Trent smiled, nodding for her to continue.

"Ellie," she said, looking up at me and then to her teacher. "This is Miss May, my kintergarden teacher."

I covered my smirk with my hand at the way she pronounced it.

"Nice to meet you," I replied as I let my hand down to shake hers.

"You as well!" Miss May said, nodding over her shoulder. "Everyone was just about to start eating."

"What did you cook anyways? Trent asked me as he placed the insulated bag on the table. He crossed his arms as he turned and watched Allie running to the group of her friends. I leaned behind him, unzipping it and pulled out a big bowl of potato salad. He narrowed his eyes at me. "Are you sure you're not going to poison us all? It wouldn't be a good first impression."

"Well, we wouldn't want them to hate your *girlfriend* would we?" I teased, my insides twisting as I looked at him from the corner of my eye. He smirked at me wrapping his arm around my waist.

He kissed my forehead. "I wouldn't care if they did, *girlfriend.*"

"Everyone, the line will start here," Miss May instructed. "Children, please join your parents."

"So when did I get promoted to girlfriend?" I asked as we moved to the back of the line waiting for food and Trent lifted Allie into his arms.

Allie beamed over at me. "Since your first date!"

I watched as Trent ran his teeth over his lower lips, and he looked down at Allie's hand over his own. "Do you mind me calling you that?"

I leaned over and kissed his cheek. "I love it."

Chapter 22

Allie yawned as she crawled into bed, and I smiled as I sat down on the edge.

"Thank you for coming," she replied, her eyelashes fluttering against her cheeks. She rubbed her belly. "Your potato salad was yummy. Trent was wrong. You're a good cook!"

Trent laughed as he sat at the end of the bed, his guitar in hand. "Who would've thought?" he teased.

"You shouldn't judge a book by its cover," I shot back, and he smirked as he stared down at his guitar strings.

She yawned again. "Play?" she mumbled as she settled down in her pillows, pulling her stuffed dog to her face.

During the play and even now as I watched Trent singing to Allie, it was apparent she was far more than just his sister. Allie viewed Trent as her dad as much as he viewed her as his child. The way Allie looked up at him as she fought the edges of sleep reminded me of how I looked at Dad as a child, and even now, with admiration and wonder. He was her hero. He would always sweep in to save her, to kiss her boo boos, and eventually, I was sure, to tease her about them. I smiled to myself as I felt my own eyes weighting down with the tone of his voice. It was less edgy than at the concert and soothing and soft just for her.

Her eyes began to shut, but she fought it as her head tilted back up. "Are you two in love?" she mumbled.

Trent's voice drifted and faded as he continued to play the guitar but left space for me to answer. My chin tucked into my neck as my heart beat rushed to my ears. I could hear every beat, flowing with the rhythm of the guitar as I stared at Trent. His eyes locked on mine, and I couldn't hold his gaze. Instead, I looked down at Allie, which wasn't much better. Her eyes were wide open as she looked at me expectantly for an answer.

"No, sweetie," I whispered. "It's a little too soon for that."

She sighed, snuggling her face into her blanket as she closed her eyes. "I think you are...you just don't know it yet," she said, her words muffled and slurred.

Trent's voice began again as he softened the strum of the guitar along with his voice until it faded out completely. He leaned down and kissed her head before following me out of the room. I sat down on the couch, pulling my knees to my chest as I looked up at him.

"Keep singing?" I asked, leaning back and closing my own eyes.

"I'm not that good," he replied, and I felt the couch indent where he sat.

I shook my head, opening my eyes and leaning to put my chin on his shoulder. "You are," I whispered. "You could be famous."

He scoffed, looking over at me with his brows knit over his eyes. "To be famous I'd have to sell out and be a pop star...My sound is too raw for that, and I don't like the idea of being turned into a pop singer. Besides, I like being a business manager—just hopefully not at a bookstore forever."

I leaned forward and kissed the edge of his jaw. "I love when you sing— it makes me feel like I'm whole again."

My voice faded as I thought back to only a few weeks ago when I thought the emptiness that filled me would never end.

"Like the parts of me aren't scattered anymore...like I can breath," I whispered, letting my cheek settle against his back as I fought tears.

Trent's fingers slipped under my chin, tilting my face up to his. He ran his thumb over my lower lip. "I will sing to you whenever and where ever."

I closed my eyes as his lips brushed against mine. He pulled me into his lap, and I wrapped my arms around his neck, my hands tangling in his hair. His lips danced over mine before traveling down my jaw line to neck. My body trembled in his arms as a sigh slipped from my lips. I felt him smiling against my skin.

"No fair," I whispered as he pulled away. I let my forehead fall to his.

"Fair," he whispered, kissing me again. He pulled away, his eyes still closed. "I'm pretty sure at some point I won't be able to stop kissing you...to control myself."

I nodded, breathing in his scent and warmth.

"I'm pretty sure you're not ready for that," he whispered, his lips teasingly close.

I kissed him once before sliding off his lap. "I'm pretty sure Allie would be convinced we were in love if I stayed the night."

He leaned forward, running his hand through his hair before looking over at me. His face was flushed, and my body warmed at the thought of him being embarrassed. "Sorry about that."

I put my head on his chest as he leaned back. "That's what Disney movies put into little girl's heads."

"You're telling me. Hopefully, she doesn't keep thinking like that when she's a teenager," he replied with a shake of his head as his hand settled on my arm. His fingers drifted over my skin, causing goose bumps.

"Don't worry; the first frog prince will fix that."

He put his hand over his eyes. "Don't remind me. I'm going to need to get a shot gun."

"Speaking of over protective dad's...mine wants to meet you," I replied, looking up at him. "Is that too soon?"

Trent's jaw was slack. "Are you sure?"

"If you want to—he's out of the private hospital, so now outside people can visit him. We moved him over to the Agave Healing Center for physical therapy—"

"Private hospital?"

My eyes froze on my painting over his television, and I swallowed. "Military."

"Your dad is military?"

I fought the urge to pull away from him and rub my temples. "Kind of...it's complicated."

Trent opened his mouth to speak but then closed it. "You don't have to tell me."

"I just don't like talking about it..." I replied, running my fingers across the top of his jeans. "It's—"

Trent pulled me closer, sinking into the cushions as he kissed my head. "Don't worry about it, El. You don't have to tell me."

"Are you mad?" I asked.

"How can I be when you asked me to meet your dad?"

I closed my eyes. "Thank you," I whispered.

He rubbed my arm as he began to sing just loud enough for me to hear, and I drifted with the sound of it. The raw edges of Dad's illness softened as I melted into the sound of it.

Chapter 23

I rubbed my jaw as I lifted my cup of coffee to my lips. My eyes locked on the desert outside the kitchen window; today it felt barren and harsh. The night before I fell asleep with Trent singing to me, and at some point he woke me up and drove me home. I was grateful he had such amazing neighbors who would help him on such short notice; because I was sure I couldn't have driven myself home. I didn't even remember the drive or crawling into bed; just the hard pounding of thoughts in my head. I spent the rest of the night in a fitful sleep with my thoughts. My hand slipped down to my chest, rubbing my collarbone as if I could release the tightness in my chest.

It didn't help.

Ironic.

That was the word on replay in my mind. It was exactly how I was going to describe Dad's job to Trent. He saved me from the explanation, but it still stuck in my mind. For years Dad moved us place to place as he tried his hardest to find a cure.

My jaw shook, causing my teeth to rattle.

The cure to what was killing him now.

I swallowed down the rest of my coffee before going into the basement to look at my paintings. Dad pulled through, and the gallery wanted three of my best paintings. I pulled them out of their bags looking at each of them, but all I could see was faults. I wasn't sure any of them were that good. My eyes shifted in the dim light to the room containing all of Mom's pictures. My eyes locked on the wood grain of the door as I contemplated opening it.

Years. It had been years since I looked through her prints. I was too afraid to find a painfully happy moment embedded in one of the images. I swallowed as I walked to the door, and my hand froze on the door knob. The coolness of the metal raced from my hand up my arm and to my face, spreading the feeling through every part of me until my hair was standing on end. I closed my eyes, listening to the click-click of the door mechanism as the knob turned. The metallic sound echoed through the basement and sent a shiver up my spine. I felt the door loosen, and I pushed it open without looking. My lids lifted slowly as the stale air of the room rushed past me and into my lungs. I flicked the light switch, cringing at the loud click and then the cascading of the light over the room. All the pieces of the dark room where still there, the individual buckets that held the different levels of developer—the pins to hang the pictures up. I felt the air stop midway into my lungs as my eyes fell on a pin with a picture still caught in its grip.

My bare feet skidded against the floor as I walked slowly up to it, unpinning it and turning it to face me. I ran my fingers over the edges of the paper, appreciating the way their sharpness reminded me it was real. I swallowed as I stared down at it. It was apparent Mom hadn't taken the picture, it didn't hold any of her style—but looked more like mine—and even more, the picture was of me long after Mom passed. I was sitting on the large rock in the backyard, looking into the distance and the sun framed me, casting soft shadows around my frame and illuminating me like a halo.

At what point had Dad changed the study back to a black room?

My breath rattled in my lungs.

And when did he take up Mom's career as a hobby?

I shook my head, and a stack of albums I'd never seen caught my eye. I reached up, pulling them off the shelf and sank to the floor, placing the sun photograph in front of me as I did. I ran my fingers over the parchment paper cover before taking a deep breath and flipping open the cover. The pictures flashed, blurring into one another as my eyes burned with each flip of the page.

"Ellie? Ellie?" Trent's voice hammered into my skull, and I flinched as I looked at the pictures spread across the floor. I hadn't even realized I pulled them out of the album. "There you are."

I looked over my shoulder at him, and he rushed forward, pulling me into his arms.

"What happened?" he whispered into my hair as he rocked me in his arms.

I pressed my eyes closed, but the images still flashed in my mind. I hugged his arm to my chest as the silent tears slipped over my cheeks and onto his skin.

"Years," I croaked as he rocked me. "Years and I never even knew."

"Knew what, El?"

I shook my head, pulling my eyes shut even tighter. "We've been hiding—all this time...we've been hiding."

"You're really confusing me, El," Trent said, and I heard the sound of the paper rubbing over the concrete as Trent picked up one of the pictures. His chest rose beneath me before he whispered, "These are amazing."

"Dad took them," I said, and my voice felt harsh and raw. "I was painting, and he was doing photography...and we kept it away from each other because we were afraid it would hurt the other."

"Funny how that works?" Trent commented, and I turned in his arms to look up at him.

He cupped my face in his hands, his thumbs wiping away the tears from my face.

"I wonder how many things we just didn't talk about because we thought it would hurt the other too much," I shook my head in his hands, his grip soft but firm. "We never really talked about the past from that moment on...and when the future looked so unclear...we didn't talk about that either. Now, we know exactly what the future holds, and we still don't talk about it."

"And what does the future hold?"

I swallowed, closing my eyes against a rush of more tears. *Death.*

Trent leaned forward, pressing his lips against my forehead. The warmth of his lips spread through me, much like the cold metal had iced me, and this provided the opposite. My body relaxed beneath him. His lips moved against my skin as he whispered, "I see a future where you're happy, El, and I'm sure that's what your Dad hopes for too."

"But what if he's not in it?" I chocked on the words, and Trent pulled me back into his arms.

I buried my head in the warmth of his chest. His lips found my ear, and his breath washed over my bare neck. "He'll always be in it, no matter if he's physically there or not. Your mom is still here—these pictures— your Dad held onto the part of her, and it became a part of him. You held onto that part of her too, and you paint them just as beautifully as she captured them. The people we love are always there, in some way, if we want them to be."

I took a deep breath, and Trent pulled me up to stand with him. He took my face in his hands again, his eyes racing over my eyes. "Thank you," I whispered as I put my hands over his.

His lips curled up to one side, nodding over his shoulder. "You want to pick out the paintings you're bringing to the gallery?"

"Can you do it?" I asked, looking down at my feet. "There's only one that's not for sale."

"You don't like any of them, do you?" he asked, rubbing his thumbs over my cheeks so my eyes moved back up to his face.

"Pretty much," I replied as I turned my face to kiss his palm before pulling away and wiping my face dry.

Trent smirked at me, and I stepped back, looking at him.

"What?" he asked, his hand going to the back of his neck.

"James Dean, much?" I asked, looking at his hair.

His hands went to his pockets and he pursed his lips, shaking his head. "He didn't have the side shaved like this."

I stepped forward, leaning up on my toes so our lips were inches apart. "And he didn't wear v-neck black t-shirts."

Trent reached up, tipping my chin up with one finger so our lips met. "Do you like it? I've been trying to grow it out for a while."

I nodded as I followed him out the room. I turned, looking at the pictures scattered on the floor. I flicked the light off and they disappeared.

The hollow in my chest remained, sharpening each time I inhaled. I pulled the door shut and headed to the other side of the room.

More knives were hidden in that dark corner, but they seemed a little less sharp with Trent's hand in mine.

Chapter 24

"What's this?" I asked as I turned from locking the door and stopped in my steps. In the drive way sat a Volkswagen beetle convertible. Trent's guitar was propped in the backseat.

Trent shrugged, pulling me towards the car. He placed my paintings in the back with the guitar and then leaned into the front seat. I tilted my head as I admired his butt, and when he turned I looked in the distance, pretending to be interested in the plane in the sky. He brought up a silk scarf and waved it in my face.

"If I'm James Dean, then you're Audrey Hepburn," he replied.

I laughed. "I need—"

He turned and handed me a pair of large sunglasses.

"Fine, you win!" I replied, wrapping the scarf over my head and then putting the sunglasses on. "What do you think?"

He leaned back against the car, crossing his arms, and I lifted my camera, popping off the cap and taking the shot.

"Very James Dean," I said.

Trent reached forward and pulled me into his arms. "Good."

"The car is kind of sissy on the other hand," I commented, smirking up at him.

"Wait until I open her up on the highway," he shot back. "It's got a turbo!"

"Oh!" I replied, throwing my hands up in the air. "So fancy!"

He narrowed his eyes at me as he opened the door for me. "You'll see."

"I'm sure," I replied, sinking down into the warm leather seats. My hands fell over the camera, and I felt a sinking pit in my stomach.

"Hey," Trent said, putting his hand on my knee and shaking it. "What's wrong?"

I shook my head, swallowing back the rush of anxiety that raced over me again at the thought of Dad's pictures. "Nothing."

"Really?" he commented.

I closed my eyes. "I never even saw him with a camera...at least not like this. Just some rinky dink point and shoot."

Trent merged onto the interstate. "You want to stop and see your Dad? Talk this through with him?"

I glanced over at him. "Are you sure?"

He smirked. "I brought my guitar for a reason."

"You're tricky, you know that?" I said, smacking his arm. "Are you going to sing him Sleeping with Sirens?"

He nodded, leaning forward as he laughed. "Hey, if I'm James Dean, you're Audrey Hepburn."

"You'll need to take the next exit," I said. "And my Dad knows SWS, so you'll get to sing that."

He used his left hand to lower the classic sunglasses he put on his face and smiled at me. I snapped the shot before he could move and looked down at the picture.

"Finally," I commented as I looked down at it.

"Finally what?" he asked as he downshifted off the interstate.

"Captured your beautiful tattoo in a picture," I commented, turning the camera so he could see it.

I watched him pale and his throat move up and down as he looked away. "Which way?" he asked, coughing.

"Left," I replied, still watching him. "What's wrong?"

He rubbed the scruff on his chin. "Is that it up there?"

I nodded, waiting for him to answer, but he kept driving in silence. When we pulled into the parking lot he turned the car off, and dropped his head between his shoulders as he flipped his arms in his lap.

"I should've brought a sweatshirt," he muttered, and I put my hand over his arm, covering the rising sun above the fish.

"It's over a hundred degrees and you should've brought a sweatshirt?" I repeated.

"So I could cover them."

His eyes finally met mine, and despite the dark sunglasses I knew they were locked on mine.

"They're beautiful, why would you ever cover them?"

He leaned forward, placing his forehead against mine. "I just want your dad to like me."

I pulled his sunglasses off, putting my hands on either side of his face. "He will. It wouldn't matter if you had a tattoo on your face...although, that would be awful."

Trent laughed, his fingers slipping up and pulling my own sunglasses off. His gaze moved from my lips up to my eyes. "Thank you."

I shook my head, leaning forward and kissing him. "Thank you...for being you."

"I could say the same to you," he whispered before kissing me again.

I wanted to lose myself in the feeling of his lips against mine, but I was distinctly aware of the fact we were in a convertible in a parking lot, and pretty much everyone could see us making out. I pulled away blushing. "You make it extremely hard to be upset."

Trent cocked his head at me. "It's the hair, isn't it?"

I shook my head as I pursed my lips to keep from smiling. I gave up as I handed him the item that completed he look. "It's the sunglasses."

Trent took them and put them on his face before leaning back to get the guitar. His shirt rode up, exposing his hip bones and the trail of hair leading from his belly button to his pants. I looked down at my hands as I tried to breath.

"And maybe the guitar," I commented as I gathered myself enough to get out of the car.

Trent lowered his sunglasses with one finger. "You're awfully flustered for sunglasses and a guitar," he commented as he put his free arm around my waist.

I chewed the inside of my cheek, glad the dark glasses hid my eyes as I closed them. They shot back open as the image of my fingers sliding his shirt up and over his head ran through my mind.

"They do a number on me," I replied through a strangled laugh.

Trent held the door, his shirt lifting as his forearm tensed against the weight of it.

God damn it. Clean thoughts!

I concentrated on un-knotting my scarf from under my chin as we walked down the hallway.

"Hey, El!" Morgan greeted from the visitor's desk. I watched as her eyes raced up and down Trent before returning to me. "Brought a musician?"

"Trent, meet my friend Morgan. Morgan, this is my boyfriend Trent," I said, and Morgan smiled as she clasped Trent's hand in a firm shake.

"My pleasure," Morgan replied, and her voice was breathless.

"Pleasure's entirely mine," Trent replied as he slid his sunglasses off and hung them on his shirt neck. "We're heading into Sedona for the day and El wanted to stop and see her dad."

"Dad wanted to hear Trent play," I explained, glancing over at him as he put his free hand back around my waist.

Trent pulled me closer, kissing my forehead. "And it's not like I could deny anything El asks me to do."

I knew my face was burning again, but I didn't care. I relished the warmth Trent's eyes sent coursing through my body.

"You two are too cute," Morgan commented, and I smiled over at her. "I'm glad to see..." she looked down at her hands, and then back up at me before continuing; "I'm glad to see you both."

I pointed at her. "Don't forget we're stopping for lunch on Tuesday after class."

Morgan nodded. "Of course, we have a lot to talk about. You guys have a good time in Sedona."

"So you guys are back on good terms?" Trent asked when we were out of hearing range of the visitor desk.

"I didn't realize while I was keeping secrets, so was she. I think it's worth getting to know her without all the walls I've always put up— that apparently *we* put up. She's studying to help people like my dad," I explained, and Trent nodded.

"I'm glad you're letting other people in," he commented as we reached the hall of glass.

"Do you have friends?" I asked, my stomach tightening as I thought about the fact I didn't really.

Trent's shoulders tensed and then relaxed. "No...Well, I guess I do—if you count the other parents. Speaking of which, we're having a neighborhood Memorial Day picnic, and I'd like you to come, if you want."

"I'd love to...maybe I'll even cook something."

"Just make sure it's not too kinky, okay? I don't want to be embarrassed in front of my friends."

I knocked hips with him. "Believe me, there'll be moms there that will love 50 shades of pie."

Chapter 25

Trent stood behind me as I signed our names on the visitor log and the nurse directed us to the garden. Dad spent much of his time out there when he wasn't in physical therapy. As we walked out the doors, the warm air washed over my skin, washing away the sticky staleness of the AC, and I knew exactly why Dad liked it outside. While we still had AC in our house, we never kept it as cold as this place did, or any place did really. Trent's hand went slick in mine and he pulled away rubbing his palm against his jeans. I stopped, turning to face him. The sunglasses were back on his face, but it was pale again.

"Are you sure you're okay with this? I mean if it's too soon—"

He shook his head, stopping me mid sentence. "No, it's not that—unless you feel that way? Do you feel that way?"

I laughed as I leaned up on my toes and kissed him. "Not at all. He's going to love you."

"I'm the bad—"

"Boy." It was my turn to cut him off. "Except not really. You're pretty soft on the eyes...and in here." I let my hand fall over his heart. "My dad knows my type usually has tattoos, so you're pretty tame compared to some."

Trent's lips went into a solid line of disapproval, and I stared down at the end of my braid running my fingers over it. My insides twisted as I waited for some sort of response.

"Tame?" he finally repeated.

"I..." I began, but the air rushed out of my mouth in a confused incoherent mumble.

When Trent chuckled, my eyes shot up to his amused face.

"Glad to know I'm *tame*," he said leaning down. He kissed my neck and my entire body flushed with heat. His lips slipped up to my ear. "Or so you think," he whispered into my ear before letting his teeth slide over the earlobe.

Holy God. Bare hips then this. I was going to melt into a puddle of all hot and bothered in a second.

"Ellie!" I heard Dad call, and Trent pulled away, his hand going to the back of his neck. It was his turn to blush.

I narrowed my eyes at him, and he smirked before I turned to Dad walking towards us.

"How long have you been out here?" I asked, kissing his warm cheek before hugging him.

"Don't worry, they make sure I don't stay out too long," Dad replied, looking between Trent and I. "So you brought a friend?"

"Dad, this is my boyfriend Trent," I said.

Trent reached forward, shaking Dad's free hand. His other was locked on the top of his cane. "It's nice to meet you, Mr. Abela."

Dad shook his head. "I'm not old enough to be a Mr. Call me Paul."

I felt my face twitch as I looked at Dad. He really wasn't that old. Forty-five. The number caught in my mind, and I felt my hands curl into fists. Still, the cancer aged him, or maybe it was the countless drugs they'd pumped into him, some of which he discovered. My mouth went dry. It would be hard for Dad to take pictures with his cane.

Trent coughed, and my head jerked up. I hadn't realized the awkward silence that fell over us as I stood glaring at the cane.

"I brought my guitar. El said you wanted to hear me sing—she must've exaggerated about how good I am," Trent commented, holding up his guitar case.

Dad pursed his lips. "I thought that could be the case, so I asked Morgan. Turns out you're quite the heart throb singer."

Trent coughed again. "Not sure I'd say that."

Dad's lips curled up as he nodded to the door we came through. "I guess I can be the judge of that. Why don't we go in? They're going to be yelling at me if I don't come in soon, anyways."

We followed Dad into the building where the nurse looked up from the desk and gave us a smile.

"Paul, it's about time you came in!" the nurse commented, and Dad tossed me a knowing glance over his shoulder before moving into this room. Trent settled on the couch, and I sat next to him, pulling my legs to my chest as I turned to him. I watched as he slipped the guitar out of the case with his hands shaking, and I squeezed his knee. Dad sat on the seat opposite of us, leaning forward as he watched Trent tune the guitar. His hair was coming in good now, and the light blonde had specks of silver shining through. Dad's eyes moved to mine and he winked before we both looked back at Trent.

Trent closed his eyes, his foot slowly counting out the beat before he began to strum the guitar. He nodded as he began to sing the song. His voice wasn't anything like the original singers, it wasn't as high pitched, and it brought the lyrics to life in a way that made me take a deep breath. I watched as Dad settled back in the chair, carefully watching Trent, his hand over his mouth to hide his expression. I watched as Dad's finger began to lift and tap its way to the beat. When the song ended I couldn't keep the smile off my lips as I looked at Dad and then Trent. Trent's eyes stayed on his guitar, and I looked back over at Dad.

"So?" I asked.

Dad nodded, leaning forward. "I remember when you convinced me to buy tickets to see those guys. It was almost unbearable...that was before your heavy music phase—and that one, as far as I know, hasn't ended yet."

I rolled my eyes, putting my hand over Trent's still tapping knee. "This version?"

"Ill," Dad commented, and I blinked at him a few times. His smile faded. "What isn't that what all the kids are saying?"

Trent coughed. "I think the word is, sick."

"Ill means the same thing!" Dad commented as his hands formed a triangle in front of his face. "Do you write music, too?"

"Yeah, most of the time I sing my own songs. That was kind of a joke between El and I," Trent shrugged.

"Now the scarf makes sense," Dad said as he looked at the scarf I had tied around my neck. "Is that your camera?"

I picked it up from the side table and stood to hand it to him. "Yeah. I really like it, although, I don't know if I'm as good as Mom...or you."

Dad's eyes shot up from the camera locking on mine. His chest moved up and down beneath the thin white shirt he was wearing. "You found them?"

I could feel my heart racing as I gave a slow nod. I wanted to say the words yes, but they trapped in my throat as his eyes fell to the camera in his hand. "They," I swallowed. "They were so nice...but I don't remember you ever having something like this."

He shrugged. "Sometimes you don't need anything this fancy...I would've done digital, but being in the dark of the black room—" he paused, running his hands over the tiny pictures on the dial. "I just felt like she was there."

Dad looked up at me, and his eyes were wet. "I was afraid it would bug you. I know it was your thing to be in there with her—"

I stopped him with a shake of my head. "No...I never really had the patience for it—waiting to see what the picture was. It never made sense to me that she still did most of it on film."

Dad chuckled to himself. "I get less and less patient with old age."

He stood and walked to his bedside table and pulled out a small digital camera.

"Nikon?" I asked as he handed it to me.

"Of course," he said as I examined it. "So where were you two headed to when you detoured off my way?"

I glanced over at Trent who was still staring down at his guitar. "Oh," his head shot up. "Sedona, dropping off her paintings at the gallery and then spending the day in town."

Dad sat back in his chair as I handed him his camera. He ran his hand over the arms of his chair before looking over at Trent. "Would you mind playing me one more song?"

Trent shook his head. "You want an original this time?"

Dad nodded, and I settled in my seat, closing my eyes as my heart beat slowed to the sound of Trent's voice.

Chapter
26

I closed my eyes, tipping my head back as the wind raced over my face, and I drifted on the happiness I didn't know still existed in the world. For so long I'd felt myself fading, disappearing, into the abyss of death that had surrounded me for so long. Everything was so numb as I prepared myself for the worst, but as I let my eyes flutter open to see Trent I realized all the parts of me I'd ignored were coming back to life. Trent's fingers intertwined with mine, and my heartbeat rushed in my ears.

There's no going back.

I couldn't ignore the depths of pain that clawed at me, because they felt that much more real when I stared at Trent. The future seemed far more relevant with him there. I closed my eyes again, ignoring the gnawing in my stomach as Dad's face flashed in my mind. At what point did that future end? How much of this would he get to see?

"Hey," Trent said, squeezing my hand. "You okay?"

I picked my head up, nodding. "Yeah, of course."

"You've been quiet since we left—I thought your Dad looked good."

I took a shaky breath as my eyes moved to the guard rails. My limbs tingled as I thought of the night that felt so long ago. The night where I felt everything spiraling out of control, and I realized there was nothing left to save any of us.

"El?" Trent's voice sent tingles like fiery fingers against my skin.

I swallowed down the guilt. Part of me felt like I was alive again, like I *could* continue if...*No!* I shook the thought free before glancing over at him. The smile I gave him felt more like a grimace and his furrowed brow showed it looked that way too.

His cheek twitched as his eyes went straight ahead of him. His eyes raced over the road in front of him as his jaw tightened. "I'm not sure if it's my place to say this, El—but," he paused, gulping in air. As he exhaled, his tongue ran over his teeth and then he finally continued; "I know you said it's going to come back...but you don't know when. Just..." he exhaled. "Cherish these moments. You have a parent who truly loves you."

A new wave of guilt washed over me as I stared at him. His vein in his neck protruded as his arms tensed, his hands firm against the steering wheel as his eyes stayed on the road ahead.

"I know I have no right to say it, El. I just come from somewhere so different," he explained, closing his eyes for a moment before letting them settle on the road again. "The relationship you have with your dad...it's so special."

I leaned over and kissed his shoulder. "Thank you."

Trent scoffed, his body shaking with the movement. "For what? I..."

"You make me remember to live...for him." I squeezed my eyes shut. "Sometimes I just feel guilty about it...and then I feel guilty for not living. I just feel guilty a lot." I bit my lip, breathing in through my nose. "You signed yourself up for something really special."

Trent's eyes drifted down to mine. "Yeah, I did."

I sat back up, putting my hand over his knee. "You won't be saying that when you have to help me study for my first test next week. I'm pretty certain I'm going to flunk it. I just can't grasp this algebra stuff."

Trent smirked over at me. "Try accounting—the opposite of everything you were ever taught in math."

I shook my head, laughing. "Ah, no thanks."

"You sure?" Trent asked, lowering his sunglasses. "It's fun."

"Yeah," I said, dragging out the word. "I'm sure it is."

I leaned forward, picking up his smart phone. "You have anything good on here?"

"Depends on your definition of good," he replied as he pressed a button on the dashboard and the phone lit up. "Pick something. I've got it streamed to the car."

"I thought you rented this thing," I commented as I scrolled through the list and settled on Our Last Night.

"I did, but I'm super smart—remember, accounting, algebra, the occasional business I run," he shot back. "Nice choice."

I smiled, turning up the volume before settling back and nodding my head to the cover song.

Chapter
27

Trent opened the door, smirking as he leaned against it. I held the pie I made in his face, fluttering my eye lashes at him as I waited for him to comment.

"You really made something?" Trent asked as he put his hands in his back pockets, tipping back on his heels as he looked down at it, brows drawn over his green eyes.

I leaned up and kissed him, ignoring his skepticism. "I had to...after all; you did help me get a ninety on my exam."

"I was sure you didn't absorb any of it," Trent teased as I walked in and put the pie down on the counter.

"Thanks," I whispered as a tingle swept up my neck and across my face.

Trent wrapped his arms around my waist from behind me, pulling my body into him as he tucked his chin into my neck. "I meant because I'm not a good teacher. I'm used to helping with kindergarten level sh—tuff," he said, catching himself as Allie ran into the room.

"What's that?" Allie asked as she stood up on her toes, putting her chin on the edge of the counter. "Pie? What kind?"

"Strawberry Rhubarb," I replied. "Just needs to be popped in the oven to bake all the way through."

Allie turned, looking between Trent and me, before glancing up at her brother. "You think it's any good?"

I felt Trent shrug and elbowed him in the ribs. "I guess we'll just have to see."

I narrowed my eyes at him as I turned in his arms, placing my forearms against his shoulders. "Are you saying just because I made it, it will taste bad? I thought my potato salad proved I *can* cook."

Trent's lips curled at the edge, the white of his teeth showing. "Cooking is much different than baking...but I was just saying you can tell when something is homemade or store-bought."

I blinked at him a few times. "One thing is for certain, either way, you're only worth a store-bought pie, but I'm trying to impress your neighbors, not you."

Allie tugged on my shirt, and my eyes went down to her. "Ellie," she said, putting her hands behind her back and swaying her hips. "Do you know how to braid other people's hair?"

I nodded, and she burst up, clapping. "Could you please," she dragged out the word; "braid mine? Trent can never get it right."

"Oh," I replied, looking over at Trent with wide eyes. "You mean he's not perfect at *everything?*"

Allie giggled as she ran into the bathroom and climbed up on her stool to get her brush and elastic bands from her drawer.

"You're amazing—even if your pie is store-bought," Trent commented. "What does the oven need to be on?"

I looked over the couch at him, sucking my cheeks in as he smiled at me, feigning innocence. I huffed as I turned back around. I couldn't be mad at him when he looked so cute teasing me.

"Ellie?" Trent repeated, dragging out my name in a playful tone.

I was glad he couldn't see the smile it brought to my lips."Four fifty," I finally replied as Allie sat in front of me with crossed legs and handed me the brush and elastics.

I pursed my lips to keep from laughing as I looked at the plastic lady bugs attached to the black elastics. I ran my fingers through her hair, pulling it over the back of her neck. "Do you want a fish tail braid?"

"Fish tail?" she repeated, looking up at me. I nodded, and her brow wrinkled. "I'm not sure what that is."

"How about I do it, and then you let me know if you like it?"

Her head bobbed, and I began doing the braid. When I was finished, I moved it over her shoulder and she squealed in response. "Trent could never do something like that!"

Trent leaned against the back of the couch, his breath hot on my neck as Allie turned to show him.

"Beautiful," he commented. "Now how long on that pie?"

"About ten more minutes," I replied, keeping my eyes on Allie.

Allie climbed up on the couch and pulled on Trent's arm. She stared down at his watch. "It's twelve already! Meg told me to meet her under our tree at twelve!"

I pulled her into my arms, tickling her. "You're going to have to wait!"

She giggled, pushing my arms away. "Fine! Fine! For your pie!"

Trent came around the couch, crossing his arms as he stared at us. "That's not very nice, Ellie."

Allie pulled away, jumping off the couch and hiding behind Trent's legs. Trent knelt down, and she whispered into his ear. He looked between me and her before standing slowly and moving his head from shoulder to shoulder.

"I think you're right," he said as he looked down at his sister.

"About—?"

I was cut off by Trent pulling me into his arms, his hands sneaking up my shirt to my ribs.

"Not! Not! Not fair!" I gasped between fits of laughter.

"An eye for an eye!" Trent said.

"The pie!" I cried through hiccups. "I'm sure it's ready!"

Allie tugged on Trent's shirt and he stood, clapping his hands against one another. "You're lucky she hates to be late to anything."

I rolled my eyes as I stood, pulling my shirt down. "Okay...as if you weren't enjoying yourself."

He pulled the pie out of the oven, smelling it as he did. "This does smell good."

I crossed my arms. "Homemade?"

He shrugged. "Just because it smells good doesn't mean it's not store-bought."

My cheeks were still burning from the tickling, but I knew they got a shade brighter as I narrowed my eyes at him.

Allie grabbed my hand and then Trent's. "You guys can flirt on the way there!" she said as she dragged us to the door.

"Where is the party anyways?" I asked as we walked out into the sun.

"The neighborhood park. The block gets together a couple times a year—pretty much any time there's a holiday where we can get the kids together to play. It's good for them to interact," Trent explained as the park came into view. It was already packed with people and Allie began to pull us forward faster. She looked up at us as we got within a few yards. "Go ahead," he said, nodding to her.

She rushed forward, pushing open the fence and running to the big Acacia tree inside.

"It's too bad we weren't closer in April. I hide the eggs all over the place," Trent said as he placed the pie on a table filled with food. He slipped his hand into mine. "They still haven't found all of them."

"You sound like my dad. I'm still finding them years later," I explained, laughing.

Trent tilted his chin up, signaling to an egg tucked in the limbs of a smaller Acacia tree.

"Are you kidding me?" I asked, my eyes widening. "How are they supposed to find them in *trees* taller than they are?"

He rolled his shoulders, winking at me. "They need a bit of a challenge."

"Unbelievable," I said as we sat down on the swings. "They're all going to think bunnies can fly."

He chuckled as he kicked off and began to swing. "A flying bunny?"

"You'd be seeing one flying at you if I had one," I shot back, kicking to keep up with his momentum.

"That's animal cruelty," he called over his shoulder at me.

I reached out and smacked him as he passed me. "I know smacking you is!"

His head tilted between his shoulders as he laughed, causing him to shake and slow. I dug my feet into the ground, stopping as well. He ran his hand through his hair, tilting his head. "So I'm an animal now, am I?"

"What does that mean?" I asked, shaking my head.

He raised an eyebrow, and I felt my whole body warm as his eyes washed over me. I stood, beginning to walk away, and he pulled me into his arms. "Not so fast!"

I turned in his lap, and he moved my bangs out of my eyes. I felt my lashes flutter against my cheeks as I resisted the urge to kiss him, mumbling, "There are children around."

He sighed, putting his forehead against my collarbone. "You're naughty."

"Don't forget that," I teased, breathless.

His head lifted, and his lips moved against my ear as he replied, "But I'm the animal."

I couldn't help the sharp intake of breath as my body tingled.

"I suppose I should introduce you to the other parents." Trent heaved a sigh, and I stood, holding my hand out.

"Make sure you tell them *I* made the pie."

"Yes, that's exactly how I was going to introduce you. Here's my girlfriend, the great pie maker."

I narrowed my eyes at him as he wiggled his eyebrows up and down before leading us towards a crowd of people.

"Gerard!" Trent called out, and a man in a police officer uniform turned around with a smile filled with perfect white teeth. "You're here! Did you just get off your shift?"

"I couldn't miss this!" Gerard replied, clapping Trent on the back.

"Gerard, this is Ellie, my girlfriend. Ellie, this is Gerard, Meg's father," Trent said as I held out my hand.

Gerard flashed me another smile, and this time it reached his honey-brown eyes. His shaved head and tall muscular physique made him daunting in the outfit, but the kindness in his smile showed otherwise. "And I thought you might be a cat lady someday..."

His voice trailed off, and Trent punched his shoulder. "Seriously?"

"Nah," Gerard replied, his chin tucking into his neck. He looked over his shoulder calling out to his wife, "Lynn— you were right. She's his girlfriend!"

A petite red-headed woman turned, blinking at him a few times before putting her hand up and turning back to her conversation. I felt my face heat up as Gerard turned back to face us. "She's always right, so no big deal to her. If I'm right though, it's the end of the world!"

"Something to look forward to?" Trent teased, looking at me from the corner of his eyes.

I laughed to myself. I was used to Dad always being right, and I was pretty sure that wasn't going to be any different in this relationship. Trent seemed to be on a similar wave length to him, which meant when he was right and I was wrong I would end up terribly annoyed by it.

"So where did you two meet?" Gerard asked before taking a swig of his root beer.

I glanced over at Trent, and his smile spread warmth radiating in my chest. "He saved me from Stew."

"Stew?" Gerard asked.

"One of my employees," Trent explained.

"So," Gerard narrowed his eyes, holding his chin with his hand as he leaned back on his heels. "You stole an employee's girl?"

I burst out laughing, leaning forward as I shook my head. "Hell, no! He let me *suffer* for over a month while Stew harassed me every time I went to the store—and I go a lot since I'm in college!"

Gerard's bold laughter rattled through the air. "That's cruel!"

"I told you!" I hissed as I glared at Trent.

"Mark it on your calendar—the first time you were wrong! The first of many!" Gerard commented.

"Doubtful," I muttered to myself, but I couldn't help but smile. There was something about Gerard's infectious personality that made it impossible to be embarrassed.

Trent looked down at me, and I leaned up on my toes to kiss him.

"See!" Allie called out, and I pulled away from Trent as she rushed towards us with whom I assumed was Meg, in tow. "I told you they love each other!"

Meg's mom was now at Gerard's side. "My name's Lynn. Nice to meet you, Ellie," she said as she reached out and shook my hand. Her hand released and patted her daughter's head. "And this is Meg."

Meg looked up at her mom just as Allie looked up at Trent. They both fluttered their eyelashes at their parents.

"What?" Trent asked, tilting his head at her.

"Can I *please* sleep over Meg's tonight?"

Trent glanced up at Lynn and Gerard who looked between each other before nodding.

"Oh!" Meg said as she jumped up and down. "You two can have a sleep over too!"

I swallowed as I felt my face, followed by my arms and legs go numb.

Trent coughed, rubbing the back of his neck with his free hand; the other tightened around my waist, causing a rash of heat to explode beneath it.

I'm going to die right here.

"You can sleep over Meg's," Trent finally replied, but his voice was gruff with discomfort.

"Well," Gerard began as he looked between us and his wife. He seemed to sense our unease as he looked over at the picnic table, rubbing his stomach. "I'm famished— you guys ready to dive in? No one likes to be the first one to head over to the food table, but there's a mighty fine looking pie over there."

"Ellie made it! Trent thinks she bought it, though," Allie commented as we moved towards the tables filled with various picnic foods.

I looked over at Lynn. "It's to die for, and made from scratch."

"I wish I could bake," Lynn said as she pulled her straight hair into a pony tail. She wrinkled her freckled nose. "I can cook, but I sure as hell can't bake!"

"You're telling me," Gerard said over his shoulder as he began to pile a plate with potato salad.

"Told you so," Trent whispered in my ear.

I elbowed him as I shot back, "I can do both!"

Trent raised an eyebrow at me, and I breathed in deeply before grabbing a plate.

"This is really smart," I commented, pointing to the inflated thing filled with ice and the containers that needed to stay cold.

"It's store bought," Trent teased, and I narrowed my eyes at him.

"Beer?" Gerard asked as he reached the cooler.

I shook my head as he handed one over to Trent.

"Mean drunk?" Gerard commented, and I shrugged.

I grit my teeth as I fought the sinking feeling in my stomach. I reached forward and grabbed a water before following Trent to a picnic table.

"Do you ever drink?" Trent asked as he took a sip of his beer. "I mean most people your age have."

"You've seen my college buddies, what do you think?"

Trent moved the chips around his plate, concentrating on them as his lips pressed together. "Just because you hang out with them doesn't mean you're like them."

I pushed my bangs out of my eyes. "I got drunk once...never again. Gerard nailed it; I'm a mean drunk."

"You? Mean?" Trent commented as he popped a chip in his mouth.

I unscrewed the top of my water before replying, "I hope you never see that side of me...I can be brutally illogical."

"Can't we all?"

I looked down at my plate filled with food, my stomach suddenly rolling. "My dad's never been."

He reached forward, squeezing my hand. "Dad's never are..." his eyes clouded, and his jaw clenched before he added, "If they're good ones."

"You are," I replied.

Trent's hand remained over mine, but his eyes went down to his food. "I'm just a brother."

"Not at all— not to her. She looks at you like I look at my dad." Trent's eyes rose to mine, and I leaned forward; "Like you're her hero, because you are."

Chapter 28

Allie hugged Trent and I before skipping hand and hand with Meg down the side walk in the opposite direction with Gerard and Lynn close behind. Trent's hand found mine, and we turned towards the apartment. I dipped my head back, pulling in a breath and letting it out slowly as I stared at the grayish night sky. I couldn't remember the last time I saw the stars. Phoenix was beautiful, but it was lacking anything like a night sky. It was something I did actually miss from New England. We lived in the country, and I was always able to see the stars. Trent looked down at me, his eyes darting over my face.

"What you thinking about?" he asked, watching my expression.

I let my eyes look back into the starless sky, my body feeling heavy. "Just remembering what stars look like."

Trent scoffed, his head jerking. "I know...I think I've almost forgotten. We should've stayed in Sedona for the night."

I let my head drop back down, swallowing as I did. I fought the urge to rub the goose bumps rising over my arms at the thought of us spending the night together. It could happen tonight. My eyes fluttered as I finally replied in a controlled voice, "Maybe next time.

"Speaking of which," Trent said, dropping my hand and speeding up so he was walking backwards in front of me. "How are your paintings doing?"

I pulled my lips in as I looked down at my feet, letting the breath I held in my lungs out. He either missed the change in my tone, or he hadn't noticed. The change of subject made a smile twitch on my lips.

"So?" Trent pushed.

"I have to get some more up there. Two of them sold already," I replied, finally letting my eyes meet him as my heart raced. "One week—and two sold!"

Trent's eyes widened and he stopped, pulling me into his arms and spinning me around. I laughed, tipping my head back as the starless sky spun around above me. "That's my girl!

He lowered me back to the ground slowly, and my shirt rose as the cotton of my shirt stuck against his. Our eyes locked on one another, and the hollow buzz of suburbia faded to nothing against the sound of my blood rushing in my ears. His hands moved up my bare arms to my face and his thumbs caressed my cheeks as his lips lowered to mine. Heat flooded my body as the kiss deepened, his lips pushing mine apart so his tongue raced over mine. A car drove by, honking, and I pulled away, my hand going to my damp lips as I looked at him. He took a shaky breath before swallowing.

"Uh...you want to," he swallowed again, signaling over his shoulder with his thumb. "Uh...watch a movie?"

I bit my lip to keep from laughing at his sudden awkwardness. "Yeah, I'd like that."

We fell into step with one another and Trent's hands remained in his pockets. I slipped my arm through his, smiling up at him until he gave in and his fingers intertwined with mine.

"You're cute when you're embarrassed," I commented as we made our way up the front steps.

"I'm not embarrassed," Trent said with his voice low as he unlocked the door.

"Nervous?" I asked, and the same feeling flooded my veins with a chill as I looked around the empty apartment.

Tonight. Us...alone. Sure, we could've taken advantage of Allie being asleep any other time—but after that kiss...My mind raced, and I bit the inside of my lip to check my thoughts.

"No," he replied, shaking his head. "You?"

I felt my mouth go dry as Trent grabbed the remote off the side table and turned on the television. He sat down, patting the empty seat next to him with one eyebrow raised. I rubbed my palms against my jeans as I sat down beside him and pulled my legs up behind me.

Deep breaths. No! I pulled my eyes shut. He'd notice if I was breathing too heavy. My mind drifted to his lips grazing my neck, his hands slipping up the bare skin of my sides. *Stop!* I curled my toes as he put his arm around me, pulling me closer to him. His finger tips ran over my arms, and I caught my breath in my throat.

Normal. Act normal.

"How's this one?" Trent asked, nodding to the television.

"Sure," I replied without even paying attention to what it was.

I tried to pay attention to what was going on, but I couldn't concentrate with his fingers skimming over my skin like that. I fought the urge to play with the end of my braid, or play with the frays on my pants, or anything—anything to keep my mind off the way his heart seemed to be pounding too hard against my ear. Was he thinking—I clenched my jaw.

He's a guy.

And you're a girl.

I felt a cold sweat dampening my neck despite the central air cooling the house to a comfortable temperature.

Finally, I couldn't take it anymore. I need to do something—or at least talk.

"So," I began, looking down at my hands. "It must be nice to live near a cop?"

Trent's fingers froze over my body, and his muscles tensed.

"Yeah," he replied, and I watched as he licked his lips before sucking his lower lip in. His free hand went to his forehead before his palm turned and he continued; "Actually, it's really nice. My dad...he's found us before. He keeps trying to take Allie— even though he knows he won't get anything from the state, and they won't let him have her. It's like he has this grudge against me for taking her away. He—" Trent paused, rubbing his eyes. "I had to put a restraining order on him. My own father...anyways, there's a warrant out for him now, and if they catch him he'd spend something like twenty years in jail. I don't see him cropping up here any time soon, but...it's nice to know that there's a cop here. It's been a couple years since I saw Dad last, I still worry, though."

"What about your mom, does she ever come around?"

Trent's eyes clouded and he shook his head. "I'm not even sure she's still alive. She was heading towards OD'ing pretty fast."

"You miss her?" I asked, cocking my head at him.

Trent leaned forward, his hands raking through his hair to the back of his neck where his fingers tangled together as he nodded. He glanced over at me. "I know I shouldn't, but I do. She wasn't a bad person, El. She just made bad decisions. I wish we'd been enough to turn her around, and I feel like an awful person for taking her daughter away—but she..." his voice drifted, and his mouth turned down as he squeezed his eyes shut. "She wasn't stable. That's not good for a kid—I should know."

I leaned forward, rubbing his back. "You shouldn't feel guilty; you did what was best for Allie, and for you."

His eyes locked on mine, ticking back and forth as he asked, and "Do you really think I'm her hero?"

I ran my hand over his curled bicep, pushing his arm down and letting my fingers trace the tattoo on his forearm. "Yeah, I do. You saved her, whether or not she knows it—you truly are a hero."

"Your dad is your hero..."

"Yeah," I began as my throat thickened. I felt myself blink hard. "He's always been trying save someone...but look where he ended up."

Trent shook his head, and I stood dropping my head back to look at the ceiling as the metallic taste filled my mouth. I walked over to the door leading to his room and pushed it open. I wanted a distraction. I didn't want to think about it. I heard Trent follow me, and I walked over to the guitars hung on the wall. I ran my fingers over the strings. I knew Trent was leaning against the door frame, watching me carefully.

"My dad used to play drums before he got sick," I explained. "I used to want to learn how to play guitar...then we could have our own band."

Trent walked forward, going to sit on his bed, and I turned to face him.

"He's a scientist. He's been trying to find the cure for different types of cancer for as long as I can remember...and I don't mean little labs somewhere. Government labs...and all those tests...and chemicals—and whatever the fuck," I replied, stopping as my body trembled; "he was handling—that's what gave him it...the cancer. He was trying to find a cure," my neck pushed forward as I fought back the tears. "And he...he basically killed himself."

"There's no cure?" Trent whispered.

I looked at the ceiling, dimly lit by the bedside lamp. "If there was, he would've found it."

Trent stood and his face came into my vision as he looked down at me. He ran his hand up my back until it reached my head, tipping it back to a normal position. He put his forehead against mine, his hand cupping my cheek as his other stayed on my lower back.

"Not all cures are black and white—not all cures save us," Trent whispered, and I felt my eyelashes heavy with tears.

"I'm dying too—every time I look at him and know that every breath he takes is closer to his last one." I didn't bother wiping away the silent tears now making their way down my face.

"It's always been that way, El. We're all going to die someday," He crushed his eyes shut, shaking his head. "That sounded harsh. I didn't—"

"You're right."

He opened his eyes, his chest rising with the deep inhale he took. "I do get it. I used to come home and wonder if I was going to find my mom dead." His eyes drifted before coming back to mine. "But every time I didn't—every time I came home and she was fine—I was thankful for it, even more so if she was straight."

I laid my head on his chest, and his hands stayed on my lower back, his own head lowering into the crook of my shoulder. We stayed like that for a moment as my heart beat evened out, my eyes drifted to his bed and the rate picked up again. My chest tightened as I stared at the neat brown and tan checkered comforter, and then my eyes drifted to the time.

1:30 AM.

My eyes suddenly felt heavy, and my mouth formed a yawn.

Trent looked down at me, and his own eyes were heavy. "Tired?" he asked.

"Yeah, and I don't feel like driving home." I ignored the whooshing of blood through my ears as my face heated.

"I can take the couch," Trent explained as he pulled away and pointed his thumb over his shoulder before going to his dresser and pulling out a pair of pajama bottoms and a plain black tee. "They might be big, but it should be more comfortable for you."

I took them from him, my hand touching his and causing tingles to run up my spine. "You know, I don't mind if...if you *don't* take the couch."

Trent's eyebrow twitched as he looked at me, and I laughed.

"Come on, we're both adults, and I'm sure you can keep your hands off of me if I'm hidden under all this," I replied, holding up the clothing that undoubtedly would be baggy on me.

"Are you sure?" he asked, pulling his own pair of pajama pants out of the drawer.

"Positive, now turn the other way so I can get undressed," I ordered, using my pointer finger to signal a circle.

He put his hands up. "Of course, but I think you'll be the one peeking."

I rolled my eyes as I turned, pulling my shirt off and replacing it with his. I paused as I heard the zipper of his pants go down. I pursed my lips as I gazed straight ahead as I unzipped mine and pulled them off. I cursed as I struggled to pull the tight bottom off. "Skinny jeans."

"You okay?" Trent asked, and his voice was deep with amusement.

"Oh, shut up! If you had to wear jeans this tight you'd understand."

I turned and flopped on his bed, putting my arms behind my head as I stared at his bare back. Between his shoulder blades was another tattoo, this one of a bird flying through the sun.

"You didn't tell me about that one," I commented, and he turned, putting his hands up.

"I didn't know you wanted to know where all of them where," he replied, smirking down at me as my jaw dropped.

There was another tattoo on the cap of his shoulder, this one a Japanese lotus in bright orange and pink. My eyes wondered to his chest, which was covered in a thin layer of hair I hadn't expected. He scratched it, his neck turning red up to his ears.

"Sorry about the hairy chest. I can put a shirt on if it bothers you," he said.

I sat up, pulling my knees to my chest as my eyes wandered again. I shook my head, putting my eyes back where they belonged, on his face. "If you have to put a shirt on it won't be because of your hairy chest."

His eyebrows twitched as he laughed. "You like it then?"

I tapped my hands on my knees as my eyes dropped to his slightly sculpted chest, down to his flat stomach and his hip bones. I lay back, pulling the pillow over my face. "Why couldn't you put on a burlap sack?" I muttered into it.

I felt Trent's body indent the bed next to me, and he lifted up the edge of the pillow, blinking at me.

"What was that?" he asked.

I rolled my eyes smacking him with the pillow before putting it back under my head and turning my back to him. Trent reached over me, flicking off the light switch, and wrapping his arm around me. I snuggled into him and closed my eyes.

Chapter 29

I rubbed my eyes as I rolled over in the bed, spreading out over the soft sheets and inhaling Trent's cologne.

Trent's cologne. My eyes shot open, and I looked at the guitars on the walls. I sat up, running my hands through my hair and pulling out the braid. I remembered Trent wrapping his arm around me, but the second the light had gone out I fell into a deep sleep. I looked to the side of me where Trent's pillow was still indented with the shape of his head before slipping out of the bed and heading into the main living area.

Trent stood at the stove, still in his pajama bottoms, humming to himself. I walked forward, wrapping my arms around his waist.

He lifted his arm, putting it around my shoulders. His lips found the top of my head before he spoke, "Hey, I didn't want to wake you up. You looked so peaceful. I hope you like pancakes."

I closed my eyes as I moved my chin so I could kiss the tattoo on the top of his shoulder. A shudder passed through his body as I moved my lips over his skin, answering without lifting them, "I love them."

I looked up at him through my bangs, and his nostrils flared as he fought to keep his eyes open. "That's not really fair," he said, his voice hoarse.

"Why?" I whispered, my lips skimming over his tattoo up to his neck.

I felt his muscles tense beneath my mouth as the stove clicked off and the sound of the pan scuffing across the glass surface filled the room. A tingle passed up my spine as he turned, pushing me up against the wall behind us. His lips crushed into mine, and my hands slipped up his back digging into the muscles over his shoulder blades. I gasped as his lips left mine, drifting down my chin to my neck. I was losing control. Fast.

How many weeks...My eyes fluttered against my cheeks as his hands slipped up my shirt.

Weeks, El. How many weeks?

Four? The shirt slipped over my head.

No, it was more than that.

Wasn't it?

His lips skimmed over my collarbone, my eyes found the ceiling as my hands buried in the back of his hair.

Six or seven?

His hands drifted up, pushing my bra strap down.

Fuck it.

His lips found mine again as his hands slid down my back and over my ass, bringing my legs up and around his waist. He carried me, one hand firmly wrapped across my back as the other felt along the edge of the wall until we got to the bedroom, where he placed me softly on the bed. I pulled his body over mine before he could lift away. Our bare skin pressed together, and my eyes rolled in the back of my head as warmth spread through my limps. His body trembled again as my back arched against his hands running up my spine to my bra clasp. He paused, his forehead against mine as both our chests heaved, his hands hovering over either of my shoulders. I leaned forward, and the bra fell down to my waist. His eyes raced over mine, and they seemed to ask if I was ready for this.

I closed my eyes, pressing our mouths together as I pulled him back to me. Our bare chests touched, and my mouth opened in a moan against his warmth. His lips moved down, and his hands slipped up my arms into my own, our fingers weaving together. My body arched again, and I loosened our hands, slipping them down his back to his pants. His eyes locked on mine again, his arms straining as he held his body inches above mine. I leaned up running my lips over the tattoo that started this intense heat.

"El," he whispered my name, a breathless gasp, and I slipped his pants down, my lip dragging up his neck to his chin.

I swallowed as his mouth found my own neck, his arm slipping under my waist and pulling me to the top of him before he pushed the baggy pajama pants down my body. His mouth traveled down my body as he did. He rolled over me again, pulling my arms over my head as our hands slipped into one another.

~~~

Trent kissed my head as I placed it on his chest, our legs still tangled beneath the blankets. I ran my fingers over the hair on his chest, and he sighed.

"Does it bug you?"

I shook my head, looking up at him as I kissed the skin beneath my lips. "It's sexy."

My sounded weak against the sound of my hammering heart in my ears. Trent's chest rose with a chuckle.

"I think you're hallucinating," Trent replied, smirking down at me.

My body warmed again, and I closed my eyes as I shook my head, cuddling into him. "It's sexy okay, stop fighting it."

Trent's fingers ran through my hair, weaving through the smooth waves until they stopped halfway down my back. My body shivered against his fingertips over my bare spine. "So is your bed head."

I leaned up on my hands, perching on his chest as I blew my bangs out of my eyes. "Now that's a bold faced lie!"

He shrugged, sitting up as he tilted my chin up with one finger. "I can think whatever I like to."

I narrowed my eyes at him and his lips found mine again, spinning me back into lightheaded happiness. My stomach rolled as I saw the time on the clock from the corner of my eye. "Lynn and Gerard probably noticed my car is still here."

"Look at me," Trent whispered. "Are you okay?"

I opened my eyes and swallowed, nodding. "Yeah."

His eyes flicked across my face, and his lips formed a tight line. "You look guilty."

I sat up, rubbing my face, before looking over my shoulder at him. The sheets had fallen down to his waist as I moved, showing his bare hip bones, and my skin heated at the thought of them pressed against my own. My eyes moved back up his flat stomach to his now pale face. His jaw clenched as his brows hung tightly over his eyes.

"How many weeks have we been dating?"

Trent's eyes widened in an instant, and he sat up further in bed.

Eyes on his face, I reminded myself, but they still drifted down where the blanket was barely covering him. My eyes shot back to his face as my own burned. I fought the urge to wrap my legs around his waist and run my fingers through his now messy hair. The top length was pulled up in an attractive tangle that enhanced the strong shape of his jaw.

"You're worried how many weeks we've been dating?" Trent asked.

"I...I just honestly can't remember," I replied as I pulled my bottom lip into my mouth, half in embarrassment, half to keep my mind off of how perfect his body felt against mine.

He leaned forward, kissing my shoulder. "Eight...and five days. Depending on when you count this relationship having started."

I let the breath out I hadn't realized I was holding. "That's not bad then."

Trent's right eyebrow lifted into his forehead as his lips lifted up on the same side. "You have a set amount of weeks before you can have sex with someone?"

I hid my head in my knees. I didn't really, because I didn't really date all that much, which meant I didn't...do this all that much either.

"Do you?" I finally asked, looking over at him.

He pursed his lips. "It doesn't usually get this far."

"You're a guy, though," I replied, fighting the shifting feeling in my stomach as I wondered just how many girls he had been with. I didn't want to know. Did I?

He laughed, scratching the top of his head. "So that means I'm automatically a slut?"

I pressed my eyes shut as I shook my head. "No—"

His finger pressed against my lips, and I opened my eyes. His finger slid under my chin, tilting our lips together before he pressed our foreheads together. "I haven't in a long time...I've been too busy being a single parent. I care about you, El. A lot...besides the fact you're extremely beautiful."

I smiled, kissing him. "Thank you."

"Now," he said, slipping out of the bed so his full body was exposed again. "Breakfast?"

My stomach fluttered as my eyes drifted from the line of hair below his belly button down. I pulled his body back over mine, kissing his smiling lips.

"Round two?" I suggested.

His eyes wandered down my body, beneath his own. "Been a while for you too?"

I leaned up, running my teeth over his ear lobe before kissing his neck. "Maybe."

Trent laughed, his lips kissing my neck as my eyes fluttered shut. "I don't know if we have enough time right now...but I promise I won't be able to keep my hands off of you too long."

I sighed as he pulled away and leaned down to pull his pajamas on. I stood, and he froze, his eyes wandering over my body. He sucked air through his teeth, and I bit my lip as I leaned down and picked up my jeans.

"Maybe..." he began as I slipped my pants on.

I cocked my head at him as I let my fingers stop on the zipper. "Maybe?" I repeated.

He stepped forward, his hands moving up my bare sides and lifting my arms to put them around his neck. Our chests pressed against each other, igniting the heat again just as the doorbell rang. He looked up at the ceiling, before pressing his eyes shut.

"I should've just left the room," he muttered to himself as he looked down.

I laughed, pulling his over-sized shirt on. "I'll get the door."

"Hello, Ellie!" Allie said as she skipped through the door.

Lynn smirked over my shoulder as I heard the bedroom door open.

"How was Allie?" Trent asked, scratching the back of his head.

He was now wearing a pair of khakis, a black tee and a black and red over-shirt.

Lynn looked between the two of us before answering, "Very good as always."

"Thanks for watching her," Trent said, and Lynn nodded, still smirking.

"Any time. Good to see you again, Ellie."

I smiled back at her, feeling the blush heating my cheeks but choosing to ignore it.

"We had pancakes!" Allie said as she plopped on the couch, still bouncing.

"We were just about to eat ours," Trent explained as he went to the stove where the last pancake looked about half done. He opened the trash and dumped that one in before taking the plate piled with already cooked ones into the microwave. "Do you want to get the laundry together for me?"

"Sure," she replied, bouncing off the couch and onto the floor. "Why are your pancakes cold?"

Trent's arms tensed as his fists clenched. "Ellie and I got to talking, and we just forgot about them."

"You must've been talking about something fun!" Allie said as she shook her head back and forth, hopping like a bunny to her bedroom.

I burst out laughing and Trent hugged me, laughing too.

"It was fun, wasn't it?" he teased before pulling away and going to the fridge to grab the syrup.

"Yeah," I replied, sniffing the air. "But those pancakes smell really good. I don't know how I missed that when I came out."

Trent blinked slowly at me, signaling to his body. "All this, maybe?"

I rolled my eyes. "I think," I replied, stepping forward and kissing him. "I could've just eaten them—but you could resist *me.*"

"Aren't we full of ourselves?" Trent shot back as he took the pancakes out and split them between the two plates and handed me mine.

Allie came back into the room dragging a pink bag with purple butterflies all over it, filled with clothes. "I got mine! You have to get your stinky clothes, though!"

Trent winked at me as we sat down, and I plopped a piece of pancake in my mouth. I closed my eyes leaning back. "You definitely cook better than me," I commented through a mouthful.

Allie sat on the couch, turning to face us. "I don't know. That pie was pretty yummy!"

I smiled over at her. "I'm glad to hear that," I said, shooting Trent a look to stay shut up.

He put his hands up. "I actually agree with Allie."

"See!" Allie said. "You can cook!"

"Not store-bought?" I asked.

Trent shook his head.

"Trent?" Allie asked, placing her cheek on her hands on the top of the couch. "You remember the quarters?"

"I sure did," he replied, nodding to a few rolls on the counter top, next to the bowl where his keys were.

"Why don't you do the laundry at my house? You can take the quarters and put them in Allie's piggy bank," I suggested.

I looked down at my pancakes, cutting them carefully as I waited for an answer. Maybe Trent had had enough time with me between the last few days and needed a break—or maybe it was a special thing between the two of them. I swallowed at what felt like an unnaturally long pause.

"What do you think?" Trent asked Allie, and I let my eyes move up slightly.

"Maybe I'll have enough to buy that owl?" she asked, clapping.

"Owl?" I repeated as she went to the counter and tried to get the quarters. Even on her tip toes, her fingers barely reached the edge of the counter.

Trent stood and grabbed the quarters. "Go get your bank." Allie ran into her bedroom, and he looked over at me. "There's this over sized owl at the craft store she saw. She's been obsessing over it since, but it's over priced."

"I think I know the one—pink—about this big?" I showed the size with my hands and Trent nodded. "I think I actually have a coupon for that store— 50% off."

"No sh—stuff," he said as Allie ran in the room with her plastic piggy.

I laughed into my hand as he shook his head at his slip up. I watched as Trent handed Allie each quarter, and she counted them as she placed them into it. When she reached the end, she counted on her fingers, her brow crunching as she tried to do the math.

"Is fifty quarters enough?" she asked. "That's how much is in here."

"That must be heavy!" I commented as I picked up Trent and my plates.

She nodded. "It is! Trent...is it enough for the owl?"

"If you help do the dishes tonight, then we'll call it even. How about that?" Trent asked.

She jumped up, smiling and nodding furiously.

"Looks like we have to stop off before laundry," I commented over my shoulder as she handed Trent the piggy bank.

Allie spun in a circle. Singing in an undecipherable voice, where all I understood was the word owl in between squeals.

Trent cringed before coming over to me and whispering, "She didn't get my talent."

Chapter 30

I walked up the stairs, pausing at the entrance to the living room. Trent sat on the couch, his arm over the top of it; Allie snuggled into his chest with her giant pink owl between her legs as they watched PBS. She could barely wrap her arms around the thing it was so big, but her face was priceless when Trent lifted it from the shelf and handed it to her. She was barely a head taller than it and practically fell over as she tried to carry it to the cash register. I had a feeling she wasn't going to let it out of her sight any time soon. I felt my muscles relax as I made my way to sit down on the other side of Allie.

"Your laundry is washing," I said, looking down at Allie. "By the way there were a few tops I think I'd like to borrow."

She wrinkled her nose at me shaking her head. "You're too big, silly!"

I clicked my tongue against the roof of my mouth as I sunk down into the couch, pouting. "Are you sure?"

She nodded with her eyes wide. "Positive!"

"Ah, well," I replied with a sigh, smiling over her head at Trent.

Trent glanced over his shoulder, using his hand to turn the photographs behind us. "Allie was right, you do look a lot like your father—but you look a lot like your mom, too."

"Thanks, but I think I look more like my dad," I replied.

Trent narrowed his eyes at the photograph, and then looked over at me. "You have her smile."

I laughed, nodding as I wrapped my hands around my knees. "Dad says the same thing. He says it's like she's smiling through me."

Allie handed me her owl, turning and peeking over at the photograph Trent was looking at. "Where's your mommy, Ellie?"

My jaw went slack, and I stared between the two of them. What did you tell a child about someone who died? I bit my lip, wondering how Trent had ever explained to Allie where their mom and dad went. I opened my mouth to speak, but Trent shook his head as he put his hand on Allie's shoulder.

"She's in heaven," Trent replied, his voice soft.

Allie looked over her shoulder at me, before crawling into my lap and wrapping her arms around my waist.

"My mommy's there too," Allie whispered, rubbing her cheek against my stomach.

I glanced over at Trent who was looking at the tattoos on his forearms. His eyes didn't move as he stared at them, his lip caught between his teeth.

"It's a nice place," Allie said, looking up at me through her eyelashes. "Trent promised it was."

I nodded. "It is."

Allie pulled away, turning the next photo around. Trent's eyes lifted to look at it, and a smile formed on his lips.

"You were a cute baby," he commented.

"Aren't all babies?" I replied.

Allie plopped back down, pulling the owl back into her lap and wrapping her legs around it again. She put her chin on the top of its head before saying, "Some babies look like aliens!"

Trent's and my gaze locked on one another as we both tried to contain our laughter.

"I guess you're right," I finally said once I thought I could control myself.

Allie pursed her lips looking at Trent and then over at me before looking straight ahead at the television. She smiled to herself. "I bet your babies will be cute!"

My eyes widened and Trent coughed into his hand, sinking into the cushions. "Thanks Allie, but you're thinking very far ahead."

Allie shrugged; her eyes still on the television. "People who love each other make babies."

It was my turn to cough. I glanced over at Trent who was covering his eyes with his hands. He lifted his fingers so I could see his eyes, and they were smiling just as much as his lips. I rolled my eyes before standing. "I'm going to change out of these clothes."

When I came back down the stairs he was waiting on the second step. He looked at me over his shoulder. "Kids say the darnedest things?"

"Allie sure does!"

Trent ran his fingers through his hair. "She's very good at observing things, but not so much at keeping her observations to herself. She calls it like it is."

I sat down next to him, putting my head on his shoulder as we watched Allie coloring in a book I got her at the craft store. "It must've been hard...telling her?"

Trent's lips pressed against my forehead, before he leaned forward with his palms up as his arms pushed against his knees. "It was hard lying to her, but I didn't know what else to tell her. It was just easier. I hope she doesn't hate me for it someday."

I cocked my head as I stared at the koi on his arms, reaching forward to trace letters hidden within the waves that surrounded the night scene.

"That's her name?" I whispered as my fingers spelled out the word *Marie.*

Trent clenched his fists and the sky around the koi contorted. "Yeah."

His hands unclenched and he ran his fingers over the day scene, his fingers stopped at the waves. The name *Allie* was hidden much the way his mother's name was.

I tucked my head in his shoulder, using my hand to turn his face to mine. "She's smart...she'll know you did it to protect her—and you never know, it might not be a lie."

Trent's face paled, and his eyes stayed on his arm. He ran his tongue over his lips before looking up at me.

"You could try to find her?" I whispered, and his eyes relaxed, his body slouching beneath me.

"That'd be selfish—" he said, shaking his head. "I need to think about Allie...and that's not good for her."

"So being a parent means you never think about yourself?" I asked, my vision darkening at the edges.

Dad always protected me. He even went to most of his first doctor appointments by himself. It maddened me he would do that, and I had been so hurt by it then. Now, I realized it must have been hard to hide it from me, and even harder to go through it alone.

"No...It just means you *should* make decisions based on what's best for someone else—even if it means you're making a sacrifice. Probably the reason Mom let me take her in the first place," Trent replied.

"You think she let you?" I asked, looking back over at Allie. She was talking to her owl, patting it on the head as she explained to him what she drew.

"She signed the papers freely...followed my wishes to not make contact with Allie."

His face turned red, and his head went into his hands as he leaned forward.

"But?" I asked, watching as his back tensed, and my stomach twisted.

"I didn't make her promise to not contact *me.* She knows where we are—she wrote me a letter...I got it a few days ago. I just worry about Dad—she makes bad decision when it comes to him. The only good one she made about him was when she made sure he was deemed an unfit parent, so he couldn't try to take Allie away. He blames me, of course."

His hands squeezed into fists, and he stretched his legs as he rubbed his knuckles over his thighs.

"You're worried she's talking to your dad?"

Trent nodded, squeezing his eyes shut as his nostrils flared. His panic leaked off of him in waves, and I founded myself holding onto the edge of the hardwood step too hard. I let go, looking down at the red marks on my palms. My stomach rolled as the image of the guard rails flying past me flashed through my mind. We were human, and humans made mistakes. It was learning from that mattered.

I swallowed. "Are you thinking about moving?"

Trent cleared his throat, and I watched as his hands tapped on his knees. "I think it's the best idea—but..." he put his elbow against the wall." I fucked up, El. I was selfish...and now she's going to pay for it. We live next to her best friend—"

"Gerard's a cop—"

"And he's not always home."

"Too bad your dad couldn't just get thrown in the slammer," I replied, rubbing his shoulder as I attempted to make a joke out of the situation.

Trent leaned his head back making a half laughing and half choking noise. "If only it was that easy."

I squeezed his knee. "Then it wouldn't be parenting—would it?"

Trent kissed my forehead before standing and holding his hand out. We walked back into the living room where Allie was whispering to the owl.

"What's that?" I asked, leaning over to look at her drawing.

"There was a free page," she replied, pushing it forward so we could see. "There's you—see the braid! And me—braid too! And Trent...and of course, Owlie!"

I pursed my lips as my heart pounded in my chest. I couldn't keep the smile off my face as I looked up at Trent. At that moment it didn't feel like a sacrifice.

Chapter 31

"Long time no see," I said to Morgan as I leaned on the visitor desk, narrowing my eyes at her.

She looked up at me, running her tongue over her teeth inside her lip. "I can't help it. I have to pick up shifts whenever I can— real life experience makes for an easier in when I need an internship," she covered the side of her mouth as she leaned forward, whispering; "Getting in good with the boss so maybe I can do it here."

"It's alright, I see how it is," I replied, looking around; "so where's the hot dude you blew me off for hiding?"

Morgan rolled her honey brown eyes. "Your dad is in the same wing he's been in his whole stay."

I gagged, crossing my eyes. "Really?"

Morgan nodded. "The nurses all love him—call him *the silver fox*. Meow!"

I blinked at her a few times before we both started laughing. "You have a few minutes to walk with me?"

Morgan looked over at her desk partner who gave her a soft smile and nodded over her shoulder. "Thanks," she said, patting the woman's shoulder as she walked around to my side.

"So how are things with book-hottie—Trent, right?" Morgan asked, looking over at me, and I knew that a blush instantly hit my cheeks. Her eyes widened. "Did you guys—?"

I felt my mouth go dry as I continued to stare ahead.

"Finally!" she said, grabbing my arm. "It's been, what, two months?"

"Yeah, I didn't realize we'd been dating that long," I replied, finally letting my eyes meet hers.

They were soft, like I had gotten used to over the past few weeks. She was here almost every time I came to visit, and she always made a point to walk me to Dad's wing, sometimes she even came in and talked with us for a little bit on her breaks. While we kept making plans over and over again, we never seemed to be able to quite nail down a time where we were both available. I smiled at her—this was nice, though. I felt like if I really needed her, she would be there as soon as I said so.

And I realized I would be there for her too.

"I couldn't have kept my hands off him that long," Morgan teased, elbowing my ribcage. "You have too much self-control."

I laughed. "I'm sure you could've—when you dated that Mark kid, wasn't it almost a whole two weeks?"

She stopped at the door to the wing, putting her hand on her hips as she pursed her lips. "Ha ha! It was actually almost a month! And he was pretty damn hot."

"As hot as Trent?" I asked, cocking my head at her.

"Yes..." she paused, looking at her white sneakers before glancing back up at me sideways."Well, he would've been if he had tattoos like him!"

I bit my lip, and she narrowed her eyes.

"What are you hiding?" she asked, leaning forward.

I looked at the ceiling. "He's got more of them."

Her eyes widened and she reached for my hands. "Oh," she dragged out the word; "tell me more!"

We walked through the doors, our heads bent together. "He has one on the cap of his shoulder—so gorgeous; it's a lotus flower—orange and pink. And in between his shoulder blades he has a bird flying into the sun."

We stopped at Dad's door. "So hot," Morgan whispered.

"Even better—he designs them himself!" I explained.

She squeezed my arm, biting the inside of her cheek as her eyebrows raised. "You should have him design you one."

"Design what?" Dad asked as he stood from his couch and flicked off the television.

Morgan grimaced, and I shrugged. "A tattoo."

"A tattoo?" Dad repeated. "For you Morg?"

Morgan shook her head, a shiver passing through her body. "No way...needles are not my friend."

"Your dad's lucky then," he replied, looking over at me with a frown. It didn't meet his eyes though, which were bright and wide. "And apparently, Trent's looking to see if he can get on my bad side."

Morgan mouth *sorry* before waving and heading back in the direction we came.

I crossed my arms, looking at Dad. He was only an inch taller than me, so I didn't have to look up at him like I did Trent. "As if you have a *good* side," I shot back.

Dad's lips curled up into a smirk before he tossed his head back and gave his best maniacal scientist laugh. "Indeed," he replied, letting his head come back down slowly as he moved his fingertips together. "Indeed."

"Laying it on thick today, huh?" I commented as I held my elbow out to link with his. He wasn't using his cane today, but I still wanted to make sure he had something to hold onto if he needed it. He placed his arm through mine, and we walked to the door to the garden. "So since you're feeling so much better...will you be coming home soon?"

I pushed open the door and we walked into the bright sunlight. Dad breathed in the fresh air, a soft smile on his lips that I knew didn't mean yes.

"It's looking better, but the doctors are still running tests..." his voice drifted, and he didn't have to say the words *to see if it's back yet.*

I swallowed the lump in my throat. "Well, soon enough I'm sure."

Dad winked at me. "With the fresh air and daily walks with my girl, I'm bound to be home sooner than later."

I smiled at him before reaching up and rubbing his head. "And you've even got hair now, like, real hair!"

He puffed his chest. "They call me *the* silver fox," he said, putting an accent on the words *silver fox.*

"You realize that's kind of disturbing, right?"

His neck jutted back as he looked over at me. "That your dad is hot? Or that your friend thinks he's hot?"

I stared back at him, blinking in much the same fashion I had with Morgan. "Seriously?"

He shrugged, and I burst out laughing as we sat down on the bench. We tipped our heads back to the sun in unison, and I let my hand fall into his. He squeezed it, and I found myself chuckling again as the warmth of his happiness filled my core.

Chapter
32

It had been four days since I had seen Trent face to face. We chatted briefly on the phone, but it seemed the problem that plagued Morgan and I now plagued Trent and me. My stomach sank as I rubbed my temples. Trent assured me the meetings with senior management would be over soon, and that the vacations his employees were suddenly taking would be over soon too. Mid June was always a heavy vacation week for his team members. Still, I wondered if the move towards intimacy in our relationship caused the shift. I sat up, pushing my hands through my tangled hair as I rested my forehead on my knees.

That has nothing to do with it! I told myself...over and over.

I didn't know if it was sleeping without Trent by my side, or if it was sleeping in this big house alone, but I hadn't been able to go to bed at a reasonable time—or stay asleep for a reasonable amount of time. I stood, pacing the room before stopping at my book shelf. I ran my hands over the bindings as I searched for one I hadn't read over the past few days. I breathed out, puffing my cheeks with air. There weren't any.

My cell phone buzzed on the bedside table, and I moved over to it, chewing on my thumb nail as I did.

It was one of my nervous habits—like not eating. I stopped, the phone in my hand as I looked straight ahead of me. What did I eat last? *When* did I eat last? I grit my teeth as I slide my finger across the screen and the text message popped up:

Trent - Allie is convinced I should be 'a man' and tell you I miss you. So...I miss you.

I tapped my fingers over the face of the phone, making the screen dance. I needed something to eat...and I needed something to read.

Trent's work could easily solve both of those issues.

I ignored the nerves jumping in my stomach as I grabbed my purse and headed for my car. I tapped my hands on the wheel as I waited for the cars to pass and made my way onto the street. My jaw clenched as the *what ifs* tried to push through the mental wall I put up. I gave in to the need to think about *anything* else and turned on a CD that was heavy enough my teeth practically shook with the angry riffs of the guitar. When I parked in the bookstore lot I didn't waste time sitting in my seat and contemplating.

You can go back. The words rushed through my brain, causing my muscles to clench as I reached the halfway mark to the door. *He doesn't know you're here.* My stomach twisted, and I realized again just how hungry I was. I glanced across the street at the fast food restaurant. *A burger might not be too gross.*

My feet were still propelling me forward though, and my hand connected with the cool metal of the door before my brain could catch up and tell me to stop. Stew raised an eyebrow as I walked in the store, speed walking to the back section where the chairs were. He shrugged it off as his eyes moved behind me. I glanced over my shoulder to see a tall blonde girl and a gaggle of other attractive young girls walking in.

I plopped down on the love seat and pulled my feet underneath myself to sit crossed legged. I took my cell phone out of my purse and text Trent:

A real man would tell his girlfriend that in person.

My phone vibrated before the screen could rest:

Trent - Too bad I have bills to pay

I smirked to myself as I quickly text back:

Find me if you can...

I stood and peered around the floor-to-ceiling bookshelf that made this area a private alcove for customers. Trent's hand was in his hair as he looked down at his phone. His brow furrowed before a smile spread across his lips, and he shook his head. I bit my lip, all nerves gone as I watched his reaction.

See! He's happy you're here.

I ducked my head back just as he began to turn towards me. My heart hammered in my chest as I waited a few seconds before peeking my head out again—right into Trent's chest.

Trent grabbed my shoulders, his hands slipping down them and over my arms to tangle his fingers with mine.

"Now, that—that was a little too simple."

I pulled my lower lip in, my shoulders lifting as I blinked up at him. "So, I'm no good at this game."

His finger lifted my chin so our lips touched. "Maybe I'm just *that good.*"

I rolled my eyes, pulling him behind the book shelf so no one could see us. He raised an eyebrow before leaning down and kissing me again. My mind slipped away, concentrating on the softness of his lips and the way his hand cupped my face while the other pulled our hips closer together. I felt my body flush with heat as I thought about exactly *how* attracted I was to this man. I was never a fan of PDA, even if we were hidden behind a wall of books, but with him I lost myself in exactly how perfect and comfortable *this* felt. I blushed, pulling away.

Trent's eyes moved over my face, and his lips slowly dipped down. "What's wrong?"

My hand went to my neck, rubbing it as I replied, "Nothing, why?"

Trent blinked at me, his head tilting. "Did you come here because you were worried I was avoiding you because we..." his voice drifted, but his eyes stayed locked on me as my face heated to levels that made me sure it was scorching red."El—come on, you have to know by now how I feel about you."

I coughed. "Yeah, I do—I just..."

Trent shook his head cutting me off, and his lips curled up just slightly at the edges. He pounced on his toes as his hands went into his pockets. "I kind of wondered the same thing about you—"

"You've been the one avoiding me!"

"But you know where I live...and work..."

"Trent," I said, stepping forward and putting my hands on his shoulders. "You have to know by now how I feel about you."

Trent's eyes came back to mine, his hands knitting across the small of my back. "Why don't you tell me?"

The word flickered in my mind, but I pushed it back. Just like I pushed the *what ifs* back. They belonged in the deep corners of my mind, not slipping off my tongue. My eyes wandered to his lips, something to help the word disappear.

"Why don't I just s*how* you?" I murmured as I leaned up on my toes.

"I'd like that," he whispered back and just as our lips were about to touch his cell phone buzzed in his pocket. He pulled away, looking down at it. His jaw clenched as he looked at the number. "It's Allie's school."

He picked up the phone, and his voice deepened with worry as he said, "Hello...speaking. Oh, okay...the babysitter isn't scheduled until one when she gets off the bus... Yes, understood. I'll be there to pick her up in about twenty minutes."

Trent stared down at the phone as it went black. "She's sick—fever and vomiting." He looked up at the ceiling before squeezing his eyes shut. "There's not another supervisor scheduled until three when my shift is over. I'll have to call and see if Mitch can come in earlier."

I put my hand over his as he went to swipe the screen. "Don't worry about it. How about I pick her up and bring her over to my house until you get off your shift?"

"Are you sure?"

"Of course," I replied.

Trent pulled me into his arms, kissing my head. "Seriously, thank you so much."

He pulled away, and his forehead creased with lines.

"What?" I asked.

"Can I just give you a spare key to the apartment? I think she'd prefer to be in her own bed." My breath caught in my throat. He coughed before adding, "If you don't mind."

"Of course. I'll go pick her up now, but you'll need to call the school and let them know I have permission to pick her up," I said as I pulled out my car keys.

Trent pulled his own out, unwinding the apartment key from the loop it was on. He paused halfway. "Don't you usually go see your dad?"

I put my hand out, my other on my hip. "I'll call him and let him know. Now, give me the key," I nodded to his phone; "Call the school, and get back to making money."

He put his hands up before dropping the key into the palm of my hand. "Yes ma'am!"

Chapter 33

Allie did not look good when she climbed into the back seat of my car. She paused, her chest heaving and her eyes heavy as she looked down at the five-point safety harness of her booster seat. I had attempted to take it out of Trent's truck and install it in mine, but ended up needing Trent to come out and help me. I leaned in, to help her and she let her hands fall to her sides as I finished buckling her up. I swallowed as I looked at her pale face and flushed cheeks, wondering if I should have given in at the five minute mark instead of the ten minute mark of the failed install. A soft smile came to her lips and her eyes fluttered.

"Thanks for picking me up," she mumbled in her baby voice.

I leaned forward, caressing her cheek with the back of my hand and kissing her forehead. "Of course, sweetie. Here's the bag the nurse gave you, if you feel sick, you know what to do?"

She didn't open her eyes as she nodded, her tiny fingers grasping the plastic.

I looked in my rear view mirror and her head lulled to the side, the plastic bag slipping out of her grip as she fell asleep. I wasn't a fan of vomit, but I realized as my eyes went back to the road, that for her and Trent I was sure I could handle it.

Luckily, I didn't have to find out. She didn't move or make a noise the trip home, and only mumbled *Owlie* as I pulled her into my arms to carry her inside. I pulled pajamas out of her drawer and she changed into them as I got her a bottle of ice water and an icepack for her forehead. Trent was fortunate enough Allie went to a school with an in-school doctor's office where they already said it was the flu and gave me specific instructions on what to do; an inhaler to help her breathe, lots of fluids and what they called "chest PT"— medical slang for firm, but gentle, pats on the back to help loosen the phlegm in the lungs.

I sighed as I sat down on the couch, pulling the blanket over me as I took out my cell phone to call Dad.

"Hey you," Dad greeted. "How's my princess?"

"I'm good, but Allie has the flu, and Trent couldn't get out of work, so I offered to pick her up and take care of her until he got off his shift," I explained, running my fingers over the stitch markings on the patchwork blanket.

"The vaccine is missing a few key strains this year—"

"Dad," I said, dragging out his name before he could launch into his scientific evaluation of the vaccine.

"Okay, I'll spare you."

"I'm sorry I won't be able to visit you today," I said, sighing. I would miss seeing him, but I was truly glad to be able to be there for Trent and Allie.

"I don't mind at all. There's bingo, and the book you gave me from Trent last week," he replied, his voice unmoved.

"Are you sure? I could always come later?"

I could hear the smile on his lips as he responded, "And spread the wealth?" My stomach dropped as I realized it *wouldn't* be a good idea for me to see *him* for a few days after this to make sure I wasn't sick. I had my vaccine, but then again, so did Allie. Dad seemed to sense my unease, his tone softening as he continued, "Do you remember what Mom used to make you?"

"Of course," I replied, closing my eyes as I imagined her at the stove. "Homemade chicken noodle soup."

"Here's the secret ingredient—I taught her how to make it. Now, go find yourself a pen and paper. You can make it for your little miss over there."

I found something to write with and listened carefully as he listed off the ingredients and instructions. It was easy, but that also made me think it would be easy to screw up.

"Oh, and El—I'm proud of you," he said as I finished writing the last piece.

"For what?" I asked as I stood and walked over to the fridge to check to make sure I could make it.

"For always putting other people first—and being so caring."

I breathed in, putting my head against the fridge. "I learned from the best."

"Tell Allie I hope she feels better. Love you."

"Love you too, Daddy," I replied.

~~~

I sat up as I heard Allie's bedroom door open. She was dragging her owl by its wing, and her eyes were half open as she stuck her nose in the air.

"Something smells yummy," she mumbled as she crawled up beside me.

186

I felt her forehead, wrapping the blanket around her as she leaned back into the couch. Her fever seemed to be going down, and I felt a little relief. She still looked so pale, though.

"My daddy says he hopes you feel better...and he gave me the recipe to Mom's Magic Chicken Soup."

She smiled faintly, rubbing her face with the owl's wing. "What's magic about it?"

I winked at her as I stood. "It always made me feel better."

Her eyes flickered open. "Can I try some?"

She nodded, and I got her a small bowl of it. For as sick as she was, she perked up when I handed her the bowl, and she ate it slowly. When she was done she handed the bowl back to me, and I put it on the coffee table as she curled into me, placing her head in my lap.

"I think your daddy's right," she said, sighing as I pulled the blanket up to her chin.

"You liked it?"

She nodded. "I love you, Ellie."

I brushed her hair out of her face, running my fingers through it as I replied. "I love you, too, sweetie."

Chapter 34

A soft laugh woke me, and my eyes fluttered to see Trent standing above Allie and me. His hand was over his mouth as the other cupped his elbow. He leaned forward on his toes and his hands dropped to his pockets, fully revealing the smirk that had been hidden beneath.

"Tired?" he asked.

I shrugged and Trent took the textbook I fell asleep with off my chest, sitting down on the edge of the couch as I carefully moved up, trying not to disturb Allie.

I rubbed my eyes. "It's hard to sleep at my house," I admitted.

Trent ran his fingers over the words on the cover. "Has it always been?"

I bit the inside of my lip, shaking my head. "When Dad's around it's fine...but it's been awhile since he's been home. It's a big house to be in all alone...and it was nice spending the night here—you make me feel safe."

Trent leaned over and kissed me, his thumb rubbing my cheek. "I'm supposed to, and you can spend as much time here as you want..." He glanced down at his sister. "She enjoys having you over, obviously."

"And you?" I asked, smirking at him.

He ran his teeth over his bottom lip, one eyebrow rising. "I have my own motives for wanting you to stay the night."

I giggled to myself, and Allie stirred, opening her eyes. They widened when she saw Trent. She climbed into his arms, snuggling her face into shoulder. "I missed you."

"Did Ellie not take good care of you?" Trent teased, looking down at me and winking as I frowned back at him.

She shook her head. "She did. But she's not you. No one takes care of me like you."

Trent smirked at me, kissing her forehead. I rolled my eyes.

"I'm hungry," Allie said, curling up into Trent's arms. "Is there more soup?"

Trent glanced over into the kitchen. "So that's what smells so good."

I nodded. "You know what goes perfect with chicken noodle soup."

"The can it came in?" Trent shot back.

I slid around him, sticking my tongue out. "Grilled cheese."

"I want one!" Allie said, perking up and smiling at me.

I leaned down, pressing my hand against her forehead. "Feeling better, hmm?"

She shrugged, pulling her blanket up as Trent settled into the couch with her.

"It's about time for more medicine. I'll go get your inhaler, and then I'll make grilled cheese for us to go with the *homemade* chicken noodle soup," I said, narrowing my eyes at Trent.

He gave me a crooked smile, his green eyes lighting up. "Just like the pie."

I came back into the room, handing Allie her inhaler. She took it, following the instructions the doctor gave us on what to do. I glanced over at Trent. "She's not going to be able to go to school for a few days."

Trent nodded, rubbing her back as his lips curved downward. "Yeah..."

"What's your work schedule for tomorrow?" I asked as Allie handed her inhaler back to me. Trent stood, and Allie tugged on his shirt, crawling into his arms. He adjusted her on his hip as he followed me to the kitchen.

"I'm the opening supervisor. There's another supervisor coming in around twelve, and I can get off then. I'll have to see if Gerard or Lynn is available until I can get out," he explained as he took the lid off the crock pot and leaned down to smell the soup.

I opened the fridge, pulling out the cheese and butter. "Wouldn't Meg get sick?"

Trent sighed, kissing Allie's head. "Yeah."

"Good thing I don't have class until two tomorrow then."

"Are you sure?" he asked as he handed me the bread from the cupboard.

"Absolutely, but you have to help me with Algebra after dinner," I replied, slathering the butter onto the bread with a bit too much force. The butter knife dented the bread, and I winced.

"Is the class that bad?" Trent asked as he went into the living room to put Allie back on the couch.

"I don't know," I muttered as I put the piece of bread onto the pan where it sizzled.

Trent came up behind me, wrapping his arms around my waist.

I sighed, placing the pieces of cheese on the bread before putting the top slice on and flipping it. "I just feel like such an idiot when I try to do math. It just doesn't sink in."

"You did so well on your last test, though?" he asked, moving my hair away from my neck and kissing it.

"That's because you helped me. I studied for that so much that I fell behind in my modern civs class," I replied, my stomach hollowing out as I thought about it. Falling behind for me was a B on a test, but I wanted to graduate Summa Cum Laude like Dad—even if it was just in English Lit.

"The book you fell asleep reading?" Trent asked, his tone hinted with laughter.

"Thanks," I hissed, pulling away from him as I put the first two sandwiches on a plate.

"Is dinner done yet?" Allie asked, peeking over the edge of the couch. "Or have you two gotten better at kissing quietly?"

I looked at the ceiling as Trent chuckled to himself. "The princess demands her grill cheese."

I concentrated on ladling the soup into the small cup on the plate before turning and handing it to Trent.

"And magic soup!" Allie called as she turned back around.

Trent paused mid-step, looking over his shoulder at me. It was my turn to smirk. "I made it—of course it is!"

Chapter 35

"Third batch of paintings?" Dad asked as I handed him my cell phone to help me pick out the next set. "That's great!"

"Yeah," I said, leaning over his shoulder. "I have to bring more each time. This time they want me to bring six. I don't know how I'm going to keep up with the demand."

Dad tilted his head as he looked at the painting, a building set into the red rocks of Sedona. "Is this of a picture you took?"

I nodded, putting my hands on his shoulder and cupping my chin so it wouldn't dig into his collar bone. He gained weight since he started his rehabilitation, but he still wasn't where I was used to him being, and he still seemed fragile.

"I think you should bring some of your photographs to the gallery Mom used to display at. They'll recognize your last name, but the style is uniquely you," Dad commented. "You should definitely bring that one. How much are you charging?"

"Three fifty."

"That's it?"

"Yeah," I said sitting back and pulling my legs beneath me. "The gallery owner thinks I should increase my prices, but I think that's why they're selling. I'm priced right at their minimums."

Dad sat back in his chair, his body slumping as he stared at the next painting, his forehead creased with thought lines. "Maybe just increase a little bit more to cover your gallery fees. If you keep going like this you won't need to be an English teacher." I tipped my head back, staring at the ceiling before letting my chin drop to my chest as I blinked at him. He smirked. "Yeah, I didn't think you really wanted to be a teacher."

"Got that right," I muttered.

Dad squeezed my knee. "You're really good with Allie, though."

I shrugged. "That's different...it's kind of...like she's my kid."

"Who knows, maybe someday she will be," Dad's voice was soft as he continued; "Then I'd get to meet my grandchild."

I felt the rash of goose pimples travel up the back of my arms as I swallowed the pain in the back of my throat.

"Speaking of Allie," I began, my voice sounding as raw as my insides suddenly felt. "It's her birthday this weekend, so we're bringing her to Sedona with us for a nice picnic."

"That sounds wonderful!" Dad said as he handed me back the phone. "The first three, then the fifth, eighth and ninth paintings, and mark them up to *four* fifty."

"Fine," I replied as I marked the photos of the paintings to sell. I shook my head as I looked at the ones he selected and then up at him. He blinked at me as he pushed his chin out. "You picked the same *exact* ones as Trent."

"Great minds think alike. When will I get to see him again?" Dad asked, standing and going to the shelf now piled with books from Trent.

"I can bring him any time you like," I replied. "But you're doing so well, won't you be coming home soon?"

Dad licked his lips, his chest rising as he breathed in. His fingers ran over the cover of the book before he turned to face me. "I've got an appointment a week from today to get my clearance to go home."

I sprung up from the chair wrapping my arms around his neck. "I can't wait!"

His muscles tensed beneath me, and I fought back the tears as his anxiety rushed over me.

Coming home.

He wouldn't be returning here even if his cancer came back, and his tense muscles and the grip of his hug told me he wasn't telling me everything.

I swallowed hard.

Coming home.

Then why did my chest feel so hollow and empty?

Chapter
36

Monsoon season.

That meant tourists wouldn't be hammering down the doors of the gallery as much as they had been in the prior months. Spring and Fall were always the busiest seasons, but monsoon really was my favorite. The days always started sunny but midday when the heat was almost unbearable, the clouds would begin to gather before exploding overhead. The rain never lasted long, and drifted away by the evening so the sky was crystal clear. I couldn't wait to see the stars dancing above us. I smiled over at Allie in the backseat next to the stacks of paintings.

Allie caught me looking back at her and gave me a huge, crooked smile with plenty of holes. Her piggy bank went almost empty when she got Owlie, but the spaces in her smile meant it was already starting to fill up again. "I'm so excited! A picnic! A real picnic!"

"We just had a picnic a few months ago," I reminded Allie, smiling over at Trent.

"Not like this! With a blanket and sitting on the ground!"

"Well, Trent's deprived you, hasn't he?" I teased.

Trent looked at the ceiling of the car, before letting his eyes fall back to the road. His fingers tapped out a beat on my thigh to the Hands like Houses album playing on his cell phone.

"Are we almost there?" Allie asked, closing the book she was reading and looking at me with wide eyes.

I shook my head. "Sorry, sweetie. It's a long ride into Sedona."

Allie's mouth pressed tightly together, and her nose wrinkled as she looked back at me. "You should've sat back here with *me* then."

"And leave Trent all by himself? He can't read and drive like you can—or watch a movie," I said, leaning over and handing her the portable DVD player.

She sighed, taking it from me and swiveling the screen. "Fine...so what did you get me?"

I narrowed my eyes at her and Trent said over his shoulder, "Presents are for after the picnic, Allie."

"Fine," she huffed as she put her ear buds in. "Make me wait even *longer.*"

Trent's voice was unmoved as he answered, "That's right."

I rested my head against the window, watching as the scenery rushed past in an ever changing blur. The drive to Sedona from Phoenix was always amazing to me. The dry yellow and brown desert drifted past us, turning into rolling mountains and then the mountains themselves transformed, to beautiful red rocks. My eyes drifted away from the window over to him, and I smiled as I admired the way his hair fell perfectly over the top of his head in that James Dean fashion, framing his classic sunglasses. My eyes fell to the way his tee shirt tugged perfectly at his shoulders and over his chest, where hair stuck out beneath the v-neck.

"It's not nice to stare," he commented, his lips twitching up at their edges as he scratched his chin. The fish danced on his skin as he did and I shrugged.

"You're always staring at me," I pointed out, nudging him.

He lifted his sunglasses with one finger, exposing his beautiful green eyes as he bit his lip. "I wonder why."

I rolled my eyes as his truck pulled off the road, parking next to the *Red Rock Pass Required* sign. Trent leaned over as he put the truck in park and pulled the pass out of his glove box. He tucked it on the dashboard before turning to look at Allie. "You ready?"

She closed the DVD player and gave several enthusiastic nods. Her pig tails bounced on either side of her head, and I laughed as I slid out of the truck before opening the door and helping Allie down. Trent came around the truck with the cooler and blanket in hand.

"We can get to the creek quickly from here," he explained as I placed Allie on the ground, and she skipped in front of us. "Within sight, Als."

Her head bopped as she slowed, and I pulled the lens cap off my camera to catch her mid skip. I breathed in as the preview quickly flickered off the screen. The clouds were already starting to gather.

"Do you think we'll get to eat before the rain comes down?" I asked as we headed up the trail. It widened and in front of us was a creek path surrounded by twisted Juniper trees. I ran my fingers over the limbs. "Is this a vortex area?"

Trent laughed as he spread the blanket out and called Allie over from the edge of the creek. It was shallow, but I could tell from the way his eyes watched her that it made him nervous for her to be so close. "One question at a time, but yes to both."

I opened the cooler and pulled out our lunches, handing them to Trent and Allie before sitting down myself. We ate in silence, admiring the beautiful surroundings while Allie hummed to herself. When she was done eating she reached for my camera, biting her lip and pausing as her hands wrapped around it. I nodded, and she pulled it into her lap, looking at the buttons before she popped off the lens cap, her eyes widening as she did so. I laughed, leaning forward and flipping the switch to ON.

"Just push that there," I said, pointing to the button.

"You're brave," Trent whispered into my ear as I leaned back on my hands.

"Not near the water, sweetie," I said as Allie stood and began snapping pictures. She watched the preview carefully before nodding, and then snapping the next another picture.

She stayed near us, and Trent laid down putting his head in my lap. "She even forgot about her p-r-e-s-e-n-t-s," he whispered.

Allie looked over the camera at us. "I can spell, you know!"

Trent laughed, looking back up at me. I smiled down at him, running my fingers through his hair. His eyes shut, and he breathed in deeply before his muscles relaxed.

Allie's giggles broke his trance, and he turned his head to look at her. He blinked at her, his eyebrows raised. "And what is so amusing?"

She lay down next to him, putting her head on his chest. "How do you get the last picture back on the screen?"

I reached down, pushing the menu button, and the screen lit up again. She looked up at me as she tilted the camera so both Trent and I could see it. "I caught something amazing—two people in love."

Trent's eyes lost focus on the picture before drifting up to mine. My fingers stopped combing through his hair as I struggled to remember what breathing was. I could hear my heart pounding in my ears as a soft smile lifted the edges of his lips.

Holy God.

He. Loves. Me.

My brain jammed, stopped working as my chest tightened, my heart went into overdrive as I tried to connect the dots of how *I* felt.

"Uh oh!" Allie screamed, jumping up and knocking both of us out of the daze. My vision seemed to cave in and I was suddenly light headed, as if I *actually* had stopped breathing. "Rain!"

Allie pointed to the screen that had timed out and gone black, and there on it was a giant water droplet. I looked up just as it down poured into us.

"In the cooler!" I instructed; opening and pointing for Allie to stick it in. She did so as I yanked the blanket up and pushed it around the edges so it wouldn't get shaken around. "Go! Go!"

Allie grabbed the cooler and rushed ahead of us, carefully carrying it over her head. Trent and I followed suit, but I fell behind.

"Damn flip flops!" I hissed as I they slipped off into the mud.

Trent stopped, leaning down. "Hop on!"

"Piggy back?" I asked as I jammed my shoe back on.

"Yes! Now move it!" he ordered, and I jumped on his back already slick with rain.

I couldn't help but laugh as I put my face up to the sky, letting the rain drip over my skin and cool it after sitting in the Sedona sun. By the time we reached Allie she was standing with the cooler at her feet, her arms crossed over her chest.

"You two are too slow!" she said as she shook her head, her lips twisted in an angry fish face.

Trent let me down and stepped forward into the muddle at her feet. The water splashed up and coated her up to her waist.

Allie's mouth dropped open, and I hid behind Trent as she stepped forward and then took one huge jump into the puddle. It sent clay tinted water flying in every direction around her, over the side of the truck, coating the cooler and finally, coating Trent's entire front. I stepped to the side, unscathed and looked him up and down. His t-shirt was stuck like a second skin, enhancing the shape of his arms and chest, catching the perfect curvature of his hips into his jeans—also stuck to him. Trent and Allie slowly turned to face me as I burst out laughing at the two of them.

"No!" I said, taking a step back and shaking my hands at them. "I'm innocent—this is between you two!"

The siblings shook their heads at me before both jumping and sending more clay mud everywhere, including all over me—from head to toe. I wiped my face with my hands, shaking my hand off as I stared at them laughing at me.

"That's not very nice," I muttered, pouting.

"Awe," Trent said, pulling me into his arms. "I'm sorry!"

"You're a jerk!" I hissed, pushing back and softly hitting him.

His eyes locked on mine and the dizziness from the picnic returned. I gave him a smile before pulling away.

"We're two hours away from home and totally disgustingly dirty," I teased, putting my hands on my hips as I looked between the two of them. "What do you have to say for yourselves?"

Trent pointed at Allie as she pointed back up at him.

I rolled my eyes. "Good thing Sedona is touristy; at least we'll be able to buy something clean—albeit outrageously priced—which, you, Mister, are picking up the tab on."

Trent put his hands up. "You're the rich artist!"

I pushed him forward. "Get in the truck and drive, boy!"

Allie put her hands behind her back, swaying her hips as she looked up at me with a wide smile. I sighed.

"See, can't be mad at me—I'm too cute!" she replied as I opened her door and lifted her in before putting the cooler below her feet.

"The same can be said for both of you!" I replied as I shut her door, and then climbed into my seat.

"You know you love us," Trent shot back.

My eyes froze straight ahead.

There was that word again.

I laughed it off, pushing his elbow. "Did you really have to team up on me?"

Trent's laugh joined mine, but it seemed hard and forced.

I swallowed as the laughing died down. I concentrated on how disgusting my wet clothes felt against my skin and ignored all logical thoughts from my head and my heart.

Chapter 37

Dad clicked through the pictures on my laptop, his eyes running over each detail in the photographs slowly. I stood, running my fingers over the collection of books he now had at his bedside, some of which I didn't recognize. I cocked my head, sitting on his bed and opening one of the books to flip through it.

"Morgan," he explained, and while my eyes moved up to him, his eyes remained on the lap top. He clicked again. "She visits me on her breaks. She's a good kid; it's too bad you two don't get to hang out much."

"We have our daily walks," I said, smiling as I closed the book in my lap. "I wish we both had time for more but between school and work, and school and Trent and Allie; neither of us has a ton of free time. We've tried a few times to meet up, but it just hasn't panned out."

Dad looked up at me over the laptop. "So you consider her a friend?"

I nodded. "We know we can count on each other."

I watched as Dad's eyes returned to the laptop, and he clicked again. "I'm glad to hear you have some solid friends."

I swallowed as his eyes locked on the image in front of him. They didn't move, but stayed set on the screen. His Adam's apple moved up and down as his jaw line tightened. Finally, he spoke, his voice soft. "You're a family now."

I stood and went to sit next to him. The picture on the screen was the one Allie had taken of Trent and I. Trent's head was in my lap, and I smiled down at him as he smiled up at me.

"What do you mean?" I asked.

Dad lifted one finger and clicked again. This time a picture of the three of us was on the screen, each of laughing as we made silly faces.

"I'm not blind, El—"

"You'd be right about that," I teased, smirking at him as my chest tightened.

"You're very much in love with both of them—you have more than just me now."

My eyes froze on him and I heard the words he didn't speak. "You can't leave me yet," I whispered.

Dad shook his head, putting his arm around my back, and I slumped in the seat, putting my head on his shoulder. He kissed my forehead as he continued to click through the pictures. "No, princess, not yet."

He was right, I did have them now, but I still desperately needed him.

I swallowed the lump in my throat.

I was sure I always would.

~~~

I looked down at my watch as I opened the door to the house. It showed Monday was the day of the week. That meant I was just in my civics class. I was so distracted I couldn't even remember what class I was in. I pushed the door shut behind me and slipped my shoes off, rubbing my face. I was exhausted from the replaying of Dad's words 'no, princess, not yet'. They sunk hard in my throat, forming a rock in my belly as I walked past the pictures of us as a family. I didn't want a new family—I wanted Dad to be a part of the bigger family Trent and Allie formed around me. I fought against the tears threatening to consume me.

I couldn't stay in this house right now.

I grabbed my purse and headed out the door. Trent's shift hadn't started yet, but it was close enough. When I got to the store I ordered a latte and peach tart before sitting down and sticking my ear buds in to listen to Fit for a King. I needed something strong with moving lyrics. I needed something, anything else, to concentrate on. I let the rhythm sink into me as I sunk down in the lounge chair, carefully chewing each bite of my food.

Yet.

Three letters that kicked my ass and soul. I could barely function because of them.

I felt the presence of someone else and opened my eyes to see Trent coming towards me. I stood, my ear buds pulling out as my cell phone fell to the ground, but I didn't care. He wrapped his arms around me, and I buried my face in his shoulder with speaking.

"You should've called," Trent said into my ear as he rubbed my back. "Is everything okay? Did something happen with your Dad?"

I wanted to say yes, but it was too hard to think about speaking the words that I knew some part of him had given up. Anger suddenly flooded my veins, heating my body to an unbearable temperature. He was giving up, and he hadn't even given me a chance to do anything. I was still partially a child. I wasn't ready to be parent-less. I pulled away and looked up at Trent.

Guilt replaced the anger, and my body went cold with the weight of it. He was parent-less because his had made bad decisions, not because God had split them apart.

The anger rushed over me again. God. This really wasn't fair was it? The hands Trent and I were dealt by that very being? I put my hand on my forehead as I shook my head, too many emotions collided together, and it felt like my head was splitting in two.

"Not going to tell me?" he asked as he put his hands on my shoulders.

"I'm sorry...Dad's fine— I guess...I'm just..." my eyes fluttered and I shook the *yet* from my mind; "having a bad day."

Trent rocked on the balls of his feet. "You're difficult," he finally said.

I smiled up at him, tilting my head. "You love difficult."

His eyes locked mine as he dropped his hands into his pockets. "It appears I do."

The three words that kicked my ass and soul. But only because I let them.

I looked down at my feet. "So, my dad needs a new book. He finished the one you suggested a couple days ago."

He looked over his shoulder, tapping his fingers on his thighs. "I've got it."

He rolled up the sleeves of the navy blue button-up he was wearing as he walked through the shelves, weaving through them with deliberate intent. I followed, watching him as I found a smile slipping to my lips. He stopped at a shelf, spotting the book in an instant and pulling it off the shelf to hand to me. "Here you go."

I flipped through the first few pages, pretending to review it before I gave a firm nod. "I approve."

Trent chuckled to himself before nodding to the cash registers. "Glad to hear. They know to give you my discount. I have to do inventories today."

I leaned up on my toes and kissed him. "Thank you. I just needed to see you."

"Any time...you staying over tonight?" he asked, his hands going into mine, and I knew from the way his tone of voice pitched he was hiding something from me.

"Are we doing something special?" I asked with narrowed eyes. "I don't want to have another restaurant incidence where I feel under dressed."

"There were people in s*horts!*" Trent reminded me.

I stuck my chin out shaking it. "I still felt weird!"

He laughed in response, but quickly covered it up with a cough when I shot him a dirty look. "Uh...wear something nice."

"How nice?"

He put his arm on the top of the short bookcase, tapping his fingers over the wood as he looked at me. "Allie's sleeping over Meg's."

"On a school night?"

"I know—I'm too lenient—whatever."

I rolled my eyes. "Enough with the mystery and changing the subject— should I wear a dress and heels?"

Trent's head went back and a full smile came to his face. "I've never seen you in a dress."

"What are you going to be wearing?"

"A casual suit."

"What's that?"

"A casual suit," he repeated.

I sighed. "When should I come over?"

"Seven, dinner first. There's a new sushi place that opened up down town."

"I love sushi!"

"I figured as much," Trent replied. "I should get going."

I shook my head. "You're a pain." He smacked my butt as I turned to walk away. "I didn't mean literally," I hissed over my shoulder.

He shrugged.

"Inventory!" I reminded him, and he sighed before heading towards the back of the store.

Chapter 38

When I arrived at the apartment Trent was outside, sitting on the front steps with an artist pad and a set of colored pencils. He was already dressed in what he called a "casual" suit, which consisted of dark wash jeans, a white button-up and thin pink tie topped off with a navy suit jacket. He didn't look up when I parked my car in the driveway, but instead kept drawing, switching colors even as my heels clicked against the cement walkway. I cocked my head as I stared down at the drawing. This was of a cherry tree, shedding its flower petals slowly to the ground, the shading around it made it look like the clouds were settling over it.

"That's beautiful," I whispered as I breathed in.

His eyes slowly rose to mine and he shook his head. "Nowhere close to as beautiful as you."

He stood, and I lifted my shoulders up, the tiny straps of my dress moving with them. Trent put his hands on my wrists, sliding them up my bare arms up to my neck. "I should've asked you to wear a dress sooner."

I looked down at the dark purple dress, a plunging cowl neckline showed more of my skin than I ever did; plus, the dress barely hit my finger tips at its shortest lengths, and the longest parts of the handkerchief cut was at the top of my knees.

"You like it?" I whispered.

Trent's thumbs stroked my neck, causing tingles to rush over my skin as my breath left my lungs. Our eyes met as he leaned in to kiss me. My fingers ran up the front of the suit, stopping at his shoulders as his lips lifted away from mine. I leaned closer, pulling his lower lip through my teeth. He pulled away laughing.

"I wish I hadn't made those reservations now," he whispered, his forehead still pressed against mine.

I brushed my lips against his again, before replying, "We do have the entire night alone."

My hand slipped down, wrapping around his tie and his chest rose against it as he inhaled. "Hmm..."

"Pink?" I asked as I let my fingers release the tie.

He shrugged. "Allie picked it, and you've seen that face, how could I say no?"

I put my hand over my mouth as I fought back the laughter.

He looked at the sky, sighing. "Go ahead, mock me."

"How can I mock you?" I asked, blinking at him. "It's a pink tie, and you look like—" I shook my head, signaling up and down his body; "*that!*"

"Whatever that means," Trent replied, leaning down and picking up his sketch. I cocked my head, staring at his ass openly. He looked over his shoulder, narrowing his eyes. "Save that for later—when you can actually undress me with more than just your eyes."

My mouth dropped open, and he winked as he hopped up the steps and opened the door to place his drawing things on the door side table before grabbing his keys. He turned back to me, and my mouth was still hanging open.

"Really?" Trent commented, crossing his arms and leaning back on his heels. It really wasn't fair that he could look so dapper and yet so *not* hipster. "You look like *that*."

I closed my mouth, chewing the inside of my lip to keep from smirking. I shook my head and gave into to the warmth spreading through my body. I smiled at him. "You're not going to blind fold me or something?"

Trent stopped mid stride, putting his hands together and rubbing as he looked at me. "I didn't think you'd let me...unless—"

"No!" I cut him off. "I didn't mean it like that."

Trent dropped his hands, snaking one into mine. "I just figured I'd check."

"Kinky!" I hissed.

He leaned over, his lips running over my earlobe as he whispered, "You're the one who bit my lip."

I smacked him before hopping into the truck. I grabbed the door to shut it but stopped when I noticed he was standing there unblinking with a silly grin plastered on his face.

"What?" I hissed as I slammed the door, crossing my arms as I sunk into the seat.

He chuckled to himself as he jumped in and put the truck in gear. He put his arm over the back of the seat, the self-satisfied look still on his face.

"Trent?" I dragged out his name as I said it.

"Let's say I'm excited to see what's underneath the dress *again*."

I looked at the gray fabric of the ceiling, staring at the imaginary patterns as my face burned.

"Jerk," I whispered to myself.

"What?" Trent shot back. "You're beautiful— I can't enjoy it?"

I slipped my hand in his. "Just not so openly."

He laughed in response.

"So, what's the special occasion?"

Trent rubbed his thumb over mine. "We haven't celebrated any milestones in our relationship...It's been a year since I first noticed Stew torturing you," I narrowed my eyes at him as he continued; "You were so nice at trying to persuade him you didn't need help, but you always took a deep breath like you were ready to smack him."

"I almost did a few times, and that's not very nice of me."

Trent shook his head. "You were always lady like; most other women would have been rude to him."

I sighed. "Yeah, I have a hard time being mean to most people."

He looked at me out of the corner of his eye as if he was waiting for me to say something else, or realize something else. I felt my heart beginning to race as silence filled the space between us. Finally, he coughed, rubbing his unshaven chin. "It's also almost the end of your semester, meaning you survived Algebra! And...We've been dating 4 months."

My stomach fluttered as my head jerked back. I wanted to say *really?* But somehow, thankfully, kept it in. Instead, I leaned over and kissed his cheek.

"You're a hopeless romantic now?"

He shook his head, his brow furrowing as he fought the idea. "Nah— I just like to do something nice every once and a while."

I nudged him. "Admit it."

His mouth opened, his eyes searching mine before his lips pursed back together and he swallowed, looking back ahead.

The unspoken words hung in the air, and my stomach fluttered again, this time in a far more uncomfortable way.

"So sushi—and then what?" I asked, interrupting the uncomfortable silence.

"Actually, sushi is *after*," Trent said, and I looked over at him as he parked in a gallery lot.

"After?"

He put the truck in park. "I saw an article on this gallery—the best photographers of Arizona."

Trent bit his lip before jumping out of the car. I followed suit, shutting the door behind me and falling into step next to him. He put his arm around my waist, his muscles tight against my skin. I squeezed his side, cocking my head at him, and the tension fell away. His eyes softened. "I hope you enjoy this."

"Why wouldn't I?" I asked as he held the door open for me.

He pulled his lips in again before, nodding inside. He followed me as my eyes lifted to the photograph as I walked in. My knees weakened as my eyes froze on the perfect framing of the sunset from *my* backyard. My chest tightened, painfully pushing all the air out of me. I grabbed for Trent's arm as my mouth moved with no words coming out. I stepped forward, my hand out but stopped when my fingers were inches from the print. They tingled, acting to trace the scene.

"Abela had this eye, didn't she? Almost ethereal," a person next to me said, and I yanked my hand in. "It's too bad she's gone. It's been almost ten years since we saw a work this amazing."

I nodded, and the woman held her hand out. "Ann Stella, gallery owner."

I put my hand in hers, glancing over at Trent, still breathless, speechless. He smiled, and I shook my head, knocking myself back into reality. "Ellie...Abela."

"Abela?" her hand froze in mine as she glanced at the picture. "As in Abby's daughter?"

I breathed in through my nose as I gave one nod.

"I should've known!" she whispered, her hand finally slipping from mine as she pressed her palms together and then folded them outward towards me. "You look like her—you have her beautiful hair."

It was in a braid, per my usual, something I favored due to Mom always having one.

"Thank you," I whispered.

Trent held his hand out. "She has her mom's talent for photography, but even more, she can capture it in acrylic paint beautifully. Trent Wentworth. El's boyfriend."

I was finally able to comprehend the thin, silver-haired woman in front of me. Her eyes wrinkled in the corners, showing the smile she wore now was something she always did. Her kindness radiated from her as she placed her hand on my back, and we turned towards the painting again.

"Have you painted this one?"

"Tried," I replied. I struggled to loosen the tightness in my chest, taking in a shaky breath. "It was...hard—emotionally. It was her favorite picture. I just could never capture it and do it justice."

"I would love to commission you for one the same size as this," she said, glancing over at me.

"You haven't even seen one of my paintings," I whispered in response, the words sounded gurgled.

"Actually, I have—" she smiled, looking over my head at Trent.

I let my gaze follow hers to him. He looked at his feet as his toes moved beneath the canvas of his sneakers. I now understood his nerves. I leaned over, placing my hands on his stiff arms as I kissed his cheek, and his arm muscles softened.

"I'd love to try," I replied as I turned to her once again.

"Excellent, I've drafted up some paperwork if you'll come this way. It'll only take a moment, you can read through it and return it later this week," she explained.

Trent and I followed, and she handed me the paperwork, squeezing my elbow as she walked passed me to greet more of her visitors. I stared at the paper, my eyes widening at the number on the page. *$5,000.00.* My eyes dried before I finally blinked and looked up at Trent.

"Am I really seeing this number?" I whispered.

Trent looked down at him, nodding. "I think so."

I threw my hands around his neck and kissed him once. "Thank you."

He rubbed his thumb over my chin. "Anything for you. I'm glad you're not upset with me."

I shook my head. "This is amazing—if I can do it."

His eyes locked on mine. "You can."

He believed it, and suddenly, so did I.

I threw my hands around his neck and kissed him once. "Thank you."

He rubbed his thumb over my chin, his eyes dancing over my face as his lips lifted in the corners, "Happy Birthday."

My mouth dropped open, and he raised his eyebrows.

"What?" he teased; "You thought your dad really wouldn't tell me?"

I inhaled, my eyes going to the ceiling. I wanted to be mad at Dad for telling him, but at the same time it was almost impossible to be mad at either of them.

"Man can't be trusted," I joked, but the laughter didn't reach my face as my chest constricted.

Trent's eyebrows dropped, framing his eyes as his smile faded. "I think I'm missing something."

I pulled away, walking past him and back up to Mom's painting. My eyes glazed over as I stared at it, waiting for Trent to come up beside me. "We haven't celebrated my birthday in a long time."

Trent shook his head, and my eyes went down to my hands that I hadn't noticed I was wringing. "Five years ago...today was when my mom died."

Trent's body tensed and he pressed his eyes closed as I watched him from the side of my vision. He shook his head. "Why didn't your dad tell me that part?"

I inhaled again, my shoulders lifting and then falling as the breath passed over my lips in a soft 'whoosh'. "I'm guessing he figured you could heal that wound by making it an amazing birthday. He tried...more than once," I replied, swallowing; "but it was hard on him too, you know?"

Trent didn't respond and I placed my head on his shoulder, intertwining our fingers. Warmth spread through my limbs as I looked up at him, his eyes filled with a mix of panic and concern as they gazed down at me. I smiled and his brow furrowed, his lips parting as he waited for me to explain.

"He was right, though—as always. You already made today amazing, plus," I dragged out the word as I swayed my hips; "we haven't even had sushi, or sake yet."

The smile returned to Trent's lips as his body relaxed, and I felt the tightness in my chest lift. "Twenty one and suddenly you're going to become a lush?"

I winked at him as we headed to the door. "We have a lot to celebrate."

I glanced over my shoulder at Mom's painting, and the tightness I expected didn't return, instead I could feel the smile on my lips. I looked back at Trent, "Including my mom's life."

Trent leaned over and kissed my head as he slipped his arm around my waist. "Exactly."

Chapter
39

I rolled over and placed my head on Trent's bare chest, breathing in his scent and relaxing deeper into the bed. I could feel myself smiling as his arm wrapped around me and he ran his fingers up and down the skin of my spine. A sigh escaped my lips as his lips pressed against my forehead.

"Morning," Trent whispered, his voice hoarse from sleeping.

I looked up at him, breathing in deeply as I put my chin over my fingers. "Morning," I said, my lids heavy.

"Sleep well?" Trent asked, his hands running up my back to weave through the waves of my hair.

I nodded, sitting up and pulling the sheets around me. They pulled down from Trent, exposing his hips bones so I found myself sucking in my bottom lip. "Do we have to pick up Allie?"

Trent closed his eyes, sinking deeper into the pillows as he shook his head. He cracked one lid open. "Lynn's bringing her and Meg to school. We have several hours of peace."

"What about work?" I asked, running my finger across the skin of his stomach and watching the goose bumps follow behind it.

"I have today off…" he said, leaning up and tilting my chin up so our lips were inches apart. "And you don't have classes."

"We can do anything we want?" I suggested, leaning in and nipping at his bottom lip.

He growled, and I laughed as he pulled me over the top of him, his mouth dancing over mine.

~~~

"So…" Trent said, placing his hands behind his head so his arms created two v's. "What were you thinking about doing today?"

I licked my lips as I looked up and down him, and his chest rumbled beneath my chin.

"Besides what we just did…again," he commented, his eyebrows wiggling in a playful motion as he smirked at me.

I shrugged as I rolled over, arching my back as I stretched. The cotton sheet slipped down my body, pooling at my waist.

"That's not very fair," Trent whispered as he leaned forward and kissed my chest. I fought the urge to pull his body back over mine and instead stood up, running my hands through my hair.

"A shower, and then, if you don't mind, seeing my dad? He went to the doctor yesterday," I began and my stomach rolled. I swallowed before continuing. "He could be coming home soon."

Trent looked around my room. "Home?"

I rolled my eyes as I tossed a pair of his jeans at him from the drawer I reserved him. "Yes, and we still have your place," I reminded him.

He grabbed the pants from the air, smiling down at them. "It'll be great to have him back."

I nodded, and he slipped out of the bed, his body fully exposed.

"That's not fair," I said, narrowing my eyes at him as he stretched, his lean muscles tempting me.

He shrugged as he dropped the pants on the bed and wandered towards me, pulling our hips together. "Isn't it?" he whispered into my ear.

I pulled away from him, running out the door giggling as he followed me into the bathroom. I turned the shower on just as he slid in, pulling me into his arms as the water cascaded over us.

Chapter
40

Morgan was at the front desk when we walked in. She was wearing pale yellow scrubs today; these ones fit her better, the top tying in the back and the pants flaring out. She smiled up at us, and the color of the clothes picked up the gold flecks in her honey brown eyes. They widened for a moment as she looked between us.

"You guys must be going on what? Five months now?" she asked as she stood, coming around and giving me a hug.

"Yeah, actually," I replied. "Walk with us?"

She glanced down at her desk partner, who nodded with a smile. She was used to this by now, and I was pretty sure it was the only break Morgan really ever took. She was a hard worker, and I was sure when she had her degree they would jump at hiring her.

"How have you been?" Trent asked Morgan, and she shrugged.

"Busy between work, family and college, there isn't much time for me. You don't happen to have a twin brother, do you?" she teased, shrugging her shoulders. Trent shook his head. "Not as if I'd have time for a relationship anyways, but you guys are too cute together."

I blushed, looking up at Trent, his eyes locked on me. My breath caught in my throat and I leaned up to kiss his chin.

"Too cute!" she repeated.

"How's Dad today?" I asked her as we turned down the windowed hallway.

She bit her lip, her shoulders tightening. "Seems a little caught up in his thoughts, but aren't we all?"

She reached out and touched my elbow as I felt the blood drain from my face. "I'm sure everything is fine, El."

I felt my jaw tightened as I looked between her and the entrance door to Dad's wing. Morgan knew Dad pretty well since he was one of the longer resident patients. Since I wasn't home much between school, it was better for him to be in a care facility like this, plus the government paid for it. I swallowed the hard lump in my throat. *They should,* I thought, because he wouldn't be here if it wasn't for them.

I knew it was unreasonable, but I didn't want to be mad at Dad for his decision to do the research that caused his cancer. It was easier to blame the government, an entity that existed pretty much just to be blamed for everything.

Morgan squeezed my elbow again, and I pulled a weak smile to my lips, my face feeling too tight as I did.

"Good to see you again, Trent, and congrats on five months," she said, shooting us both a smile before turning back down the hall.

"You okay?" Trent asked as he held the door open for me, and I hesitated.

"Of course," I replied, but it was a weak whisper instead of a full answer. I rubbed my arms as I walked passed him. "Of course."

I knocked on Dad's door, and he looked up from the book he was reading, his glasses perched halfway down his nose. He pulled them off his face, tucking them into his polo shirt pocket. "Good Morning, princess, and I see you brought the boyfriend!"

Trent laughed as he followed me into the room, holding his hand out for Dad. "Mr. Abela."

Dad shook his head. "Paul, call me Paul."

"Good to see you, Paul," Trent replied and Dad pulled him into a 'man hug'—one arm, two claps on the back.

Dad pulled away and rubbed the top of his head, his hair now filled in. "And I have hair since the last time you saw me!"

I rolled my eyes as Trent laughed. "Silver fox, right?" Trent joked.

Dad nodded. "You know it!"

I flopped on the bed, rolling onto my stomach as they went and sat down in the lounge area of the room a few feet away.

"How was the gallery?" Dad asked Trent as they sat down, and I narrowed my eyes at the two of them.

"You knew?" I asked.

Dad rolled his shoulders. "Perhaps."

"Perhaps?" I repeated.

"Trent called me to ask me what I thought about the idea," Dad explained.

"I didn't want to upset you," Trent began, chewing the inside of his cheek. "And I wasn't sure if seeing your mom's photography in a gallery would or not, so I checked with him."

"Very thoughtful," Dad commented as he looked between us.

I inhaled, rolling onto my back and looking at the ceiling before rolling back over again.

"You mad?" Trent asked, and I laughed at his stoic expression—eyebrows framing his eyes, and his lips in a thin line.

"No, it was very sweet of you to check...speaking of checks—how was your check up?" I asked Dad.

He pulled his glasses out of his pockets, unfolding and refolding the arms as he stared at them. His lips curved downward as he shook his head. "Fine."

"So," I asked, sitting up as my heart began to pound. He wasn't acting very excited for a check that went good. "Do you get to come home?"

Dad continued to concentrate on his glasses. "I have to go for another check-up next week, and then we'll see."

"Why?" I asked, my eyes moving rapidly over his nonchalant frame.

He shrugged, acting as if it was nothing. "They just want to be sure before they give me an answer."

He didn't say what they were giving him an answer on, and I felt myself blinking too quickly as Dad turned to Trent and started talking to him about the latest book he read. My mind raced as I stared at them, not listening to what they were saying. Why was he avoiding the conversation?

Was he hiding something?

Chapter 41

"Ellie!" Allie called, running across the front yard as I shut the door to my car. She jumped into my arms, burying her head in my hair. "I missed you!"

I laughed as I walked towards Trent with her in my arms. "It's only been two days."

Allie's lips wrinkled as she squeezed them together, her eyes slits as she thought. She shook her head, holding up four fingers, then lowering one. "Three days!"

"Well," I said dragging out the word as Trent held the front door open for me. "We have the whole weekend to make up for it!"

"You don't have to study?" she asked, pouting as I put her down.

I pulled my backpack off my shoulders. "A little bit, but Trent and I will try to do it after you're asleep."

Trent's eyebrows twitched and he leaned over and whispered, "I'm going to be studying you..."

I elbowed him, and he smirked over at me as I shook my head.

"You two are weird," Allie said, blinking up at us. "Really weird."

Trent bent down, his arms on his knees so he was at eye level with her. "That's not very nice, Allie."

Allie shrugged, her head going back. "It's not?"

Trent shook his head slowly, and Allie sat on the floor, her face crumbling. "Jeremy said Meg and me were weird. We were just having fun like you and El. I don't want to be weird if it's not nice."

Trent's shoulders tensed as he stared down at his little sister and one of his hands weaved through the top of his hair, gripping it as he reached the back. I leaned down, putting my hand on Trent's shoulder.

"Weird isn't necessarily bad. It just means you're different, and there's nothing wrong with being different. It means you're uniquely you, and wouldn't you rather be you than anyone else?" I asked Allie, and her trembling chin lifted as she looked at me. Her eyes were wide and round as she nodded.

I reached forward, rubbing her cheek. "But...why isn't it nice to say it then?"

"It all depends on how you mean it," Trent said, looking over his shoulder at me.

"Then how do I know if I'm a good weird or a bad weird?" Allie asked as she looked down into her lap, her tiny fists balling in her lap.

Trent's shoulders hunched and I realized he didn't know what to say again.

I walked around, sitting beyond her and pulled her into my lap. She tucked her chin into my arms as Trent stood, his jaw clenched as he waited for my response. I moved her hair out of her ear. "Do you like who you are?"

Her chin bobbed up and down against my arm, and I kissed her head. "Then it's a good weird."

Trent looked at the ceiling, pinching the bridge of his nose as he rocked on his heels. Allie turned in my arms, looking up at me. She put a finger up. "I've got something for you!"

"For me?" I repeated as she crawled out of my arms and ran into her bedroom.

"Thanks for that," Trent said as he helped me stand.

I leaned up and kissed his cheek. "First of many awkward conversations I'm sure."

Trent laughed. "Will you handle '*the*' talk for me too?"

My mouth parted as I stared at him, his smile weakened and froze as our eyes locked on one another. My mind stopped when he asked, although I knew he was joking, because that was so long term. Like Allie was as much mine as she was his. Allie's feet jumping up and down below me as she pulled on my shirt knocked reality back into me. Trent turned into the kitchen and started making an enormous amount of noise with pans, and I looked down at Allie, the room spinning. I sat down on the couch as she crawled into my lap and held the paper out in front of me, looking anxiously between me and the picture. My mouth froze yet again; open as I stared at the picture of four people, three adults and one child. Across two of the adults were Trent's and my names, the little one said Allie.

"Who's that?" I managed to choke out, my voice sounding strangled.

"What's your daddy's name?" she asked, slipping out of my lap and grabbing a crayon from her bin on the coffee table.

"Paul," I whispered, leaning forward and putting my arms against my legs as I watched her scrawling his name across the top of the last adult. My nose burned with my eyes as the lump formed in my throat.

Allie turned. "It's done now! My family!"

The clanking pans had stopped, and I looked over my shoulder at Trent. His head was tilted back, his lips pushed inwards against each other as his neck corded. Allie crawled back into my lap, and my body shook with shock as she looked up at me.

"When can I meet your daddy?" she asked, and I heard Trent curse behind me as he dropped the lid to a pan.

"As soon as he's home," I replied, running my hand through her hair.

"Where is he?"

"He's been sick," I explained, staring at the picture clutched in her grasp.

"Sick?" she repeated, and I nodded as she cocked her head at me.

"Yeah."

"Is he going to be better soon?"

"Allie, why don't you go get ready for dinner?" Trent said from the kitchen.

She looked over my shoulder, frowning at him. She sighed, sliding out of my arms and handing me the drawing.

"I bet he'd like this picture then," Allie said. "Tell him I can't wait to meet him."

"Okay," I whispered as I watched her run into the bathroom, pulling the string Trent put on the light switch to help her turn it on and off. She climbed up on her stool, leaning forward and squirting the soap into her hand before turn the handles, each halfway and counting in her head. Her nose squished up as she lost count and sighed before putting her hands under the water. My eyes drifted down to the paper; at the bottom it said "My Family Portrait" in text, obviously, an assignment from school. The smiled twitched at the edge of my lips, and I jumped when I noticed Trent standing in front of me.

He sat down on the couch, rubbing his hands together as he slid his teeth over his lower lip. His eyes stayed on his hands as his eyes fluttered. "I know you didn't sign up for this..." I shook my head and he continued; "No, I get it's not..." his eyes closed as he exhaled through his nose."I get it's not something someone your age wants."

"My age?" I snapped.

The water shut off in the bathroom and Trent leaned back, his head bouncing against the back of the couch as his hands tightened on his thighs.

"I didn't mean it like that—hell, who knows where I'd be if things were different."

"Trent—"

He shook his head, cutting me off. "I get it if this is too much, between your dad, college and...Somehow adopting my sister—my daughter, by dating me."

"You're wrong," I whispered back. "You're exactly what I needed."

His eyes locked on mine just as Allie came back in, holding her hands out to him. "Hand check?" she asked.

Trent coughed, nodding as he looked at them. "Perfect."

~~~

After dinner Allie plopped in front of the television, scooting close to it as her favorite cartoon came on the screen. I sat on the couch, and Trent sat next to me, putting his arm over my shoulders.

"Listen, I'm sorry I put you on the spot like that. I just hadn't thought about how this affected you until now," Trent explained.

I leaned up and kissed his cheek. "Don't worry about it."

Trent reached forward, rubbing my cheek. "Thank you."

The doorbell rang, and Trent's brows furrowed as his body tensed. He stood, rubbing his hands over his pants as he headed to the door.

"You're going to go blind sitting so close to the television, why don't you sit up with Ellie?" Trent suggested as he put his hand on the door knob. He waited until Allie was next to me before opening the door. He slammed it shut almost as soon as it was open.

"Come out and be a man Trent! Be a *real* Wentworth!" a voice yelled from the other side of the door.

Allie jumped into my lap, wrapping her arms around my neck.

"Mother fu—" Trent's eyes flashed down to Allie, and he stopped with his hands behind his head as his body trembled.

Allie tucked her head into my shoulder, her body wracking suddenly as she sobbed against me. I stood, pulling Allie tightly in my arms as Trent pulled his cell phone out of his pocket. The door shook as the man slammed his fists against the wood.

"I want to talk to you Wentworth!"

"Who?" I mouthed.

Trent opened his mouth but no words came out as another scream explained it. "Afraid of your own father!"

My eyes widened as Trent handed me his cell phone. "Speed dial one—it's Gerard."

"Trent—"

He shook his head. "Go hide in the bedroom closet."

"Wait," I whispered, pulling Allie tighter to me. "Wait for Gerard."

"The second he sees a cop he's going to flee. I want his ass in jail—where he can never find us again," Trent replied.

I opened my mouth to try to convince him otherwise, but his chin was set in a firm line, and I realized he felt this was the only way to protect Allie.

"Closet—please?" he asked again.

I nodded, turning and running into the room. I locked the door behind us before slipping into the closet. I held the speed dial down as my hands shook.

"Hello?"

"Gerard?" I asked, breathless as panic caused my limbs to go numb.

"Ellie? What's wrong?"

"He's here—" Goosebumps traveled up my arms as I said it. "His dad is here."

"Mother fu—" Gerard began but the rest was muffled. "I'm five minutes out. Where's Trent? Please tell me he didn't do anything stupid?"

"How dare you? How dare you steal my *own child* from me?" Trent's dad hollered outside. "What makes you think you're a better father than I am? I want her back—back!"

"Ellie? Is Trent doing something stupid?"

"I'm about to," I replied, the phone slipping from my hands. I put Allie on the ground.

She stared up at me with red eyes. "What you going to do?" she asked.

My eyes caught movement outside through the window. Trent's father was falling to the ground, and Trent was shaking his fist. He hit him.

Fuck.

Something stupid.

Something very stupid.

I locked eyes on her tiny frame, shaking with fear. "Is Trent going to be okay?"

I nodded. "Stay here—do not come out until I come back for you—lock the door behind me."

Allie's head bobbed before I turned and ran out the door, grabbing my keys off the door side table, pausing only to make sure I heard the click of the bedroom door locking. Trent and his father were rolling on the ground, and I watched as his father rolled on top, punching Trent in the face so blood flew across the ground in a sickening black streak. They were too busy fighting to notice me, and I opened the car door, every movement becoming too slow as I unlocked the glove box. I grabbed the gun and everything went too fast. I slipped the safety off, running around the car so Trent and his father were directly in front of me. Trent's father was still on top of him, and I wasn't sure he was conscious anymore. My hands stopped shaking as I took my stance, his father's right shoulder perfectly in my aim.

"Stop!" I yelled.

Trent's father looked over at me. "What the—"

Trent had his eyes. I swallowed.

"I swear to God, I'll fucking shoot you!" I shout. "Get on the ground!"

I could hear the sirens in the background as he dropped to the ground, putting his hands behind his head. Trent was motionless on the ground behind him, and I fought the urge to go to him. Instead I leaned down, digging the gun in between the man's shoulders.

"Who are you?" his father asked, his voice muffled by the dirt. He moved, and I dug the gun in deeper.

"It's loaded," I hissed.

"Why should I believe you?" he shot back.

"You really want to test the theory?"

Tires squealed against the asphalt, but I kept my eyes on the tattered plaid shirt beneath my gun's muzzle.

Trent. Trent.

I fought to keep my dry eyes open as I heard the feet on the ground, handcuffs jingled as another set of tires squealed and then another. Gerard pried my hands off the gun, and I fell back, watching as the man was put in cuffs.

"Send an ambulance," someone was saying as my eyes moved to Trent.

His face was covered in blood. He wasn't conscious.

Screaming. There was screaming.

Allie!

My head turned as she ran out the front door screaming. I grabbed her before she could reach Trent.

"Trent! My daddy!" she screamed, fighting my arms. "I need to make sure my daddy is okay."

My eyes followed hers.

To Trent.

Her daddy.

Chapter
42

It's funny how things can become so fucked up so quickly.

That was my life.

A constant circle of the fucked up.

This situation was no different. Trent woke up just as the ambulance made its way down the street, and Lynn took Allie so the EMT could examine him. Allie was still over Lynn and Gerard's now as I shut the door behind the EMT. I put my forehead against the cool door.

"You still sure we're what's best for you?" Trent asked, and I turned, putting my back against the door as I looked at him on the couch.

The two black marks around his eyes made the green of them pop, and I cocked my head at him as I breathed in, my chest rising as I did.

"I would've shot him," I said, and my voice was flat despite the fact the idea frightened me.

Trent tried to sit up, but swore as he winced, the butterfly bandage over his stitches on his temple stretching as he did. The pit in my stomach knotted tighter as I walked over to him slowly, picking the ice pack off the coffee table and placing it over his eye.

"Thank you," he whispered, sighing as he sunk back into the cushions.

"Don't worry about it," I replied as my eyes raced over his face. It was some sort of miracle his nose wasn't broken, but it still didn't look good. My eyes drifted up to the stitches and then down to his cracked lips as they moved.

He put his hand on my wrist, eyes locking on mine. "I'm sorry, El. I just—I needed to protect you and Allie...Yet you ended up protecting us instead. I thought I could hold my own—"

I shook my head, cutting him off. "It's fine—"

"No, El—it's not."

My jaw clenched before I spoke, "I don't have more room in my heart to lose the people I love, Trent. I have a gun. I know how to use it. It's that simple—and it wouldn't have killed him. Just made it so he couldn't beat you to death."

Trent scoffed, his head jerking so his eyes squeezed shut in pain. "How *do* you know how to use a gun?"

"Dad thought it was important I be able to protect myself," I explained. "And I'm a damn good shot."

"I'm honestly glad I didn't have to find that out," Trent said, shaking his head.

I felt my chest tighten, and I looked away, biting my lip as my head spun. Being willing to shoot someone wasn't something I should be proud of. I felt a shiver pass through my body.

Trent squeezed my knee. "More because I always thought I'd be able to kick his ass...not the other way around."

"And then your girlfriend saved your ass," I mumbled.

Trent rubbed my back. "She sure did."

I looked over my shoulder at him.

"I've never been so scared in my life," I whispered, my lashes fluttering against the emotion.

Trent reached up, pulling my head to his chest as he kissed the top of my head. "I love you, Ellie."

I closed my eyes as the words slipped off my lips, far easier than I thought they would, "I love you too."

"We should probably go collect Allie— she freaking out?" Trent asked as I sat up.

"To say the least. She called you her daddy," I replied, looking down at him.

His eyes moved back and forth over mine as his lips parted. He ran his fingers over them. "She did?"

I nodded. "She wanted to know if her daddy was okay, and she was running towards you screaming it," I said, pausing as I let the air in my lungs fill my cheeks. "I grabbed her, and I couldn't even see what was going on with you because I was trying to calm her down."

"Exactly why I love you," he replied, attempting to sit up, but moaning and falling back. "Fucking Christ! Who would've thought that old man could do that much damage?"

"Why don't we just call Lynn and tell her to bring her home."

"And tell Gerard to give you your gun back," Trent added, smirking at me as he rubbed his forehead.

"Ha ha," I replied as I went into his room and picked his cell phone off the floor—the same spot it had fallen to what seemed like hours before.

"Hey, El, how's Trent doing?" Gerard asked.

I looked at him on the couch, his eyes now half shut. "Sore."

"Two Excedrin and two Motrin."

"I'll have to get him that. Trent's anxious to see Allie—"

"And she's anxious to see him. She just calmed down ten minutes ago," he explained, and I could hear him sigh. "We'll bring her over—and I'll bring your gun back, too."

I cringed at the word, wondering if he felt different about me having seen me with a gun in some guy's back. I coughed before replying, "Thanks."

"See you in ten minutes."

I walked back into the living room before turning into the bathroom and grabbing the medicine and a glass of water. I handed them to Trent as I sat down on the edge of the couch again.

"That should make you feel a little better," I said, running my fingers through my hair. "Is anyone going to let me live this gun thing down?"

Trent shrugged as he tossed the pills in his mouth. "Probably not."

"Just don't tell my dad."

Trent shook his head. "I'm pretty sure he wouldn't approve of me after that."

"I'm pretty sure he'd be happy I actually do go to firing practice every other week," I replied, smirking at him as his eyebrows rose. "Yup."

"You're full of secrets, aren't you?"

I winked at him as I stood at the knock at the door. Trent winced, his nostrils flaring before he rubbed his forehead. I knew it was just Gerard, but the twisting in my stomach still happened as I slowly turned the knob. Allie pushed the door open before I could react all the way, running in and jumping onto Trent's chest. He managed to keep in the swear I was sure he wanted to say as he crossed his eyes, hugging her.

I slipped out the door, closing it behind me. Gerard held out my gun, one eyebrow raised into his forehead. "Good job."

I shook my head, taking it and heading to my car. "For what?"

"Handling that gun," he explained.

I shook my head as I checked the safety, which was, of course, already on. I put it in the glove box before saying, "All you saw was me digging it into that tool box's back."

"You know what you're doing with it, though, don't you?" he asked, putting his hands behind his back.

I ran my tongue over my teeth. "Maybe."

Gerard leaned on his toes. "I may have seen you on the range a few times...you know what you're doing."

I inhaled through my nose, looking up at the night sky. "I was shaking so bad when I was in the house—when I didn't know what was going on, but the second that gun was in my hands it stopped. I just wonder if it's a good thing I could've shot him so easily."

Gerard reached forward and squeezed my shoulder. "You didn't though— you didn't react too harshly. You gave him a chance to give in. You did what you needed to do to protect your family, and now you and Trent have one less thing to worry about. Mark isn't getting out of jail any time soon."

"I should probably go make them something to eat—"

"Or order Chinese."

My stomach growled at the thought.

Chapter 43

"Do you have to go home?" Allie asked as she slipped her back pack on. "I like it when you're here a lot."

I patted her head. "I'll be back by the time you get home."

"You will?" she asked, her shoulders perking up as she looked at me. I nodded as a toothy grin spread across her face.

Trent came out of the bedroom to lean against the door frame, shirtless. His eyes were tired as he rubbed his forehead, cringing slightly. I put my hand in Allie's, and we walked out to the bus stop.

"Can we have game night today?" Allie asked as we waited.

"Of course, what should we play?" I asked, looking down at her.

"Memory," she suggested as the bus rounded the corner.

"Sounds good," I replied, and she squeezed my hand as the bus stopped.

She used her finger to signal me to lean over. I bent down and she kissed my cheek. "Take good care of my daddy. I know he likes me to call him Trent, but...all the other kids call their daddy's daddy."

"I'll take good care of him," I replied as I stood back up.

"Promise?"

"Promise."

I watched her get on the bus, take a seat and wave at me out the window. I walked back up the steps slowly, breathing in as I opened the door. I walked in, leaning my head in the bathroom where Trent sat on Allie's stool. His heads were in his hands.

"How can I go to work when I look like this?" he muttered, his hands tangled in the top length of his hair.

I rubbed his bare back. "It's called makeup, love."

He looked up at my reflection in the mirror, blinking slowly. "Makeup?"

"The good stuff is at my house, so we'll have to go there first— are you sure you feel well enough to go to work?"

Trent's lashes fluttered against his bruised cheeks. "I'll just do some book keeping."

"No inventory?"

"Nope," he said as he stood and kissed my forehead.

"Good, what time do you have to be at work?"

"What time do you have to be at class?"

"Ten," I replied. "So let's get going."

~~~

"No shit," Trent commented as I handed him the mirror. "What is this triple strength?"

I laughed, putting the foundation back in the drawer and shutting it. "No, just really expensive. You get what you pay for."

Trent shook his head, standing and cupping my face in his hands. He ran his finger over my nose. "You have beautiful skin, especially these little freckles."

I rolled my eyes. "Freckles—"

"Are adorable," Trent finished my sentence.

"If you say so," I muttered as I walked into the living room and grabbed my messenger bag off the couch.

Trent grabbed my wrist, pulling me into him and kissing me. "I say so," he whispered.

My body tingled as I stared up into his eyes, and I knew he truly felt that way. "Good thing, because your makeup took all my time, and now I have to go all natural to class."

He chuckled. "Hopefully, I don't have to hear you ever say that again."

Chapter 44

I slipped into class late, and Morgan narrowed her eyes at me. I signaled for her to keep quiet as I took a seat behind her. I tried to concentrate on the class, but my mind kept wandering to Trent and how he was doing at work. My phone buzzed in my pocket, and I pulled it out beneath the desk.

Missed Call - Dad 9:00AM

I swallowed, my hair forming a curtain so the professor couldn't see what I was doing. I must have missed his call while I was driving over. My blood pounded through my ears. He knew my schedule. I flicked my finger across the screen as another missed call showed.

Missed Call - Hospital 10:10 AM

The hospital called.

The phone shook in my hand.

The hospital called.

My body numbed as I stood, my books falling to the floor. Morgan's eyes met mine.

"El—?"

I shook my head as my vision blurred, my chest heaving.

The hospital.

Fuck.

I thought we were past this—past me having to keep my phone ringer on.

"El!" Morgan called at my back as I grabbed my bag off the floor. It was caught on the desk.

"God damn it!" I swore as I yanked at it.

The tears were streaming down my face as my chest hammered so hard it made it impossible to breathe.

Was I breathing?

"Ellie!" Morgan grabbed my shaking hands, lifting the desk so the bag pulled free. "What's wrong?"

Everything.

Every fucking thing.

I shook my head rapidly as I turned, rushing out the door and running to my car. I paused at it, my chest rising rapidly as my fingers shook over the screen of my cell phone.

Call. Hospital.

"Paul Abela," I whispered. "I don't know what room."

"One moment," the operator said.

I slipped into the car, putting my head against the steering wheel as my whole body trembled.

"Hey, princess," Dad's voice came over the line, and I thought I might faint.

"Daddy?" I gasped, choking on the name.

He could speak.

He's speaking.

"Can you skip class today? I need you to come to the hospital and speak with the doctor and me," he said and his voice was flat, devoid of emotion.

I knew he was holding something back. Something he wanted to tell me this morning.

"Yes," I choked.

"El—don't drive like an asshole. Nothing is going to change no matter how fast you drive," he said.

I grit my teeth. "Yes."

~~~

I tightened my grip around the steering wheel as I stared at the hospital door, opening and closing for the visitors and patients going in and out. None of them looked like I did.

None of them knew what was coming.

When I lifted my hands from the steering wheel, they were trembling so bad I could hardly remove the key from the ignition. My vision blurred again, and I bit the inside of my cheek before yanking the door open. The warmth of the air smacked me in the face, causing a thin layer of sweat to form on my skin from the previous coolness of the AC. It evaporated almost instantly, only to form again as I entered the cool of the hospital. My stomach spun, and I stopped as nausea washed over me.

"Miss?" the receptionist said, and I looked up, wishing it was Morgan's warm face. Instead I was greeted by an older woman I didn't know with knit brows. I glanced at the sign to the side of her.

"No," I replied, the words tumbling out of my mouth. "I haven't been out of the country."

"Are you okay?"

I blinked at her.

It's a fucking hospital, what good happens here? Who is actually okay when they come here?

I nodded, swallowing before asking, "My dad is here, Paul Abela. I'm not sure where."

She typed on the keyboard before telling me what wing, floor and room to go to. I pressed my shaking hand to my forehead, letting the cold of it sink into my overheating body as I walked to the elevator. Everything was in slow motion again, and I felt my muscles spasm as I watched the red numbers tick away.

Come on. Come on.

When the door finally opened I fought the urge to run down the hall to the room where I knew Dad was.

Dad.

The tears pooled in the corner of my eyes, and I quickly wiped them away as I walked at what felt like a crawl to the room. I looked at Dad sitting on the bed, nodding to the doctor. It was the same doctor who suggested I take anxiety pills. I looked down at my shaky hands and for the first time, I thought he might be right. My heart was so small now, shrunk inside the tightness of my chest. I could barely breathe as I watched them speaking. Dad's eyes lifted and met mine, his mouth stopped moving and the doctor glanced over his shoulder, giving me a sad smile.

I fought the urge to slam the door open and start yelling for no reason. Instead, I opened it slowly and stepped in, closing it behind me. I stayed near it as I stared between them, my vision tunneling on Dad.

He didn't look sick.

"Take a seat," Dr. Williams suggested.

I did so without saying anything.

"El, I'm sorry if I scared you. I just wanted you to be here for this discussion."

This discussion. My fingers dug into my sides as I nodded.

"Sometimes these things happen—" Dad began.

"Sometimes?" I asked, cutting him off. "Sometimes?"

"El, calm down, you don't know what I'm going to say."

"I don't?" I snapped. "Like hell I don't."

Dad swallowed, looking down at his hands as his jaw shook. The tears pummeled down my face. I didn't want to be like this.

I didn't want to be so angry.

But God, I was.

I was so angry at everyone in this room.

In the world.

"Your father has therapy-related myeloid neoplasm— resulting from the various therapies used to treat his Leukemia," Dr. Williams began, looking between me and Dad. "It's a mutation that sometimes happens, in your father's case the deletion of chromosomes five and seven."

There was that word again — *sometimes.*

"It's far more resistant than the Leukemia he originally had—"

I licked my lips, gasping out the words. "How. Much. Time?"

My vision blurred as I stared between them. Dad ran his hands through his newly grown hair.

"Eight months at the most," Dad whispered the words, and my head slowly drifted back as my nails dug into my skin so hard I was sure there was blood seeping through my green tee. My eyes widened.

Eight months.

"Can we have a moment?" Dad asked. Dr. Williams nodded, watching me carefully before exiting the room.

Dad waited for the door to shut before jumping off of the gurney and coming to bend down in front of me. He pried my hands off of my sides as the tears fell in their silent wet sickness over my cheeks and to our hands. My eyes were unblinking as I stared at him. Anger and pain mingled far too strongly for me to speak.

"I'm sorry, El. I'm so sorry."

"How," I swallowed, shaking my head as I struggled to speak. "How long have you known?"

Dad looked down at our hands, his nostrils flaring as he breathed in and out. "We had our suspicions. I wanted to be under constant observation, that's why my stay at Agave was so extended."

Should. Have. Known.

It wasn't normal for a person to stay in a recovery center for several months. I ignored it, though, hoping where my mind constantly went was wrong. It was so much easier to ignore with Trent there.

"Why did you keep going?" I whispered; letting my eyes fall to our hands as the sobs suddenly wracked my body. He went to put his arm around my shoulders and I pushed him away, standing. He followed.

"Princess—"

"Don't princess me, Daddy! Why did you keep going with that research? You *had* to know what it could do to you!"

Dad rubbed his face before his hands fell to fists at his side. He stepped forward, reaching out for me. "I saw them—these families without a parent— like you had been without your mother. I wanted to help them!"

My jaw trembled as new tears formed, angry, and hot. I pushed his arm away.

"Now—" the words strangled me, I shook my head as I spat them out, pointing to my heaving chest; "Now *I'm* going to be one of those statistics you were trying to prevent! Except I have *no one.* When you're gone—" I squeezed my eyes shut, tears catapulting as my chest caved. "I have no one."

Chapter 45

The guardrails were just silver blurs as I hammered the gas.

Too fast.

I'm going too fast.

This ticket would be one that cleared out the savings account. Worse than the first one. The one where I knew there was no cure for Dad, or for me.

That seemed so long ago.

Between now and then I had developed hope.

Hope that was shattered in a moment's time, with some medical term I had no understanding of.

I grit my teeth.

I just didn't give a fuck.

Tingles sped up my spine as the engine whined at me, telling me to slow down. To stop acting stupid. The tingles spread across my cheeks, and the small metal cross cupped in the indent between my collarbone burned.

I wanted to believe.

A part of me *needed* to.

But at that moment all I could feel was anger fueled by pain. The heat from the cross spread across my body and I gripped it, the edges cutting into my flesh as I yanked it off, throwing it as I screamed. The scream hollowed out as the rain catapulted down, unexpected, in true monsoon fashion.

I couldn't tell if the rain was blinding me, or if it was the bitter tears slipping into my gasping mouth.

I wanted to believe.

My eyes settled on the dashboard as the dial slowed, my foot easing from the petal as I stared at the silver cross.

But how could I?

I kept driving; driving towards the edge of the Earth.

There was an edge, and I felt my soul plummeting off of it.

Chapter 46

I stared across the flat desert, my hands grasping the cooling guardrail. There wasn't much at this scenic stop; not much besides cacti, tumbleweeds, the occasional road runner and even less occasional armadillo. The rattlers weren't so rare, but right now they were settling into their holes. It was too cold for them to be out at night. I shivered slightly against the chill of darkness setting in. I stared at the horizon, watching as the moon popped up over it. There were a few stars I could see; I was miles away from the city, but the smog still polluted the air to the point only the brightest stars could be seen. My face was dry of the tears now, my lips cracked against the salt, and I licked them to try to offer some reprieve. I was pretty sure no matter how much water I drank they would split by the time morning came. I breathed in, and my tight chest ached. I rubbed it, but it did nothing to loosen the pain. My head was pounding, but I kept my eyes straight ahead, letting the moon build the pain to the point it was almost blinding.

The gravel crunched behind me, but I kept my eyes straight ahead. The headlights illuminated me, casting my shadow over the sand as a tiny mouse ran across it. I wished I could skitter into the dark as he did. The lights turned off, and I heard the feet on the ground.

"He sent you?" I asked; my voice hoarse.

"He wanted to come himself, but thought it'd be better if he let you calm down a bit," Trent replied, stopping just behind me. "He knew you'd be here."

I closed my eyes, my chest rising to my chin. "Of course he would."

"Morgan left class after you, showed up at the store in a panic. Thank God your dad texted me."

"He texted you?" I whispered, finally giving in and turning to face him.

His eyes rushed over my face, and his fists clenched at his sides. "Warned me you wouldn't take what he had to say well."

Some of the makeup had worn from his face, and he looked tired again as he clasped a handful of his hair.

"You got it wrong, huh?" I choked on the words as I stared at him. His forehead creased as he shook his head. "I'm the one who's bad for you."

Trent pulled me into his arms, and while I wanted to fight it, I couldn't. His warmth engulfed me, threatening to make me lose it again.

"I'm not going anywhere, El. You can try to push me away if you want, but I'm not going anywhere. You are *not* going to be alone."

I pulled away, looking up at him, and his hands slipped to my face. He pressed his forehead against mine.

"I know you're scared—hell, I'm scared, too," his voice cracked, and I saw his eyes glisten. "I'm scared about this whole thing. I think it's wrong you have to go through this over and over—that such an amazing human is going to be taken from this Earth, when there are such crappy ones that keep walking it."

I swallowed. "I'm sick of being scared all the time, Trent. I'm sick of feeling like my insides are rotting."

Trent's eyes dropped, before slowly coming back up to mine. "Have you ever thought you don't need to feel like that?"

I scoffed. "He's dying Trent, and there is nothing I can do about it. I fell into this norm— going to see him, seeing him healthy again. I fooled myself, Trent. I thought he was going to get through this, now...he's dying."

Trent pulled away slowly, putting his hands on either side of the guardrail beside me. "But you're not, El. And your dad needs you to live. I plan on keeping the promise I made him today."

"What's that?"

Trent tilted my chin up before he said, "Being your cure."

Our eyes met, and I felt the hardness chip away. "Thank you."

I leaned up, wrapping my arms around his shoulders as I kissed him and then put my head on his chest, breathing in deeply as I closed my eyes. Trent's hands weaved together, cupping my spine as the slow ache inside of me eased away, at least for that moment.

Trent kissed my head, and his chest rose against my cheek as he sighed. "You want to go home?"

I nodded, my whole body washed over with fatigue, and I realized home was at least 50 miles away.

Why had I driven out so far?

"You want to drive with me, and we can pick up your car tomorrow?"

Yes. I shook my head, pulling away. "No, but I could really go for a burger and fries right now."

Trent laughed, his hands still supporting me on the guardrail. He looked down at me, breathing in, and I raised an eyebrow.

"We should probably pick something up for your dad and Allie, too," he replied, his voice muffled by his hand scratching his chin.

"Are they together?" I asked, my eyes racing over his face that was starting to redden from the neck up.

"Your dad wanted to go home—which was fine with the doctor, by the way—and I needed someone to watch Allie while I came out here to you. He offered," Trent replied, his body pulling away from me as he cringed.

"Well," I replied, slipping under his arm as I jumped off the guardrail. "Just remember you have to get me extra fries, and Dad will want extra bacon on his burger. He likes a lot of bacon."

Trent turned on his heels, his hands in his back pockets as he cocked his head at me. "You're not mad?"

I chewed on the inside of my lip, watching as his eyes concentrated on my reaction. "I will be if you forget my extra fries."

Trent shook his head as he chuckled, and my body spread with warmth. The idea of walking into my house with Dad and Allie there made up for some of my sadness. My stomach growled; the promise of a burger helped a little bit too.

Chapter 47

I barely had the door open, and Allie was already wrapped around my legs. Dad stood in the kitchen doorway, his arms crossed as he tried to look stern, but he had trouble hiding the smile on his face. I raised an eyebrow at him as I held the bag of food over Allie's head.

"Your daddy is awesome!" Allie said as she looked up at me. "We made cookies!"

"Cookies?" Trent repeated.

Allie nodded as she pulled away from me so I could continue inside and Trent could come in. She leaned up on her toes, and Trent bent down as she used her hand to signal him to come closer. "Don't worry, Trent. You're still the best daddy there is."

I watched as Trent swallowed hard before standing and rubbing her head. "Thanks, Bee."

"Bee?" I asked.

Dad took the bag of food from me. "You're the princess, but she's the queen bee!"

"Got that right!" Allie said, her cheeks crunching into her eyes as she smiled up at me.

"I see how it is," I replied as I followed Dad into the dining room.

Trent squeezed my hip, whispering into my ear. "Quick like a bee—buzz buzz."

I rolled my eyes, stopping at the threshold of the room I hadn't used in over a year. It had been that long since Dad started the various therapies that kept him away from home. He sat at the table, looking at me expectantly as Allie crawled into the chair next to him, scooting it closer to him. I swallowed as I watched him lean down so Allie could whisper something in his ear. His eyes widened, and he smiled at her nodding. I imagined him many years earlier, a bit heavier with no gray in his hair— that was once him and I. I always scooted closer to him at the dinner table, if I didn't Mom always knew something was wrong. Even as an adult I was always drawn to the chair closest to him; the one Allie now occupied.

Trent's hand on my back propelled me back into reality, and I stepped into the room.

"Had to dust the table off," Dad commented as he began unloading the bag of food. "It's not good to eat in front of a television."

I took the seat across from him. "Don't worry, we typically don't. Trent makes us all eat together," I replied as he handed me a burger.

"Extra fries are this ones," Trent commented as he sat next to me, his hand on my thigh.

Dad smirked. "Why doesn't that surprise me?"

I narrowed my eyes at him as he handed me the big carton of fries, and I popped one into my mouth.

We settled into a comfortable family dinner, one where we laughed and listened to Allie tell stories I wasn't sure were true. One where I concentrated on memorizing everything about the moment—the warmth in Dad's smile, the way Allie looked up at him with wonder before smirking over at me, her chin pointing out as if to say *see you should've introduced us earlier.* A part of me wondered how good this would be for her, when in so short a time he would be gone. How would I explain it to her, when I could barely wrap my adult head around it? Trent squeezed my leg, and I glanced over at him.

His brows tightened and his eyes darted over my face as he mouthed, "You okay?"

I ran my fingers around the rim of my glass, before nodding.

He raised an eyebrow, and I looked over at Allie and Dad again. She was listening to him intently, her hand cupping her chin as she nodded. She titled her head back, giggling, and the table moved as she kicked her legs happily. I couldn't help but smile at them.

"I'm going to get some more ketchup," I said as I stood.

"Hey," Trent said as I turned with the bottle in my hand. "You sure you're okay?"

I closed my eyes, breathing in. "Yeah, I'm just worried about Allie— she's already so attached, not that I can blame her."

"When the time comes, we'll explain it to her," Trent commented, reaching out and rubbing my cheek. "I think it's good for her...and for him."

I shook my head, looking at him so calm and collected. "You act like it's going to be easy to explain."

Trent frowned. "I know it won't be easy, but I think it's important for your dad to live as normally as possible."

I bit the inside of my cheek. "I know."

"Did the ketchup run away, or is there none like everything else in this house?"

I laughed as Trent winked at me, and I pushed passed him back into the dining room. "Ha ha, Dad," I shot back, wagging the ketchup before squeezing a glob on my fries and handing it to him.

"I keep trying to get her to grocery shop on a regular basis," Trent commented as he sat down and took the ketchup himself. I smirked as he squeezed it only to realize there wasn't any left. "That's not surprising."

I wagged a fry covered in ketchup in his face. "Karma sucks, doesn't it?"

"I'll go shopping tomorrow," Dad replied as he finished his burger. "Get some real food in here besides granola and almond milk—I mean really, can't even buy real milk?"

"I like almond milk *better* than regular milk," I shot back.

Dad's gray eyebrows raised into his forehead. "Sure you do."

"It's actually tasty," Allie said, taking a sip out of her glass. "Yummy!"

"Lasts longer," Trent explained.

"Shut up!" I said, elbowing him.

"She can actually cook," Dad said. "Despite her lack of grocery shopping skills."

"So the pie was real!" Allie commented, looking between Dad and me.

Trent burst out laughing. "I guess so!"

Dad pulled his lips in his mouth as he tried to keep from laughing, but him and I both gave in and started laughing with Trent and Allie.

Chapter
48

I watched as Trent carried a sleeping Allie to the car after I kissed them goodbye. I closed the door behind me, turning to look at Dad sitting on the lounge chair. He smiled up at me, and I fought the urge to go over and sit on his lap like I did as a child. Instead, I flopped down on the couch as I yawned.

"She's a good kid," Dad commented as he leaned forward, placing his weight on his forearms against his thighs. "Must be weird for you to be here alone."

"I'm not alone," I replied smiling over at him. "You're home, speaking of which, let me go get some fresh sheets for your bed."

"Seriously?" Dad commented, blinking at me. "Fresh sheets?"

I stood, putting my hands on my hips. "Ones that smell like they're fresh out of the dryer."

He moved his lips to the side before shrugging. "I guess that wouldn't be too bad."

I squeezed his shoulder as I walked passed him. "I'm glad you're home."

Dad sighed, and I looked down at him. "Seems a little less home-like without Trent and Allie here, though."

"What are you saying?" I asked as I went to the closet and pulled a fresh set of sheets down. Dad rubbed his hands together as I held the fresh scented cotton to my chest, the smell comforting my racing heart.

"It's a big house just for the two of us...maybe Trent and Allie might want to move in?"

My jaw dropped, and I grabbed at the sheets as they slipped from my hands. "Are you sure?"

"Do you think they'd want to?" Dad asked as he scratched the back of his head.

"You'd be okay—"

"You're an adult, El; if that's the part you're worried about. You can share a room."

A nervous giggle bubbled out of my lips before I could hold it back. "Okay. I can ask Trent."

"Allie would be in the same school district, and I could get her on and off the bus," Dad said as he stood and followed me to his room.

He helped me pull the sheets off the bed. "I'll talk to Trent about it tomorrow."

"You're almost done with your semester, right?" Dad asked.

"I have finals next week. I can't believe this semester is almost over, and I'm actually doing really well in math thanks to Trent." I replied as I handed him one side of the sheets, and we began to put them on together.

"Are you going to take more classes this next semester?" Dad asked, concentrating on the sheets, his eyes darting up to me briefly.

I paused before finishing pull the sheets over the edge of the bed. I sat down on the bed and Dad joined me, putting his hand over mine.

"El?" he asked.

I breathed in, my chest rising to my chin. My body felt numb as I thought about it. "I hadn't thought about it—especially..."

The words never made it out of my mouth.

I saw Dad nod from the corner of my eyes. "I'd like to see you graduate," he whispered.

"I want to spend time with you—"

"You can't stop living because of me."

"I want you to see me graduate too—maybe I can take a few of my classes online?" I suggested, putting my head on his shoulder.

He kissed my forehead. "I think that's a good solution. That way, we can take care of each other."

I nodded, breathing in deeply as I closed my eyes. "All of us."

Chapter 49

I ran my fingers over the book bindings, pulling one out and thumbing through its pages without actually paying attention to the contents. I put it back as Stew came over, crossing his arms over his chest. I felt my head go back as I stared at the black metal band on his left ring finger. I opened my mouth, my hand still on the top of the book I was looking at it, but nothing came out. I shut my mouth as he tipped on his heels, chuckling as he pushed his glasses back up his nose.

"Yeah, I know, right?" he commented, looking down at his hand. "Who would've thought?"

"How—who— when?" I mumbled.

"Jen, we started dating a few weeks after you and Trent—so about what, six-seven months ago?"

My face burned. "Yeah. I guess I've lost track of time."

"We got married about two weeks ago—nothing big, you know? Kind of packed up our bags and headed to Vegas," Stew explained, scratching underneath his chin. "Anyways, are you looking for anything specific? Besides Trent?"

I laughed, the tension easing from my muscles. I nodded to Dad talking to Trent. "That's actually my dad talking to him. We were going to the grocery store, and he wanted to stop in and pick up a book...or see Trent, not sure which."

"Guy's got a way with people," Stew said, smiling at me. "Is your dad an artist like you and your mom?"

I swallowed as my vision narrowed on him. "How—?"

"I saw your painting in that gallery down town— freaking epic— especially since it's your mom's photograph. Jen was amazed. She wanted to pick up a print of both of them, but the gallery owner said they didn't have any prints of your painting."

I rubbed my temple. "Dad's a photographer, too. I guess we all kind of are—no one knows where I got the painting thing from, though."

Stew's nose twitched, moving his glasses up on his face as he looked down at his shoes. He cleared his throat, his eyes coming back up to mine. "I know this is a bit odd of me to ask...but it'd be awesome if I could get a print of yours for Jen for a wedding present?"

"A print?"

Stew nodded, his cheeks reddening above his beard.

"How about I do you one better and actually paint you something?"

Stew's eyes widened. "I don't know that I could afford that."

"You'd be surprised. What's your budget?"

He put his hands in his pockets looking around the store. "Two hundred?"

"Most of my paintings are split canvas. I could do a smaller scale one, say two canvases, about this big?" I said, holding my hands out. "Anything in particular you were thinking?"

Stew blinked at me a few time before shaking his head in shock. "Oh—yeah—that'd be amazing. She loves sunrises."

"I'll look through my photographs and find one for you. You'll get a copy of the photograph with the painting, too."

"Are you sure?" Stew asked.

I nodded. "Of course."

"I really appreciate it; I mean I know how busy you are—"

"I love painting," I cut him off. "So it's no big deal."

"Wow, yeah...thanks so much."

"Give me two weeks?"

Stew's head jerked up and down, his jaw still slack.

"I should probably go check on them, get Trent back to work before he gets himself in trouble—with himself."

I walked over to them slowly.

Married.

Stew was married already.

I dragged my teeth over my lower lip as I looked between Trent and Dad. Dad only had so much time left. I shook my head.

Crazy. *That's crazy, Ellie.*

"Hey, love," Trent said, pulling me into his arms.

I breathed in his scent.

So why didn't the thought scare me?

Not having Dad walk me down the aisle was far scarier.

Marriage.

I closed my eyes, keeping my head in his shoulder.

Not so crazy.

Chapter 50

I scrubbed the dish, concentrating on the bit of cheese that seemed to have adhered itself to it permanently.

"Whoa, don't snap that thing," Trent commented, making me jump. Suds flew off my hand and covered his front. He wiped them off before blinking at me. "You okay?"

I breathed in through my nose. "I've been meaning to talk to you about some...stuff."

"Stuff?" Trent repeated, cocking his head at me as he held his hand out for the dish.

I handed it over, leaning against the sink.

"Yeah," I replied as I looked passed him into the dining room where Dad was playing a game of go fish with Allie.

"Dad and I were talking..." I looked down at my feet, concentrating on the leopard print of my canvas slip on sneakers. "And we'd like it if you and Allie would consider moving in with us."

Trent stopped drying the dish, and I let my eyes slowly rise to his as my shoulders tensed up to my ears.

"Really?"

"Yeah—he could get her on and off the bus—she wouldn't have to change schools—and this house is plenty big—and—"

Trent put the dish down and put his hands on my shoulders, pushing them down. "Yes."

"Yes? You don't need to like think about it?" I repeated.

Trent laughed, tucking his face into his bicep. "Well, I do have to discuss it with Allie, but judging by how much she loves your dad, I think that's a good selling point."

"You think it'll be okay with her?"

"Definitely...but your dad is okay with us—"

"Sharing a room? Yes, surprisingly."

"Are you sure you're ready for this?" Trent asked, cocking his head at me.

I swallowed as I moved the other thoughts out of my mind. The ones I was sure I shouldn't say.

"So," I began turning back to the dishes. "Did you notice Stew's new ring?"

"Ha," Trent coughed. "Yeah, crazy right?"

"Yeah."

I concentrated on washing the dishes, blanking out my mind and ignoring the warmth that spread through my body each time Trent's body grazed mine as he stood next to me, drying the dishes I handed him. I chewed on my lip as I scrubbed dish after dish, my hands pruning from the length of time in the suds.

"What are you thinking about?" Trent finally broke the silence.

I shrugged, keeping my eyes on the last dish. "Nothing."

"Nothing?" he repeated, wrapping his arms around my waist and putting his chin on my shoulder. He kissed my ear. "Usually you like talking to me."

I laughed, sighing as I leaned back, giving into the feeling of being in his arms. "I'm trying not to think."

"Why?" Trent asked as I turned in his arms so I was facing him.

I exhaled, and my chest rattled, the tightness not freeing. "I just keep thinking about all the things my dad will miss…" I chewed on the inside of my cheek. "Walking me down the aisle, his grandchildren growing up…"

Trent tilted my chin up with his hand, so our eyes met. "Who knows, maybe he won't miss either of those."

I closed my eyes, moving my face so I could kiss his palm. "You think?"

I watched as Trent licked his lips. "If we got married, then Allie would be his granddaughter, technically."

My eyes locked on Trent's. I hadn't thought of that. I looked over his shoulder at Allie and Dad. My mind suddenly racing to what our wedding would be like—Dad walking me down the aisle after Allie threw the flowers down and Morgan waiting to take my bouquet. Something small and intimate, where we could spend the night talking and laughing with friends and family.

"Did Stew get you thinking about this?" Trent asked, knocking me out of my day dream.

I shook my head. "Not really—he just made me think it wasn't *that* crazy. You don't think it's crazy?"

Trent put his forehead to mine, and I closed my eyes as he whispered, "No, but you'll have to wait for me to ask."

I opened my eyes, narrowing them at him. "How long?"

He shrugged. "First, let's live together—you might hate me and my nasty habits."

"Like the fact you walk in the door and your socks fly to wherever you are?"

He pursed his lips. "As if you don't have nasty habits Miss I floss my teeth two inches away from the mirror so my spit splatters everywhere."

Chapter
51

I shook my head as I watched Allie being swung between Dad and Trent. She giggled as we reached the door to the hardware store, dropping their hands as her feet touched the ground. She turned with her face red from excitement as she babbled on about what color she wanted the room to be. I was pretty sure by the time we reached the color swatches it would change another five times. Purple, pink, blue, yellow, green—she wasn't really sure. She did know she wanted butterflies all over the room. As we reached the area with the paint colors she tugged on Dad's pant leg, putting her arms up for him to pick her up. I smiled as I watched, but as he went to pick her up he cringed, his face paling as his eyes squeezed shut. My heart hammered in my chest as I stepped forward, but Trent had also seen, and he pulled her up into his arms instead. The pressure in my head built, but Dad's face gained its color back as if nothing happened, and he smiled as Allie put her hand on his shoulder. I stood next to them as Allie cocked her head at the colors.

"I want one with a cool name! Eeyore's Bow!" she said, pointing at a fuchsia pink. "I want that one!"

"A bit bright, don't you think Al?" I asked, leaning forward and picking up the paper.

She shook her head, eyes convinced with her lips set in a smile I couldn't deny.

"Grampy, what do you think?" she asked as she took the color from me, and held it in front of Dad.

My mouth dropped, and Dad smirked, seeing my expression from the corner of his eye.

"I think it's beautiful, Bee—what does Dad think?" Dad looked over at Trent.

"Very bold just like you," Trent said, putting his hand on the top of her hair and rustling it.

"I'm not a boy! Don't mess up my hair!" she said, pushing away his hand, but she was giggling. "See I want a pink bedroom!"

"Alright, let's go get this paint," Trent commented, stepping away with Allie and leaving me standing shocked next to Dad.

He rubbed the back of his head as he looked at the paint colors.

"Grampy?" I commented, cocking my head at him.

He shrugged, picking up a sage green as if he was interested in it. I was sure he wouldn't ever change any of the other paint in the house, since Mom picked the colors. "She asked me if she could call me it—I figured why not."

I put my arm into his, settling my head on his shoulder. "I'm glad she has you."

"And I'm glad we have such a wonderful family," he replied, kissing my forehead. "Now, do you think the living room would be better in this color?"

I shook my head. "I like the steel gray—it's contemporary."

Dad chuckled. "You sound like your mom."

I smiled over at him as he smirked.

"Just as stubborn, too."

"Nailed that," he shot back.

Chapter 52

"You sure you want to do this?" Trent whispered to me as he poured the bright purple-pink paint into the tray.

I leaned back on my hands, staring around the now empty room that was once Mom's office. The yellow was bright—cheery, just like Mom always was. It *did* remind me of her warmth and caring. I let my eyes settle on Dad and Allie. He was showing her how to apply the paint with a roller in a W shape, and she was smiling with her shoulders tight as she waited her turn. I breathed in, letting the air out with a sigh as a smile came to my face. I nodded, knowing Mom would've loved to turn this room into Allie's— she would've wanted us to make it her own. I watched as the paint splashed into the tray; I was pretty sure Mom would've loved the pink anyways.

"You ready, Allie?" Trent called over her shoulder.

She looked up at Dad. "You think I'm ready to do it for real, Grampy?"

My heart fluttered at her calling him that, and I felt the tickle in my nose. I pursed my lips as I watched him nod, tossing me a quick smile.

"Let's do it!" Allie cheered as she came forward and dunked the white roller into the paint. Color rolled over it, and she glanced at Dad again. "Is this enough—or too much?"

Dad came over and looked down. "Perfect."

"Let's roll together?" she asked him, and he nodded, dipping his roller in as she moved to her place at the wall.

"You two better do a clean job on the trim!" Dad commented as he moved to stand next to Allie.

"1-2-3!" Dad said and Allie and he rolled in sync with one another.

Trent's eyes found mine. "Thank you," he said.

I shrugged. "It's our home now—all of us."

Trent chuckled as he dipped took his plastic cup of paint and handed me mine. "You start on that side with them, and I'll start on this side, we'll meet in the middle?"

"Sounds good," I replied, standing and taking my paint cup and brush before leaning up on my toes and kissing Trent's cheek.

I moved to my side of the room, carefully concentrating on the trim to make sure I didn't get any paint on the ceiling.

"Uh oh," Trent began, his voice sounding guilty; "I think I might be doing this wrong."

I rolled my eyes. I was positive that he wasn't. I kept painting; that was until Allie squealed and Dad started laughing.

"What did you—" I began as I turned on the step stool to face him. My jaw dropped as I looked at the wall.

Allie and Dad were suddenly quiet, or I had lost all sense of sound as I stared at Trent. He was bouncing on his toes to his heels, the paint brush in front of him in his crossed arms as he raised an eyebrow at me, a crooked smirk growing across his face. The words written across the wall were what were now making me dizzy and breathless.

Will you marry me?

Trent's smirk grew into a full blown smile as he pulled the ring out of his pocket and went on one knee. I slowly stepped down from the stool, keeping my hand on the arm of it as I tried to steady myself. The sun streamed in through the window, hitting the diamonds at the top of the ring and sending rainbows of light cascading across the newly painted walls.

"So?" Trent asked as I took one step at a time until I was standing in front of him, and he was looking up at me.

I nodded, and the sound in the room erupted as Allie squealed and Dad started clapping. Trent slipped the ring on my finger before pulling me into his arms.

"Is this crazy?" I whispered into his ear.

"Life's crazy," he replied as he moved my bangs out of my eyes. "And you make me crazy happy—so why not live crazy—life's too short to worry about what's normal—or what's crazy. Besides I'm pretty sure neither of us is really *that* normal."

I laughed as I leaned up and kissed him. There was a flash, and I turned to look at Dad, camera in his hand.

He put his free hand up. "What, you thought I didn't know?"

I narrowed my eyes at him as Allie rushed forward, hugging Trent and I's legs together. "Grampy! Group hug!"

"Yeah, get over here old man," I shot at Dad.

Dad leaned down pulling Allie up in his arms, and my stomach dropped, waiting for him to cringe, but he didn't. He stood, kissing my forehead before wrapping his arms around us all.

"Group-selfie?" Dad suggested, and all I could do was laugh as I nodded.

Chapter 53

My stomach shifted in unease as I sat in the waiting room of the dress shop. Dad reached over and squeezed my hand. I watched as he looked over my shoulder at Morgan with Allie in her lap. I looked ahead as I let a breath I hadn't realized I was holding out. My cheeks puffed as I squeezed his hand back, and I resisted the strong the urge to tap my foot as we waited. It felt like it was taking forever, and beside the fact it felt like the AC wasn't working in the building. My palms felt slick, and I rubbed them over my jeans.

Dad coughed, and my head shot up. He blinked at me a few times before looking over at Morgan. "Can you give us a second?"

"Of course. Allie, let's go check out that rack of flower girl dresses we saw when we walked in," Morgan said, standing with Allie on her hip.

"Princess," Dad said, the word coming out slowly. "Breathe, please."

I squeezed my eyes shut.

"In, out, in—"

I cut him off. "I'm fine, Dad."

"Are you?" he asked as he shifted in his seat, his arm over the back of my chair. "You don't have to put your life on fast forward because of my cancer."

"It's not because of—"

"El—"

"Okay, so it is *partly* because of it. How can I not put my life on fast forward? I want you to be a part of as much of it as you can, and you only have so much time," I replied.

Dad leaned forward, looking at his hands as he pulled his lips into his mouth. His eyes locked on mine as he asked, "Do you really want this?"

I looked around the store, my eyes running over the beautiful array of dresses as my heart raced. My eyes stopped on Allie who was holding a dress up to her body, sashaying back and forth as she looked at herself in the mirror. My mind drifted to Trent, and I felt the smile building on my lips. My gaze fell to my hand, where I was playing with the ring on my finger.

I locked eyes with Dad as I nodded. "Positive."

"Would you marry him in two months if I wasn't dying?"

I kept my eyes on him despite the angry chill that rushed up my spine at the inevitable truth of Dad's situation. I didn't like hearing him say it.

"Yes," I replied, my voice as set as my eyes.

A smile came across Dad's face, and he put his head back against the wall, his eyes drifting back over to me. "Would've been awkward if you'd said no."

We both started laughing, and he rubbed my back.

"So, what the hell are you so nervous for?" Dad asked as our laughing subsided.

"You only get to do this once, how will I know what dress is *the* one?"

Dad shook his head. "Really? All these nerves over a dress?"

"It's one of the most important things about the wedding, aside from the location."

"Speaking of which, have you thought about where? We need to book the church and venue as soon as possible."

I bit my lip as I looked over at him.

He smirked. "Money is no object here—within reason. It is just one day, albeit it a very important one."

"We don't need anywhere big, so I was thinking—" I paused before finally letting the words roll out in such rapid succession I wasn't sure Dad would understand; "There are these elopement packages this destination wedding place does for Sedona—it covers everything, and there are different ceremony types we can do, but I don't want you to be mad that we're not doing it in a church. I wanted to do it at the Chapel of the Holy Cross, but they don't do weddings, and I really want it to be in Sedona—"

"Slow down," Dad said as he put his hands on either of my shoulders. "Breathe. Yes, we can do that, but elopement? Am I not invited?"

"You are—and fifty other people, it just means we can plan it super quickly," I replied, finally breathing in.

"Sounds perfect, sunset in Sedona—beautiful," Dad commented leaning forward and kissing my forehead.

I put my hands over his and closed my eyes as my stomach settled, and my muscles relaxed.

"Any dress advice?" I asked Dad as he sat back in his seat.

His eyebrows scrunched as he blinked at me rapidly. "Just don't do what your mom did and get something very," he held up his hands and did quotes; "in-fashion. It won't be by the time your kid gets married."

I covered my mouth as I tried to cover my chuckling. "It's not that bad."

Dad cocked his head. "Then why are we here?"

I flipped my braid over my shoulder, playing with the end of it, flicking it through my fingers. "Well, okay, it's a little bad."

A *little* didn't really cover it. The dress was more of a *thing* than a dress— all chunky lace and shoulder pads, poof in all the wrong places. Mom still looked beautiful in it, which said a lot for how gorgeous she was.

"Ellie! Ellie! What do you think of this one?" Allie asked as she ran forward with a deep purple dress in her hands. Morgan grabbed the back of her shirt just as she was about to trip over it.

"Careful," Morgan said to her, and she nodded before power walking the rest of the way towards me.

"What do you think?" she asked, twirling with it in front of her.

"Beautiful," I replied. "Are you going to try it on?"

Allie's eyes widened. "Can I?"

"That's why we're here—you can try a bunch of them on if you want," I commented, and her eyes got even wider as she shook with excitement.

"Speaking of which, I think your dressing assistant is coming," Morgan commented as a woman in her early twenties came over.

"I'm Angela," she said, shaking each of our hands, including Allie's. "Who's the bride?"

Everyone pointed at me, and I blushed. "Me."

"Great, so are we going to have you go first, or save you for last?" she asked, looking down at Allie and winking.

"Last sounds good," I replied.

She smiled. "Most brides aren't patient enough to go last!"

I shrugged. "I'll take a look around while they try stuff on. I have no clue what I'm going for!"

The girls didn't take much time to pick their dresses. Allie settled on the dress she showed me the second she slipped it on. She loved it; especially when Angela told her to spin in it. Allie giggled so hard when the tulle of the bottom flew in circles around her that she fell to the ground. Morgan was easy going in her personality, something I never realized until a few months ago, and her curvy frame looked good in just about anything. She settled for a dark purple satin dress with a sweetheart neckline and diagonal ruching that stopped at the cinched waist where a small flower sat. I rubbed my hands on my jeans as she slipped back out of the dressing room and handed Angela her dress to log the size and design. They both turned to me, and Dad looked at me with crossed arms from his chair.

"Now, you," Angela said, pointing her pen at me. She cocked her head. "Anything particular in mind?"

I bit my lip. "Lace?"

Angela's eyes went over my body and she turned to Morgan. "Are you thinking what I'm thinking?"

Morgan put her finger on her chin as she replied, looking between us so my stomach fluttered as I wondered what she was thinking. Despite the fact I got used to her scrubs, I knew she knew how to look sexy, and I was wondering just how sexy she was planning on *me* looking.

"Nothing too provocative," I said just as Morgan opened her mouth.

She pressed her lips together as she narrowed her eyes and then looked back at Angela. "Tulip."

"Exactly!" Angela said as she pulled Morgan passed me.

"Tulip?" I repeated as I watched them beginning to go through the dresses.

Morgan nodded but didn't look back at me as she pushed against the enormous weight of dresses so she could see each one. "Tight all the way down to just below the hip, and then it flares out."

I looked over my shoulder at Dad who looked up from his phone and shrugged.

Allie sat next to him on the floor coloring. I sighed.

Maybe I should've looked at some of those wedding magazines Morgan had bought me the week before. I just hadn't had time between school and spending time with Dad and Allie. School was out, so it was nice to have Dad around to help with Allie when Trent was at work, or I was at school, and he genuinely seemed to enjoy every moment of it. I felt the warmth spreading through my chest at the thought of the way Dad's eyes lit up when she called him Grampy. He adored her, and she adored him. I fought the sinking feeling that began to invade my happiness at the thought of how we would explain the inevitable to Allie. Before the thought could spread Morgan turned with a dress in her hands.

"I found it!" she commented, her voice high pitched.

I reached for it and she shook her head, pointing to the dressing room. I huffed but obediently followed her in, she placed it on the hook, unzipping it and turned to face me as my mouth dropped. She put her hands on her hips as she shook her head. "Not a word; just put it on."

The words *low cut much* never made it out of my mouth, at least not for her to hear. She pulled the curtain closed behind me, and I stood staring at the dress. It was gorgeous with its sheer lace sleeves and satin bodice covered with yet more lace and crystals that danced in the light. I didn't bother to turn the price tag, I was pretty sure I would die if I did.

Instead I stepped forward, running my fingers over the lace, surprised at how soft it could actually be. I undressed and slipped it on, stepping into it carefully as I held my breath.

"You okay in there?" Morgan called through the curtain.

I nodded, and then realized she couldn't hear a nod. I zipped up the back myself—it dipped so low that there wasn't any zipper I couldn't reach. I closed my eyes before turning and throwing open the curtain. I wanted to see their reactions first, especially when I felt so self-conscious I barely wanted to leave the fitting room. When I stepped out Dad's eyes shot open, and Morgan covered her mouth as she jumped up and down.

Angela had a few dresses in her hands that she looked down at before hanging them back on the rack, as if to say, *there's no competing with that.* Allie looked up from her drawing, and smiled.

"You look like Cinderella," she replied, leaning on her hand. "I want a dress like that someday."

I looked up at the ceiling, breathing in and out before turning to the 360 degree mirror. Morgan stepped forward and spread out the train of the dress, the lace fluttering over the satin as it settled on the ground and my eyes finally rose to my reflection. I felt the air catch in my throat as my hands settled on my stomach. It fit like a glove, slipping over the curves of my petite body in a way that was both sexy and elegant. I *felt* like Cinderella.

Allie came forward peeking around my hips. "You just need glass slippers with butterflies on them, just like the movie!"

I laughed as I put my hand on her shoulder.

"So?" Morgan asked with her hands clasped in front of her chest as she looked at me in the mirror.

I swallowed, looking back at my reflection and nodding.

"Does that mean this is *the* one?" she pushed.

My body trembled at the thought, and the hair rose on my neck as I glanced over at Dad. He was shaking his head, his hand over his mouth.

"Daddy?" I whispered.

He stood, coming forward and taking my face in his hands. "Perfection—you truly look like my princess—my Cinderellie."

Chapter 54

I looked in the mirror, breathing out as I pressed my hands to my chest. It was amazing how quickly the weeks passed between Trent and Allie moving in to now. My eyes fluttered as I fought back the tears. I looked at the ceiling before my eyes fell back to the mirror where I saw Dad's reflection in the mirror. I turned slowly to face him, looking down at the white lace covering my small frame.

"What do you think?" I whispered.

He leaned against the door frame, resting his head against his hand as he shook his head. "Like Cinderella, of course."

I laughed as the lyrics to a song he used to sing echoed through my head. "Do you remember that version of the Cinderella song?"

Dad's laughter joined mine as he walked forward. "How did it go?"

"Cinderellie, Cinderellie you're so fat and you're so smelly!" Dad sang using his hand as the musical baton. He ran his hand through his gray hair, which was thinning out again. I grit my teeth against the thought. "It was so wrong on so many levels to teach you that."

I shrugged as I sat down in the chair by the window that overlooked the beautiful red landscape of Sedona.

"You could've done a lot worse," I replied, smiling over at him as he took the seat across from me.

His chest rose as he breathed in, and then let the air out in a heavy sigh. "It's almost time, princess."

I held my hand out for him and nodded as we stood. He pulled me into his arms, and I closed my eyes.

"I wish your mom was here," he admitted, his voice shaking.

I hugged him tighter.

"But you're here," I whispered; "and I'm so glad for that."

"Are you ready?" he whispered into my ear.

I looked up. "Are you?"

He scoffed. "I don't think I'd ever be ready for you to be grown up—a family of your own."

"You're a key part in that family," I reminded him. "Allie thinks you're the best babysitter slash Grampy ever."

"Eh," Dad replied, linking his arm with mine. "That's only because she doesn't know better."

"That's for sure," I shot back as he winked at me.

Morgan stood just outside the door with Allie and Meg who were making sure they each had an equal amount of petals in each other's baskets. They stopped as soon as they saw Dad and me.

"You look so pretty!" Meg gasped, and Allie nodded so fast I wondered how she wasn't seeing stars.

"Thank you," I replied, leaning down and kissing each of them on the cheek. "You remember from rehearsal last night what to do?"

Allie put a hand on her hip. "Throwing flower petals isn't *that* hard—at least not as hard as you and Morgan not falling on your faces in those shoes you're wearing."

I glanced over at Morgan who wiggled her dark eyebrows as she lifted her dress to reveal her God-only-knew how tall gold stilettos. She even convinced me that stilettos were the only way to go, and not just any pair, five inch tall ones that captured my need for something blue with their pale blue satin and crystal encrusted flower on the front.

"Someday this is going to be us!" Meg said as she linked arms with Allie.

"Yeah," Morgan commented. "Someday soon she's going to be a teenager—and then you'll be begging me to come over for margaritas."

I cringed, and Dad squeezed my arm. "I'm sure she's going to be an amazing teenager, you were only a little bratty."

I rolled my eyes as I looked over at him. Emotions rushed over me, an onslaught of sadness of what the not so distant future held, and I fought back the tears again. Dad reached up and touched my cheek. "No, princess — don't think about that now."

Again, I found myself looking at the ceiling, but this time it was much harder to fight the tears. I could see the drops hanging on my lashes.

"Trent's out there waiting for you, and the girls are anxious to get out there," Dad reminded me. "Plus, you don't want your makeup to run, do you?"

Morgan squeezed my arm, nodding over her shoulder. "It's time for me—then them—and you," she said, giving me a sad smile.

My lips formed an O as I breathed out, watching her walking towards the door. The ushers pulled open the doors and Morgan stepped out, a breeze wafting her dress around her legs before the door swung shut again. In what only seemed like second later, the doors opened again and Meg and Allie went through hand in hand. I closed my eyes as I waited for the music to change.

I fought the urge to keep my eyes shut when I heard the change in the piano, and the rustling of people standing from their chairs. When I opened my eyes I looked over at Dad, who was the same height as me in these heels, despite his own dress shoes adding an inch to his height.

Dad coughed before looking ahead and saying, "I guess I'll let Trent steal my Cinderella."

I shook my head. "No one could ever steal me way from you, Daddy."

His eyes were soft as he looked forward and took the first step. He glanced over at me as I paused before falling into step next to him. My heart hammered in my chest, and the music faded against the sound of it and my breathing. Was I really breathing that loud? I tried to stop it, but got light headed.

I'm going to trip!

The doors swung open and there Trent was in his perfectly fitted gray suit over the purple vest and tie that matched the girls' outfits. His eyes were on his shoes, but as Gerard elbowed him, they moved up. His mouth dropped open as I whispered to Dad, "Don't let me fall."

"Never," he whispered back.

The night before the walk up to the alter overlooking the creek seemed so short, but now, with all these people staring at me, and these super high heels, it felt like it stretched on forever. When I finally reached the end Dad leaned over and kissed my cheek before turning and shaking hands with Trent. They exchanged a look I realized both of them understood, but I hadn't a clue what it meant and Dad went to sit in his place.

Trent bit his lip. "I wish I could kiss you," he whispered.

"Save that for the end," Morgan commented as she stepped forward to take my bouquet.

I bit my lip to stop laughing, but couldn't help the fit of giggles that came out of my lips.

Stop! I pressed my eyes shut and breathed in before opening my eyes as Trent's hands slid into my own. I exhaled as our eyes locked on one another, and the officiant started talking. The ceremony passed in a blur, and the part I feared the most was suddenly happening—kissing Trent in front of our closest family and friends. In that moment I forgot they were there and gave into how much I loved the man in front of me. A whistle made me pull away, my face burning with heat as Morgan pursed her lips to keep from smirking. She handed me the bouquet, and Trent nodded ahead of us.

"Shall we?"

"I present to you Mr. and Mrs. Trent Wentworth!"

I was Mrs. Trent Wentworth.

I glanced over at my husband, and I couldn't help but laugh.

Mrs. Trent Wentworth.

Chapter
55

"I can't believe how good this is," I commented as I ate the last piece of my salmon dinner. "And how beautiful everything looks."

I glanced around the small banquet room we reserved at the hotel. The wall behind us was all glass, facing out to the creek where we said our vows, and the sky was already darkening, stars popping out as the moon lit the room.

"You did an amazing job pulling it together," Trent said as he leaned over and kissed my hand. "And that dress...yeah, it's breathtaking."

I narrowed my eyes at him. "You have to say that!"

Trent shook his head. "No, but I do have something I have to do."

"Like what?" I asked as he stood. "Trent?"

He put his hands up. "Don't worry, I'll be right back."

"Get me another Shirley Temple while you're at it," I called at his back.

"Do you know anything about this?" I asked as I turned to Morgan beside me.

Her shoulders went up as she tried to contain her smirk and keep a serious face. "No, not at all."

"Gerard?" I asked as I leaned passed her.

He dabbed his mouth as he put down his steak knife. He frowned. "Nah, not at all."

"I bet Allie would tell me," I huffed as I looked for where Trent disappeared to.

"No, I wouldn't! Grampy made me swear not to," she said as she plopped down in Trent's seat.

I cocked my head at her. "So Grampy has something to do with this."

Her eyes widened, and she shook her head, zipping her mouth shut with her hands. "I'm going back to sit with Meg—you're trouble, El!"

I burst out laughing as I watched her skip back to her place beside Meg.

The music quieted, and I looked over at the DJ. Trent had a microphone and his guitar. My muscles turned to jelly as he turned to face the crowd, looking straight at me.

"Normally, the bride and groom get to do the first dance—but I'm not really a traditional kind of guy," Trent began, winking at me. "I'm also not a country singer; despite the fact that my father-in-law thinks I have a shot at it."

Dad closed one eye as he pointed at Trent, and stood, walking towards him. Dad took the microphone, and I felt myself swallow as he smiled out at the crowd.

"Now, typically, the bride gets to choose the father-daughter dance, but in her haste to plan this whole thing, she kind of forgot about it," Dad explained, and my jaw dropped open as panic raced over me.

I told Trent to handle the DJ and the music, because he was the musician after all. I hadn't thought about any of the dances or the special songs that are associated with them. I could feel a cold sweat building on the back of my bare neck.

"Well," Dad continued. "She just told Trent to handle it—and handle it he did. Princess, would you join me on the dance floor?"

I sat glued to my seat for a second before the solid nudge from Morgan woke me up, and I stood and walked to the dance floor. It was another walk that felt far too long for the actual distance. Dad handed Trent back the microphone and Trent placed it on the stand as he began to strum the guitar. I wasn't much of a country fan, but there was no mistaking the Chuck Wick's song, *Stealing Cinderella* and the meaning behind it as Dad's hand slipped into mine.

Dad was right. Trent handled choosing it perfectly, and not only that, he sang the song just as well. Dad pulled me into his arms, one hand in mine the other at my waist.

"Is it everything you dreamed of?" Dad whispered in my ear.

I nodded, squeezing my eyes shut as I placed my head on his shoulder. "Am I allowed to cry now?"

He kissed my head. "Only if it's because you're happy."

"I am," I whispered back.

Chapter 56

I stared around the thinning crowd of people. There were only a few people left; most had already gone up to their rooms or returned home. I smiled as I watched Dad on the dance floor with Allie, she was asleep on his shoulder, but he kept swaying her to the beat. Morgan was on the dance floor with her date, and I smiled as I kissed Trent's shoulder beneath my head.

I looked up at him, and he gave a soft smile, his eyes fluttering with fatigue. "I can't believe it's done," Trent whispered.

I nodded.

"One last dance?" he asked as he stood, holding out his hand.

I smiled as I took it, even though I was pretty sure my feet would fall off in the morning at this rate. My limbs were numb as I settled my head against Trent's chest, one hand on his shoulder, and the other entwined in his as we glided across the dance floor. When the music ended, the lights lifted, illuminating the room, and I tipped my head back before laying down on the floor. Trent looked down at me, crossing his arms as his brow furrowed.

"You going to make it?" he asked.

I shook my head as Morgan collapsed next to me, putting her head on my stomach and looking over at me. "Amazing."

"Mhmm," I muttered as I half-closed my eyes. "I can't feel my legs."

Morgan laughed. "Me neither! Being able to walk is overrated."

"Did you have a good time?" I asked as I watched Trent go over and shake hands with the DJ, Morgan's date joining him.

"Yes," Morgan replied; turning and putting her head in her hands as she looked down at me. "What did you think about Ryan?"

"I like him—you seem so happy. I just can't believe you found time to date someone between college and work," I replied.

"And, don't forget," she said, nodding over at Trent and Ryan; "they actually like each other!"

"The most important part!" I commented as I sat up on my elbows. I looked down at my hands, tapping them against the floor before looking back up at her and leaning forward to wrap my arms around her. "I'm so glad you're around, Morg."

She squeezed back. "Who would've thought the two of us would become so close?"

I laughed as I pulled away. "All we needed was to get away from Erica and Andrea to actually get to know one another. I bet they were pissed when I didn't invite them."

Morgan shrugged. "Who cares, it's your wedding. I haven't talked to them for months—since we don't have any classes together anymore, and they're still partying it up even though this is senior year of *college* and not high school. I wonder if the real world will hit them any time soon?"

We locked eyes and started laughing as we shook our heads.

"Speaking of the real world, I still don't understand why you and Trent decided not to take a honeymoon. If anyone deserves to get away from the real world for a while, it's you two."

"With midterms coming up, and Dad...I just don't want to spend time away from him."

Morgan nodded. "He looks like he's doing well."

"Looks and is, are two different things. Every once in a while I'll catch him wincing while doing something little, like picking Allie up or even bending down to get something off the floor. He's tired all the time, and I know it, despite the fact he won't admit it," I said, watching as he smiled over at us. I fought the way my stomach flipped as I saw the bags under his eyes.

That's normal. I told myself. *All of us are tired.*

But in the three months that passed, he was beginning to lose weight, despite the fact he was eating to try to make up for it, and his hair was thinning out. Even though he was no longer taking treatments, his body appeared the way it did when he first took them. This time it wasn't temporary effects of therapy, but the signs the cancer was working its way into his system. At past midnight, I wondered how the wedding would affect him, and I had to squeeze my eyes shut and press on my stomach to keep the wave of nausea away.

"I'm going to head up to bed with Allie," Dad said, and my eyes shot open.

I stood, leaning up and kissing her forehead. She mumbled something inaudible, cuddling closer to Dad, and he smiled down at her before looking up at me. He reached out with his free hand and traced my chin. "You did an amazing job. I'm glad I was here to see it."

I fought back the tears, swallowing as I nodded. "Me too."

I leaned forward and gave him a kiss before watching him slowly make his way out of the room.

"You two look like you're ready to pass out," Ryan commented as he walked over, pulling Morgan up into his arms.

She sighed as she leaned up against him, nodding.

Ryan clapped Trent on the shoulder before they left. It was only Trent and I now, the DJ was already packed up and leaving. I stared around the room as Trent wrapped his arms around my body, tucking his head into my chin.

"What now, Mrs. Wentworth?" he whispered into my ear, sending a rash of goose bumps over my skin.

"You carry me to bed?" I suggested as I leaned back against him.

He swept me into his arms, and I squealed in surprised as he winked at me.

"Aren't you tired?" I asked as I put my head against his chest.

"Never too tired to take care of you," he whispered into my ear, his tone and double meaning making my body spread with warmth.

I breathed in, a smile plastered on my face as I closed my eyes.

Chapter
57

Returning to *real life* as Morgan described it, was hard even after just a weekend, and I knew we made the right decision to delay our honeymoon until some other date when there wasn't so much going on. I fought the sleep threatening to take me over as the professor went over something, what? I really wasn't sure. I was still exhausted, even after two nights resting, for the most part, in Sedona. Morgan kicked the back of my desk as my eyes drooped.

"Stay awake," she hissed at my back, but there was laughter in her voice.

I glanced over my shoulder at her, and her head was in her hands, her cheek stretching against her hand as she herself fought sleep.

"You should talk," I shot back.

She rolled her eyes, and I turned back around, trying to figure out what the hell the professor was even talking about. I knew it was my business management class, because it was the only class Morgan and I shared. The last class we would ever share. I swallowed, the thought causing my chest to tighten. I glanced back over at her, and her eyes fluttered as I smirked at her, raising an eyebrow.

"Can't wait for this class to be done," she whispered, and I leaned back in my seat so I could hear her better. We were at the back of the class so we wouldn't disturb any one.

"Maybe after college is done we might be able to actually hang out outside of here and," I paused as the words caught in my throat. That part of my life was ending too; "the hospital."

Morgan squeezed my shoulder. "He recovered from the wedding yet?"

I shrugged. "Allie spent the weekend taking care of him, whatever that means. Neither him or Allie would allude to what that meant."

"Maybe they just relaxed and she did exactly that, took care of him because he's her grandpa—*officially* now," Morgan replied, her voice soft. "You know she likes taking care of people."

I breathed in, looking at the ceiling and nodding. Morgan was right. Allie loved taking care of everyone and everything, especially Dad.

"I guess I'm just worried, you know? He has a doctor's appointment tomorrow, and I can't stop thinking about it," I admitted.

The professor stopped talking and students began to file out passed us.

"Free!" Morgan said, linking her arm in mine as I stood up.

We walked in silence until we reached outside. The Arizona air, now back in the eighties for the Fall, warmed our chilled skin, and I tilted my head up to the sun as I tried to keep my mind from racing. How many months did we have left? I felt the pit in my stomach form; would Dad get to see our first Christmas as an official family?

My chest tightened, the emotional vice grip squeezing the air from my lungs.

The numbers already made it unlikely he would make it to my graduation. Seven months.

According to the original estimate he only had five months left.

"Still thinking about it?" Morgan asked.

I rubbed my face with my hand, sounds coming out of my mouth but no words. My lungs felt like they were collapsing.

Five months.

Morgan was suddenly in front of me as my vision began to blacken around the edges. "Ellie," she said with her voice firm as she grabbed my shoulders. "He's still here. Stopping think about what's going to happen months from now. Just enjoy today. I know it's hard to think about it that way, but if you don't start, you're going to end up driving yourself insane."

I squeezed my eyes shut, balancing my weight against her arms as I counted to ten. I nodded as I opened my eyes.

She cocked her head before pulling me into a hug. She didn't need to say anything else. We stood there for a minute before Morgan pulled away.

"Call me tomorrow. If you need me, I'll get off my shift—okay?"

"I can't ask you to do that."

Morgan stared back at me, her lips in a stern line. "Call me if you need me, don't think about my work. Just call me—they'll understand; they know you and your dad."

I didn't respond, and she lowered her head.

"Promise me, El?"

"Promise," I replied.

Chapter
58

Fighting the inevitable parts of life is a losing battle, feeble and pointless. Denial is easier, but at some point, there's no denying it. Death isn't always stealthy; sometimes it's bold, digging its feet in the sand as you try to push against it. It's too powerful, though. It bears down on you, grinds everything in its path down.

Hopes.

Dreams.

My whole body numbed as I stared at the results of the tests on the screen. Even I knew the pattern of the cells on the screen was not good; there were too many white blood cells. The room around me seemed to buzz as my eyes moved to Dad. He stared at the screen without a need for explanation. He knew this all too well. He looked at cell samples like this every day at work. I watched as his face paled, and he looked down at his hands.

"Um... Trent, Ellie—can you give me a moment with the doctor?" he asked, his voice flat.

"Daddy—"

His eyes locked on mine, wet with sadness. "Please, Ellie?"

I felt the tears forming in my eyes as Trent stood; his hands still in mine and nodded to the door.

The horrible emptiness filled my body, hollowing out my emotions and weighing down my limbs. I stood as my vision blurred, and followed Trent out. I watched Dad shaking his head, his hand raking through his thinning hair as Trent closed the door behind us.

"He has less time than we thought," I whispered, and my chest tightened, knocking the breath out of me as I stared up at Trent.

He took my face in his hands, pressing his lips against my forehead before pulling me into his arms. We stood there until the door opened, and Dad appeared. I pulled away from Trent and stared at him. Dad's eyes darted away from mine, down to his feet.

"Ready?" he asked Trent as his hands went into fists at his side.

Trent's face paled as he looked between us. Trent took a shaky breath, biting his lip as he squeezed his eyes shut. When they opened they landed on Dad's, who looked up when neither of us replied. Trent breathed out through his nose before finally speaking, "Nothing, Paul? You're not going to tell us?'

Dad licked his lips. "Nothing is going to change if I tell you."

Trent's throat moved up and down, he shook his head. "We deserve to know."

Dad rubbed his palms together, his lips pursing. "Three months or less...less," he swallowed; "is highly likely."

I felt my eyes blinking rapidly as I turned on my heel and walked or ran; I wasn't sure which, to the door. I wanted out of this place. Out of the hell this cancer created.

Dad would never make it to my graduation.

He would never see the birth of our child.

He wouldn't grow old.

He wouldn't...He wouldn't.

I stared at the car in front of me, waiting for the sound of it unlocking, my body trembling as tears coursed down my cheeks.

Dad slid into the car, and my throat ached as I looked over at him, his own cheeks wet. "I didn't really want to say it out loud."

I nodded, moving to the center seat and buckling up before sinking down and putting my head on his shoulder. Dad put his arm around me, kissing my head as the tears continued to flow. When we got to the house Trent put his head down on the steering wheel.

"Hey," I said, reaching forward just as his shoulders shuttered with a sob.

His knuckles turned white against the steering wheel, and I looked over at Dad, but he was already getting out of the car. I watched as he walked around the car and opened Trent's door to pull him into his arms. Everything slowed as I opened my door and got out of the car. Dad was whispering something in Trent's ear, and he was nodding, his head hidden in Dad's chest.

Trent pulled away, breathing in rapidly as he wiped his face. "Sorry, El," he whispered.

Dad squeezed Trent's shoulder before turning to me and pulling me into a hug. "I'll be inside," he whispered. "This is hard on him, too."

"I know," I whispered.

Trent and I watched Dad go inside before Trent leaned back in the seat, looking up at the ceiling.

"This is worse," he finally whispered. "So much worse."

"What do you mean?" I asked as he got out of the car.

He shut the door, his forearm flexing as he leaned against the car. He turned, crossing his arms over his chest as he stared at his shoes.

"It feels so cruel, that he has to suffer—that you—"

"We—"

"We have to watch it," Trent began, his voice trembling as he put his shaking hand over his mouth. Fresh tears streamed down his face. "I've had a dad— a *real* dad for months, El—months, and now," he shook his head. "Now, he's going to be gone."

The selfishness of my own sadness sunk in as I stared at him, his body trembling as he closed his eyes against the onslaught of emotions. His shoulders caved, and another sob racked his body as I pulled him into my arms, and we sunk to the concrete driveway. We cried together until there were nothing left but raw emotions.

Pain that I was positive would never go away.

Chapter 59

I stared at the shingles beneath my feet, the bottle of beer hanging from my hand in between my knees. Trent hadn't noticed me take it as I headed outside. Sitting on the roof drinking alcohol wasn't a responsible thing to do, but there were worse things I could do. Especially when the house was a ranch, and the roof meant I was barely ten feet off the ground. In that moment, I couldn't be more far away from reality.

Reality sucked.

The tree I used to climb up shook and Morgan appeared.

"Hey," she said as she crawled up to the peak where I was and sat next to me.

"Hi," I muttered as I took another sip of the drink.

Morgan blinked at the bottle before looking up at me with her lips in a line. "Beer?"

I shrugged as I drained the bottle. "Tastes like shit."

"Then why are you drinking it?"

I shrugged again, and she heaved a sigh. "You never texted me."

I swallowed, leaning back against the roof. "Never...the word on repeat in my head."

Morgan looked down at me; her cheeks red as the wind picked up her curly hair and blew it around her face. "Trent told me there isn't much time left."

I looked up at the sun as it cascaded down the horizon as it set. "I'm trying not to be selfish about my pain—I know Trent is having trouble dealing with this too."

Morgan looked straight ahead, and I realized there were tears in her eyes. She rubbed her face, leaving a trail of mascara. "Your dad is a great person."

I sat up and put my head on her shoulder. "I don't want to be so sad—I want him to enjoy his..."

The words choked in my throat, and I stopped as Morgan nodded. I didn't need to say anything else. In the short time Morgan knew him, he influenced her, too.

"I'm sorry—" she whispered, her voice hoarse. "I know he's not my dad."

I squeezed her shoulder. "Thank you."

"For what?" she whispered as she wiped her face again.

"For reminding me how many people care—how many people he's affected, and for reminding me how lucky I am. You, Trent and Allie reminded me of that—that I'm lucky to have had him my whole life while you guys have only had him for months."

Morgan's chest rose as she breathed in. "How sick is he going to get?"

I looked ahead as the sun dipped down and darkness spread through the desert. "I don't know. He...he was barely able to tell us how many months he has left. We'll be lucky if he makes it to Christmas."

Fresh tears began again.

Our last Thanksgiving was only a week away.

Our last Christmas only a few more weeks.

Last.

Another word that ate at my soul.

Chapter
60

I stared at the ceiling, counting as I breathed in and out.

One. Two. Three. Four. Five.

I sighed, closing my eyes as I turned on my side, looking at the dark air separating Trent and I. He mumbled in his sleep, and I smiled to myself thinking of how he always said he didn't snore, and then, as I thought it, he did.

Okay. Counting.

One. Two. Three. Four. Five

How high did they say to count?

I grit my teeth as I thought of the day ahead of me when I woke up, or more like, when I was *supposed* to wake up. I'd been up for...I turned over, pulling my phone off the bedside table and swiping my finger across it. Yup, two hours. It was almost five o'clock—almost, but even if it was five, it was still too early. I closed my eyes, snuggling closer to the cool spot on the pillow. If I got up too early I would wake Dad up. He never was a light sleeper, until now. It seemed any noise would wake him, or perhaps, he was having as much trouble sleeping as I was. It was hard to believe, though, because at the end of each day he seemed so exhausted. His skin had become drawn over the last few weeks, tightening over his cheek bones and hollowing out beneath his eyes.

Another sign his body was revolting against him. I knew he was in pain, but he never complained. There wasn't much besides taking more pain killers that could help.

My stomach rolled, empty and upset. I felt absolutely helpless as each day passed. After the doctor's visit with the bad news of a shortened time frame I pushed myself into my studies, and I would be graduating in a few short weeks, right before Christmas. I buried my face deeper into the pillow, fighting the pricking at the corner of my eyes. Dad would live to *know* I received my degree, but not to see it; the ceremony still took place in June.

The tears spilled over.

Dad wouldn't make it to June.

Trent rolled over, slipping his arm around me and pulling me into his chest. I tucked into him as he kissed the back of my head.

Moments before he was snoring in a dead sleep, but somehow, like always, he knew I was up and needed him. He never said anything, just pulled me tighter.

I inhaled, letting my chest rise against his arm before I clamped my eyes shut.

Count.

One. Two. Three. Four. Five. Six. Seven. Eight...

Again.

One. Two. Three. Four...Four. Five...Five. Seven—

Chapter 61

Thanksgiving.

I let my eyes flutter open against the light streaming through the window and dancing over the bed. I sat up slowly, looking over at the empty half of the bed. Trent was already up, which wasn't unusual. He always seemed to be up first, despite my constant tossing and turning as of late. I slipped out of bed, pulling open the curtains to let in the sun. It was officially sweatshirt weather in Arizona, some days not making it above sixty-five. Today looked like it wasn't going to be one of those days. I grabbed my phone off the bedside table and pulled down the weather.

Seventy-five and sunny.

I smiled to myself. We could eat dinner out on the patio; Dad's favorite place.

Dinner—what time was it?

Ten? Ten! I hurried out of the room, yelling down the hall where laughter was coming from the kitchen, "Why didn't anyone wake me up?"

Dad poked his head around the wall, giving me a tooth-filled grin. "Blame it on Trent. I was going to tickle you awake, but he forbade it!"

I stopped, crossing my arms as I laughed. "Forbade it?"

Dad nodded, his eyes widening.

"Trent!" I yelled.

Dad smirked at me as Trent leaned passed him. "Yes, dear?"

I blinked at him a few times as I fought the laughter. "You forbade Dad from waking me up?"

Trent looked at Dad who shrugged and went back to Allie, who was calling him back into the kitchen. "*He* forbade me!"

I rolled my eyes. "You two are both on my shi—"

"Ellie!" Allie ran around the corner, holding up a spatula covered in orange-brown goo. "Taste this!"

Trent put his finger over his lip, chastising me for swearing, and I narrowed my eyes as I shook my head before leaning down to Allie.

"What's this?" I asked as I took the spatula.

"Grampy is teaching me how to make his famous pumpkin pecan pie!" she replied, clasping her hands together and putting them over her mouth as she bounced on her toes. "How does it taste?"

I licked the spatula and closed my eyes. I wasn't exaggerating for her; it really was amazing. I waited all year for a piece of that pie.

"Is it good? Does it taste right?" she asked, her hands going to the bottom of her pink tulle skirt, underneath she had silver polka dot black leggings.

I nodded as I bent down to her level and handed her the spatula. "Did he tell you the secret ingredient?"

She smiled, bopping her head up and down as she took it back.

"What is it?" I asked.

Her head jerked back, eyes widening. "You don't know it?"

I shook my head, and she bit her lip, leaning forward to whisper to me. "I can't tell you then!"

I let my jaw drop open, and she ran back into the kitchen giggling.

I closed my eyes as I stood back up.

Today was going to be okay.

I'm going to be okay. I promised myself. It was a promise I needed to keep for all of us.

After showering I joined the rest of the family in the kitchen, stopping at the opening and putting my hand against the wall as I looked at the mess. Dad looked up from the island where Allie and him sat, a smile plastered on his face as I stared around the room. The island beneath the bowl they were stirring didn't show a hint of the dark counter beneath; in fact, it was pretty much white with flour. Trent was at the oven, basting the turkey.

"Did you guys leave anything for me to do?" I asked.

Trent looked over his shoulder at me. "Potatoes need to be peeled."

I pouted at him and he shrugged, his shoulder hiding his smirk before he turned back to place the turkey in the oven.

"Fine," I huffed as I rolled up the sleeves to the light sweater I put on. "I'll do potato duty."

I picked up the peeler and moved to the sink to begin peeling the potatoes. Trent elbowed me lightly as he came up next to me and grabbed his own potato to begin peeling.

"I thought this was my job," I commented, looking up at him.

His shoulders raised, but he continued to concentrate on his bottom. I watched as he swallowed, and he tensed. "So..." he began, still looking at the potato. I glanced down at it, completely white and then back up at him wondering if he was going to peel it down to nothing.

"So—?"

He dropped the potato, shaven to an inch of its life, into the pot. He leaned against the counter, his shoulders tense as he coughed. "I have some paperwork I wanted to...uh...talk—show you?"

"Sure," I replied, leaning over and dropping my own potato into the pot before picking up another. "You should've had me sign the prenup *before* getting married. The pre stands for before."

Trent choked, shaking his head—well, more like twitching. "No, uh, nothing like that."

I turned, dropping the next potato into the pot as he continued to kill another. I pointed the peeler at him. "Then why are you so nervous?"

He dropped his potato into the pot. His jaw clenching as his eyes widened, and he looked over at Allie. "Let me just—let's go into the living room?"

I nodded, signaling for him to lead the way. I followed him as he pulled a folder from drawer in the end table and sat on the couch. I sat down beside him as he stared at the folder, tapping his foot against the ground.

"I..." his nose twitched before he began again; "I'd like it if you..." he swallowed, his cheeks puffing as he exhaled.

"Spit it out, Trent!" I joked, bumping shoulders with him.

He sighed, before flipping open the folder with some very legal looking documents in it. My stomach sank as I tried to read the tiny print. "I'd like you to officially be Allie's mother."

Tingles rushed up my arms as I stared at him.

His eyes locked on mine as he pushed the folder to me. "They're adoption papers."

I put my hand over my mouth as I stared down at the papers. I nodded without speaking. He wanted me to *officially* be Allie's mother. Being married was one thing—this was a whole other level of trust I couldn't quite describe. My eyes shot up as Trent leaned over and grabbed a pen. His chin tucked to his chest as he held it out to me, his hand shaking. I took it and leaned forward onto the coffee table before firmly placing my hand down on the paper and signing.

Ellie Wentworth.

Mother of Allie Wentworth.

I glanced over at Trent, and the stern look on his face finally broke into a smile.

"What?" I asked; looking over my shoulder at him as my lips tugged tightly into my cheeks. "You thought I'd say no?"

He put his hand on his head, his tattoo stretching. "It's a lot of responsibility...you know, to know officially, you're a parent. I know how scared shitless I was when I signed the same document."

I leaned back, kissing his cheek. "You were doing it alone— I know I'm not."

His eyes fluttered and he pulled me into a tight hug. "Now I'm not."

"What's that?" Dad asked as he walked in the room drying his hands.

Allie rushed in, jumping onto the couch beside me and bouncing on her knees. "Yeah, what's that?"

I glanced over at Trent, and he nodded.

"Paperwork that officially makes me—" the tingles returned as the word rolled off my tongue; "your mom."

Allie's brow furrowed as she looked between us, then over at Dad who was chuckling to himself and back to us. "I don't get it—but, yay!"

She leaned forward, wrapping me in a tight hug. She looked up at me, chewing the inside of her lip before asking, "Does that mean I can call you mommy?"

My throat made a noise, but no words came out as I opened my mouth. Instead, I just nodded.

Allie's hesitant smile grew. "Now I can tell everyone at school I have a mommy!"

All I could do was laugh and nod.

I'm a mother.

I looked up at Dad, and he leaned forward and squeezed my shoulder before kissing my forehead.

"Congrats," he said. "Something to be truly thankful for."

Looking around the room, I realized there was a lot to be thankful for.

Even if these were *lasts*, they were *lasting* memories, and that was what truly mattered.

Chapter 62

I stared down at the last question on the page.

This was a last I couldn't be more excited for.

The last question, on my last final, in my last class, in my last semester of college.

This was it. I inhaled, filling my lungs with air until stars popped in my vision before exhaling and circling the correct answer.

Done. *I was done.*

I looked up at Morgan's back as I put the pencil down, and my eyes drifted to the professor sitting grading another class' tests. Morgan glanced over her shoulder at me, and I nodded as we both stood together. She linked her arm in mine, and we walked up to the front placing our tests on the pile in front of the professor. He looked up and nodded at us before we turned and walked back to our desks. We picked up our bags and headed to the door.

"So that's it," I said as we reached the hallway.

Morgan nodded, biting the inside of her cheek. "I thought it'd feel a lot more epic than that."

I nodded. She was right. I thought I would feel this utter sense of relief, but instead my muscles felt tight, and I could feel my heart beat in my throat.

"Maybe when we have our diplomas in hand?" she suggested.

I felt my feet slow without me telling them too, and I tripped slightly over them as my muscles twitched. "June is a long way away," I mumbled.

Morgan squeezed my elbow, her eyes soft as she looked at me. I didn't have to say it. She knew exactly what I was thinking.

"Technically, we're graduates as soon as those grades post," Morgan reminded me. "Are you still up for some shopping?"

Two weeks until Christmas, and I still hadn't done any shopping. My stomach growled, and I grabbed it to stop the noise. I glanced over at to see Morgan smirking.

"Lunch first?" I suggested.

She grabbed her keys from her purse. "My treat."

~~~

I gritted my teeth as I looked down at the knitted sweatshirt tossed over my arm. What did you get a person who was dying?

I ran my fingers over the soft cabling. A sweater just didn't feel like enough. I sucked my lip in as I thought of how the gray of the shirt would pull the steel flecks in Dad's eyes out. When I saw it I immediately thought of him and how handsome he would look in it.

If he ever gets to wear it.

I squeezed my eyes shut. I promised myself to handle things better, and I had been doing a good job until today. Today just seemed like a constant reminder of everything I was losing. It was everything good dragged down by everything bad. Finishing college only reminded me Dad wouldn't see me receive my diploma, and the perfect way this sweater would fit him only reminded me he may not get to wear it.

I shook the thought from my head. I knew Dad. He would take it out of the box and put it right on because he wanted me to know how much he loved it.

"Hey," Morgan looked over the rack she was standing at, her brows drawn tight over her eyes. "You okay?"

"Yeah...the tuna roll isn't sitting well," I lied. It was easier than telling her I wanted to have a breakdown right there in the store; that her form of distracting me was actually plummeting me into despair.

She didn't ask me how Dad was doing anymore; instead, she always made sure to come to the house a few times a week to see him. Sometimes she stayed for dinner, sometimes she just stayed for a few minutes. Morgan knew more about his medical condition than I did, but she had trouble hiding what she thought from her face. When she picked me up in the morning she stopped in and talked to him for a few moments and hugged him before leaving. While they were close I never saw her do that, but then again, they didn't usually stop talking as soon as I came into the room. I swallowed as I looked at the jeans. I hadn't thought about why until now. Maybe he told her he wasn't doing well.

My body went cold, and I glanced over my shoulder at her looking through the graphic t-shirts. She was acting normal today, though. She couldn't keep that from me if she knew. Could she?

I walked over to her, feeling a cool sweat building beneath my sweatshirt.

She pouted as she looked at the shirts. "I can't imagine Ryan wearing anything but band t-shirts."

"Trent wears them under his plaid shirts most of the time," I commented, lifting Dad's sweater to reveal a few plaid button-ups. These ones were thicker for the cooler weather that had set in.

"Nice. I like that sweater, is it for your Dad?" she asked as we walked to the register.

I nodded, the blood rushing through my ears. "Speaking of which," I began, smiling at the clerk as I put the pile of clothes down. "How do you think he looks?"

Morgan looked down at the jeans in her arms, playing with the tags, and the whooshing in my ears strengthened to the point where I wondered if she ever answered if I would be able to hear her. She shrugged, her eyes slowly coming up to mine. "Tired, weak...but not bad."

I swiped my card as the clerk told me my total. I didn't even hear what he said, but it wasn't like it really mattered anyways. I needed to get my shopping done. He handed me the bag of clothes, his smile lingering on me in a way that made my eyes go down. Morgan started talking to him, but I blocked it out as I wondered what *not bad* meant in her medical background. We fell into step as we headed to the trendy store with too much black and a lot of t-shirts with skulls.

"Dad doesn't tell me how he's feeling," I blurted out, and I glanced over at Morgan from the corner of my eyes.

"Yeah, he doesn't really tell me either," she replied, her chest rising as her eyes darted down to her feet and then back up again to look at me. I moved my eyes forward as she continued, "I try to get him to be honest, but he always says *he's fine*."

I scoffed. "Whatever that means."

She linked her arm in mine. "That's what I say to him, but he still doesn't budge. Says it means he's fine."

"He's a pain in the ass," I muttered.

"Got that right," Morgan said, laughing as she glanced over at me.

"Anything I can help with?" a girl with piercings on every inch of her ears, several on her lips and a few half dozen between her eyebrows.

Morgan's typical smile froze on her face, her mouth hanging open as she looked at the girl's black lipstick. It was a bit overkill even for this store. She blinked a few times as the girl's chest lifted against her now crossed arms. "I'm looking for a few specific band shirts?"

"Cool," the girl replied, her lips pursing. Her eyes widened when Morgan didn't continue. The girl's chin stuck out as she asked, "Which are?"

"Oh," Morgan said, shaking her head. "Yeah. Sorry. For Today, Fit for a King and—"

Morgan looked over at me, knowing I liked the music even though she didn't. I smiled as I finished for her, "Legend and Deftones."

The girl headed to the wall of shirts, staring up at them. "I thought we had a Deftones one, but none of the others."

I looked up the wall. There definitely wasn't anything that said Deftones. Morgan looked over at me, and I shook my head.

"Have you checked online?" the girl asked as she turned back to Morgan.

Morgan shook her head, no words coming out as her face reddened.

"Try online, there's a few different merch places the bands usually put their stuff. Check out their websites or social media, it should say on there where to get them," the girl suggested. "Have a good one."

Morgan's nose squished as she tilted her head to the ceiling. "Now what am I going to do?"

I slipped my phone out of my pocket. "Come on, I know where to look. I know you wanted to see them first, but this online place has a ton of cool shirts, usually."

"Are you sure?" Morgan asked as we sat on a bench. "I don't usually buy stuff online."

I glanced over at her. "Seriously? Are we from the same generation?"

She stuck her tongue out. "Yes, I just like to touch things first."

"Do you want to get Ryan some kick ass shirts?"

She sighed, scooting closer to me. "Fine," she said, dragging out the word.

I smirked over at her. "I want to order some, and I already have an account, so you'll just need to stop at the ATM."

"Ryan has work until five, though," Morgan said, winking at me as she looked at my phone.

"Since when do you take money from the guy you're dating?"

Morgan rolled her eyes. "He's set on spoiling me—doesn't let me pay for anything. That's why I want to get him a bunch of these t-shirts—oh, I like that one! There isn't too much blood-like-looking stuff on it."

I laughed. "One soft-core metal shirt coming up!"

Chapter 63

"Hey, sleepy head," Trent greeted me as I rolled over, yawning. He was already dressed, sitting on the edge pulling his socks on.

"Shouldn't you be at work by now?" I asked as I sat up, looking over at the clock. I shot up as I looked at the time. "Why do you guys keep letting me sleep so much?"

"I slept in too," Trent said, leaning back on his elbows. He looked down at his tattoo on his left arm, sun stretching over the koi.

"Again, back to the original question. Shouldn't you be at work right now?" I asked as I went to the closet.

Trent coughed. "Put something nice on."

I turned slowly, my pulse quickening as I crossed my arms and narrowed my eyes at him. Trent had a tie on. A *tie* on, and he had another one in his hands that he kept looking between myself and it, smirking. I didn't like how his eyes were locked on mine now, teasing me, his lip curled up in the corner.

"Trent?"

The smirk turned into a smile as he flicked the end of the tie in his hand. "That is my name."

"What's going on?" I pushed.

"Just get ready to go out," Trent commented as he stood, kissing my forehead before heading to the door.

He was wearing his nice black jeans, and the new sneakers I bought while shopping but couldn't help but give him early.

"Trent Wentworth," I hissed as I looked over my shoulder.

He stopped at the door. "Put something nice on and meet us in the living room."

"Who is *us*?" I asked, my mouth going dry.

"The family," Trent replied, his tone seeming to say it was obvious. He looked down at his watch. "You have half an hour to get ready, you think you can do that?"

"Only if you tell me what's going on!" I shot back.

Trent pointed at me, his shoulders going up. "Just get ready."

I huffed before turning to the closet. It was hard to get ready when I didn't have the foggiest idea what was going on. Where would we be going at ten thirty in the morning that I needed to look nice?

I settled for a black cotton maxi dress and a light green sweater with animal print flats. I weaved my fingers through my hair, pulling it to the side into a braid as I concentrated on getting ready instead of whatever the *hell* my family planned only a few days before Christmas. If we were going out to brunch everywhere would be swamped with last minute shoppers, besides the fact I couldn't think of a brunch place were looking nice wouldn't be out of place amongst the people in their pajamas. At least not that we usually went to, not that we actually ever went to brunch.

"Is this okay?" I asked as I walked into the living room where Trent, Dad, Allie and Morgan were.

Morgan?

"Beautiful," Dad said, glancing over at me from the couch. He was dressed up too, in the gray sweater I gave into giving him early.

I was no good at surprises, which was one of the reasons I always ordered last minute gifts online. If I received them the day before Christmas, then I wouldn't be tempted to give them to someone early. It did make wrapping a giant pain in the butt, though, because I always ended up wrapping late into the night.

I smiled; it looked as amazing on him as I thought it would. He also wore the beanie I made him in the plethora of spare time available to me since school ended. It was a hunter green that looked nice against the gray, bringing some color back to his pale face. I let my eyes drift to Allie in a puffy purple dress, with a bodice of sequins and then finally to Morgan.

"What are you doing here?" I asked, walking forward and hugging her.

She shrugged. "I just stopped by, and your dad invited me to go out with you guys."

I bit the inside of my lip as I crossed my arms, looking at the pink and white sheath dress she was wearing. "And you just knew to dress up?"

Trent stood, holding up his spare tie. "It's a surprise, El."

I stepped back, putting my hands up as my body flushed with heat. "Don't you dare!"

He stopped mid stride, then smirked and took another step forward. I stepped back again in response. "Don't make me pin you down!"

"Trent Wentworth!" I hissed as I backed into the wall behind me.

He shook the tie in my face. "We can either do this the hard way, or you can be a big girl and let me tie you up."

Dad choked, and it turned into a coughing fit that sent my already frayed nerves on overdrive.

"Dad?" I asked, looking around Trent.

Morgan handed him his glass of water, and he waved me off. "I'm fine; now let him put the *blindfold* on."

Trent chuckled. "As if that's any better, Paul."

"You're all sick!" I shot as I stepped forward and let Trent put the tie over my eyes. "And I hate you!"

~~~

Being blindfolded made everything seem to take way too long. I tapped my knee in the back of the car as I sat in darkness. I stopped questioning if it was necessary after the first ten minutes. It was pretty obvious everyone would be pissed if I took it off, and it seemed important to them all that I didn't. When the car finally stopped, and I heard the gears shift into park, I lifted my hands only to have Morgan put her hands on mine.

"Not yet," she said, and I heaved a sigh.

"This sucks," I muttered to myself as I felt Morgan move away from me and scoot out the other door. I felt my door open, and I unbuckled myself, waiting for Trent to help me so I didn't slam my head on the car frame. He shut the door behind me, locking the car and put his hands on my shoulders before guiding me forward.

Somehow, where ever we where managed to have handicapped ramps pretty much everywhere, so Trent didn't have to risk killing me by trying to tell me where steps were. I wasn't coordinated when I could see, and I was getting pretty frustrated with how uncoordinated I was when I couldn't see, even without steps. Finally, Trent stopped me.

"Sit," he ordered, and I did so.

"Now?" I begged, not bothering to try and figure out what direction to pout in.

Trent slipped the knot out, and I was finally able to see again.

My mouth dropped as my hand shot up to it, my body going rigid as I stared at the stage in front of me. The Dean stood at the podium in his full graduation attire. I turned to Trent who had a cap and gown, along with my honors cords in his lap. I felt myself breathing heavy as he handed them to me. I didn't hear him, but read his lips say, *put it on.* I stood and so did Dad. I handed him my cords as I slipped into the gown and saw the flash of the camera as he put them on over my head and then took my cap and put it on, straightening out the date on the tassel. Everything felt robotic as I sat back down, Trent's hand entwined in one of mine as Dad's went into my other. The Dean, smiled, and I glanced behind him.

I hadn't noticed all the professors where here too. Morgan coughed, and my eyes widened. She was in her cap and gown too, and passed her sat her parents.

We were graduating.

I glanced at Dad.

And he was here to see it.

Chapter
64

I stared out at the small crowd, my family gathered there for Morgan and I; all these people here so Dad could have this moment.

So I could have this moment.

I swallowed down the lump in my throat as my hand froze in the Dean's. His stern lips turned into a soft smile as he held out the diploma, and my eyes fell to it. I reached out for the leather encased paper, and I watched as the loose sleeve pooled at my elbow, exposing the hairs on my arm as they rose up. I took the diploma, and his hand left mine, slipping to my back and turning me back to the few seats filled in the auditorium. I was aware there was clapping; I could see Trent's hands moving, and Morgan's mouth open as she smiled, whooping for me—but I heard nothing. I saw the flashes of cameras, but I couldn't tell who was taking the pictures. The room buzzed around me, spinning slowly as I turned and made my way down the steps. I was moving, but I barely felt it. As I came up to Dad, the noise collapsed on me, and he wrapped his arms around me as my knees threatened to give out. I stood between Trent and Dad as Morgan's name was called, echoing off the walls of the barren room. I wondered if it was the same experience for her, and I realized as she came down the stairs, her face and neck a blotchy red-pink, that it was.

We took our seats again and the Dean returned to his podium. He lifted his hands up, and the professor's behind him stood.

"It is my pleasure to give to you the class of 2015!" he said, and my skin prickled again as Morgan turned in her seat and reached across to my tassel.

I reached for hers, and we moved them to the opposite side before standing and pulling one another into a tight embrace.

"Thank you," I whispered, and she didn't respond, just nodded into my shoulder.

I glanced over at Dad, and Morgan and I lifted our arms so he could join us.

He kissed both of our heads. "I'm proud of you both—and thankful you found one another. Thank you for arranging this with Trent, Morgan—truly amazing."

I shed so many tears in the past few months I barely felt them as they rushed down my cheeks, but I knew these ones were different. Morgan pulled away to talk to her parents, and I turned to Trent. He took my face in his hands, using his thumbs to dry my cheeks.

"Good tears?"

I nodded. "You're always responsible for the good ones."

He tilted my chin and kissed me. "I'm glad to hear that."

I laughed, closing my eyes as I held the diploma to my chest, and when I opened them the Dean and professors were funneling down the stairs towards us.

"Are you going to tell me how you convinced them to do this?" I whispered to Trent, and he shook his head, winking down at me as his hand went to my back.

The next few minutes were as surreal as my journey up the stage to receive my diploma. The professors swarmed around us, offering congratulations and asking us what was next. I found myself dazed as I shrugged each and every time.

I don't know didn't seem like an appropriate answer, but I didn't. For months I had been selling my paintings at the galleries in Sedona, and more recently, in Phoenix. I had a degree in literature, what the hell did someone do with that?

Nothing. I laughed to myself.

"Oh, I'll probably do something in graphic design," I said over and over again. It seemed like a good answer.

When the crowd had thinned out Trent looked down at me. "Graphic design?"

"That's my minor," I replied with a shrug.

"Don't mention you're doing amazing *already* as an artist at all, though?" Trent asked, his brows rising into his forehead.

I rolled my eyes. "I can't make a living off of that, plus, it's good to put on a graphic design resume."

"Stuck in a cube all day?" Trent reminded me.

I sucked my lip into my mouth as I thought about it. I hadn't ever had a real job.

"I think I'd like to try it," I replied, smiling up at him.

He cocked his head, partially closing his eyes as he tugged at his tie. "That's right, you don't have to wear a vice grip around your neck if you work in a cube!"

I pushed my tongue into the corner of my cheek as I looked at him. "So what else do you have planned?"

Trent put his hands up, stepping back as if innocent, but he couldn't hide the smile as Allie pulled on his shirt. He picked her up and put her on his hip. "What's next, Bee?"

Allie put her hands on top of Trent's shoulders and smiled at me. "Lunch!"

I glanced over at Morgan, who was just saying goodbye to the Dean. "What?" she asked as she walked over.

I put my hands on my hips. "I don't think this is going to be just *lunch*, is it?"

Morgan put her pointer finger on the top of her nose as she dragged out each syllable of her answer, "Maybe..."

I huffed as I crossed my arms, glancing over at Dad. "I really don't like being the only one not knowing."

"Actually," Trent said, leaning into my frame of view. "He doesn't know what's next either."

Dad shrugged.

"And see, he doesn't look like it's going to kill him," Allie added, her little smirk made my mind go blank. I wanted to say something smart, but I couldn't think of anything I could possibly say in front of a five year old.

Trent held up the tie, and I shook my head. "No way. Not again."

He chuckled as he stuffed it back in his pocket. "Fine," when no one but me was looking he mouthed, *later?*

I looked up at the ceiling, pushing my cheek out with my tongue.

"Alright," Trent said, clapping his hands. "Morgan, are you going to meet us there with your family?"

"For sure," she replied, and before I could make a comment they were making their way out of the room.

Chapter 65

Suddenly, in our rush to experience everything, I felt we pushed fast forward on Dad's life. The feeling sunk inside me as I watched Dad looking up at my painting of Mom's photograph, now on display in a local restaurant and gallery. His arm locked in mine, and beneath the soft sweater I could feel he was too thin. I could see the illness eating him away, and the smile on my face as I laughed with him seemed external to the screaming inside of me. I was screaming for everything to just stop.

Please stop!

I wanted these moments to last forever, for the proud smile plastered on his face as he put his free hand over his lips to stay with me forever.

I laughed as he made a joke about his kid being more successful than him.

Would I be able to memorize everything about him?

The way his voice deepened when he was both upset and proud of me? The tenor of his laugh, and the way he tipped his head back when he did?

I watched as he did those very things.

Slow down.

Please slow down.

My mind kept screaming as I smiled, nodding and laughing with him.

"This is a truly amazing experience," Dad said, and my vision tunneled on him. I felt like a little girl again as he looked down at me, soft smile pulling at his hollowed cheeks. His eyes were still bright, vibrant—like his laugh. "I'm so blessed to have these lasting moments with you."

Lasting moments; not last moments—lasting moments.

A shaky breath rattled in my chest as I glanced over my shoulder at Trent, Allie, Morgan and her family at the table just behind us. Trent shot me a smile, nodding as if he knew I was fighting an internal battle with how amazing this moment was, coupled with how hollow it somehow felt.

Dad squeezed my forearm where his hand lay, and my eyes returned to him.

"You have the best pieces of the both of us."

I shook my head as my eyes began to prick at their inner corners.

"Your mom's creative vision, and my drive for success—plus," he smirked; "my eyes and her hair."

"You do beautiful photography, Daddy," I reminded him.

He pursed his lips, shaking his head. "She gave me that, princess. I didn't have it naturally."

I looked down at his hand, aged beyond his real years and placed my hand over it before locking eyes with him. "How are you feeling, Daddy?"

He bit the inside of his lower lip as his nostrils flared and his eyes became distant before coming back to me. "You know, princess, so why do you ask?"

I turned back to the pairing of art, Mom's photograph and my painting, and fought against the burn in my throat.

"I want to be wrong," I finally whispered, closing my eyes. "Because I'm scared."

Dad stepped in front of me, taking my hands in his and kissing them. "I am too, but I know this isn't the end, Ellie. This is just the beginning."

My chin trembled as the tears tumbled over the edges of my eyes. "Of what?"

"Your life," he stepped forward, pressing his forehead to mine. "And I promise," he sucked in breath, his hands falling to my trembling shoulders; "I promise I am *not* leaving you. I can't describe this to you, but your mother never left us. Never. I promise you. And I won't either."

Chapter 66

For Dad's sake I tucked the little girl inside of me who kept screaming for everything to stop, because it wouldn't. Our lives catapulted forward, far too fast for me, but there was nothing I could do, except try to memorize everything about the man who raised me. I tried my best to ignore the things the disease and morphine were doing to him—the small twitching he developed as the doses of pain killers increased, and the fading of the brightness of his eyes as he fought constant fatigue. There was a constant box of tissues by his side for the unexpected hemorrhaging from his nose, and he needed assistance to move around more and more with each passing day.

I had a constant box of tissues in our bedroom, because in moments like now, I sobbed for hours. I heard the door click behind me, and I tipped my head back against the mattress. I felt the mattress move as Trent crawled across it before sliding down beside me and putting his arm around me. I curled into him, tucking my face into his shoulder as he kissed my head.

"Allie and Dad are asleep. Did you have a good Christmas?"

I had excused myself after tea and dessert, saying I was tired from wrapping presents all night. While it was true, I knew from the look on Dad's face he knew it had been too much for me.

It had been too good.

Dad worked extra hard to make it the best Christmas he could and with Trent's help it was amazing.

It just reminded me exactly *why* they were doing it.

"Yes," I finally mumbled into his shirt. "Amazing."

"Good," Trent replied as he pulled me up to stand.

"Thank you," I whispered as he wiped my cheeks.

He nodded, his chest rising and freezing before he slowly exhaled. "I know it's hard."

"I keep trying to remember what Dad said— lasting moments, not last moments. It's just hard when he's becoming frailer by the moment."

Trent sat on the bed. "Yeah, he mentioned a nurse would be coming everyday from now on."

I swallowed as I squeezed my eyes shut. "That bad?"

Trent shrugged as he reached forward and rested his head on my stomach. "You know he doesn't say."

I ran my hands through his hair and a knock came on the door, too small to be Dad.

"Come in," I called, and Allie peeked her head in.

"I thought you were asleep," Trent said as he wiped his eyes.

Allie crawled up on the bed, coming to sit between us. She looked at Trent's face, creased with lines of worry and pain, and then up at mine before reaching her small hands up for me. I tilted my head down and she looked in my eyes, her small blue ones racing over my own.

"It's okay, Mommy. Grampy says heaven is nice—and your mommy is waiting for him."

Shock coursed through my system, and the screaming inside my head was silenced as I stared at this little girl with more of a grip on this than I did as an adult. I blinked rapidly at her, my chest rising and falling quickly as she continued to give me that soft knowing smile. I nodded, more like twitched before kissing her forehead.

"Do you need me to sing you another song?" Trent asked as I pulled away from Allie.

She shook her head. "I knew mommy and you were upset. I wanted to check on you. Grampy says this is hard on you."

I stared at the ceiling shaking my head.

"Come on," Trent said, standing and pulling Allie up into his arms with him. "I'll tuck you back in."

I flopped on the bed as they left with my eyes still on the ceiling. I concentrated on the patterns in the stucco; anything to keep my mind from screaming. Trent returned and sat on the bed, looking down at me.

"Don't be mad," he said.

"Why would I be mad?"

"I should've told you your Dad and I already talked to Allie about what was happening. She has a good grip on it."

I covered my face with my arms. "I noticed."

"El," Trent whispered, pushing my arms away from my face. "Are you going to be okay?"

"How do you measure 'okay'?"

Trent's eyes fell to his hands, his jaw clenching. I sighed before sitting up and turning, taking his face in my hands and kissing his cheek. "Yes," I replied. "Now, let's go to bed."

I crawled under the sheets and Trent shut off the light before crawling in after me and wrapping his arms around me. His voice drifted over me as he sung softly to me. The hard edges of pain softened, and I fell into a deep sleep.

Chapter 67

Trent.

I looked down at Ellie, her curls cascading over my bare chest as she slept; something she rarely did now. She mastered crying silently a few weeks after the final prognosis was announced, but I knew every night she cried herself to sleep. I wrapped my arms around her each night, hiding my own tears in her hair.

This wasn't easy. Pretending to be happy every day, watching Paul fading so quickly. Being strong for him, for Ellie and for Allie, and the same could be said for Ellie—being strong for Allie and me.

We had gotten Christmas, and I was so thankful for that.

I helped Paul to hand pick out the gifts, knowing they would be his last. I slowly let the breathe out of my chest as hot tears rushed down my face. I hadn't let Ellie see me cry since the day Paul told us he didn't have much time left. Not because I felt it wasn't manly, but because I knew how guilty it made her feel.

"Daddy?" Allie poked her head in the room, and I sat up slowly, not to wake Ellie. I wiped my face quickly as I nodded for her to come in.

Her calling me that always sent a shock to my system, but now it was worse. Her voice was pained, and I knew something was wrong.

"Come in," I said.

She shook her head, and I could see the wet trails going down her cheeks. My stomach dropped as her chin trembled and she looked over at Ellie asleep before looking back at me.

"Allie—?" I whispered as I slid out of bed and went to the door. I knelt down, and she buried her head in my shoulder before turning her head so I could hear her whisper.

"Grampy's with the angels."

Chapter 68

Ellie.

My eyes fluttered open as I heard the voices outside.

I knew.

No one needed to tell me.

I felt the disconnect between myself and the world.

I knew.

I felt the hollow that had been growing break open completely, and the tears fell from my eyes without any sound.

Gone.

He was gone.

The door creaked open and the bed indented. Trent sat motionless for a moment before reaching over and touching my shoulder.

"Ellie, honey—" he whispered, his voice cracking as he struggled to keep the emotion in. "Wake up."

I shook my head unable to form any words.

"You're awake?" he asked, and I nodded, pulling my legs to my chest as my entire body began to tremble out of control. "You know? How do you know?"

I just did. A part of me was missing, gone softly with the night.

"El," Trent whispered, and I gulped in a deep breath before sitting up and facing him. His eyes locked on mine, and his body shuddered as his shoulders collapsed with his own sobs.

I pulled him into my arms, knowing exactly why he sent Allie away.

This was going to be a long day.

The long day merged into an even longer night, then two days, three days.

Four days: a wake and funeral.

The pain was intense, blinding. There is no way to describe the burning hole left in your soul when someone you carry so closely to your heart disappears from the Earth—into the Earth.

My eyes burned from the tears as I watched the casket being placed into the ground. Again, I fell into the motions of doing what I should while inside my mind, heart and soul screamed. Person after person walked up to me and shook my hand—told me how Dad's work had saved their lives, or the lives of their spouse, or even their children and with each of them the screaming calmed until it stopped completely.

Dad saved lives.

The realization sunk in and comforted the aching parts of me until I was numb. I wasn't sure what to feel in those moments as the dirt was tossed over and final goodbyes were whispered until the only ones left were Trent and I.

I looked over at him and he put his hand into mine. "Are you ready?"

I nodded.

We walked in silence to the car, but when we were inside, Trent didn't start it. He looked down at his hands, running them over his slacks.

He swallowed before speaking, "A few weeks ago your Dad and I had a private conversation," his eyes fluttered against his cheeks, and his hands clenched into fists; "He said I was everything he prayed for...that I saved him by saving you. I feel like he saved us, though, you know?"

I leaned over, kissing his cheek. "Yes— he brought me you."

Epilogue

Sometimes, guardian angels aren't beings that we can't see, touch or feel—sometimes, they're beings as solid as you or I. They work in the same mysterious ways, though—a silent guardian there to help us when we're scared or lost. Dad was exactly that—in life he was the angel guiding me, silently showing me the right direction to go, without telling me how to do it. He guided me to the person I was; to not taking everything for granted and realizing the cure to everything was life and living it to its fullest. When Allie climbed the tree, I never expected her to come down with that egg. I never expected to hear from Dad again, except for in my dreams and memories. But there he was again as I popped open the hot pink egg from when I was a child that had faded to almost completely white.

"What's it say?" Allie asked, peering up at me.

I leaned down, the tears filling my eyes as I wrapped my arms around her and unfolded the small piece of paper.

"I will always love you both as long as the sky is blue and the red rocks make you smile," I whispered before kissing her cheek.

"Mommy, is that Grampy's writing?" Allie asked as my lip trembled.

"Yes," I replied.

She turned. "I told you he's our guardian angel."

I smiled at her and nodded.

He always was.

About the Author

Cassandra doesn't remember a time when she wasn't writing. In fact, the first time she was published was when she was seven years old and won a contest to be published in an American Girl Doll novel. Since then Cassandra has written more novels than she can count and put just as many in the circular bin. Her personal goal with her writing is to show the reader the character's stories through their dialogue and actions instead of just telling the reader what is happening. Besides being a writer, Cassandra is a professional photographer known for her automotive, nature and architectural shots. She is happily married to the man of her dreams and they live in the rolling hills of New England their dogs, Bubski and Kanga.

Cassandra can be found on Goodreads, Facebook and Twitter.

Other Books

New Adult
Love Exactly (Sticks & Stones, #1)
Flawed Perfection (Beautifully Flawed, #1)
Contemporary Romance

In Between Seasons (The Fall, #1)
Dystopian, Post-Apocalyptic Romance

Young Adult
Walking in the Shadows
Romantic Suspense

Children's:
The Adventures of Skippy Von Flippy (Skippy Tales, #1)
Mystic Mayhem (Finding Freckles, #1)

COMING SOON
Behind the Lens (A Metal Life Novel)
Pieces of Perfection (Beautifully Flawed, #2)
New Adult Contemporary Romance

www.ingramcontent.com/pod-product-compliance
Lightning Source LLC
Chambersburg PA
CBHW070640180626
46817CB00006B/2184